WE ARE INEVITABLE

ALSO BY GAYLE FORMAN

WE ARE INEVITABLE

GAYLE FORMAN

VIKING

VIKING

An imprint of Penguin Random House LLC, New York

First published in the United States of America by Viking,
an imprint of Penguin Random House LLC, 2021

Copyright © 2021 by Gayle Forman

Visit us online at penguinrandomhouse.com.

LIBRARY OF CONGRESS CATALOGING-IN-PUBLICATION DATA IS AVAILABLE.

Printed in the United States of America

ISBN 9780425290804

1 3 5 7 9 10 8 6 4 2

Design by Rebecca Aidlin
Text set in Minion Pro

For the Heathers, the Kathleens, the Mitchells, the Beckys,
and all the booksellers,
who give us a great good place.

A town isn't a town without a bookstore. It may call itself a town, but unless it's got a bookstore, it knows it's not foolin' a soul.

—Neil Gaiman, *American Gods*

Every act of creation begins with an act of destruction.

—Pablo Picasso

Home is where I want to be, but I guess I'm already there.

—Talking Heads, "This Must Be the Place"

WE ARE INEVITABLE

The Rise and Fall of the Dinosaurs

They say it took the dinosaurs thirty-three thousand years to die. Thirty-three millennia from the moment the asteroid slammed into the Yucatán Peninsula to the day that the last dinosaur keeled over, starving, freezing, poisoned by toxic gases.

Now, from a universal perspective, thirty-three thousand years is not much. Barely a blink of an eye. But it's still thirty-three thousand years. Almost two million Mondays. It's not nothing.

The thing I keep coming back to is: Did they know? Did some poor T-rex feel the impact of the asteroid shake the earth, look up, and go, *Oh, shit, that's curtains for me*? Did the camarasaurus living thousands of miles from the impact zone notice the sun darkening from all that ash and understand its days were numbered? Did the triceratops wonder why the air suddenly smelled so different without knowing it was the poison gases released by a blast that was equivalent to ten billion atomic bombs (not that atomic bombs had been invented yet)? How far into that thirty-three-thousand-year stretch did they go before they understood that their extinction was not looming—it had already happened?

The book I'm reading, *The Rise and Fall of the Dinosaurs* by Steve Brusatte, which I discovered mis-shelved with atlases a few months back, has a lot to say on what life was like for dinosaurs. But it doesn't really delve into what they were thinking toward the end. There's only so much, I guess, you can conjecture about creatures that lived sixty million years ago. Their thoughts on their own extinction, like so many other mysteries, they took with them.

※

Fact: Dinosaurs still exist. Here's what they look like. A father and son in a failing used bookstore, spending long, aimless days consuming words no one around here buys anymore. The father, Ira, sits reading in his usual spot, a ripped upholstered chair, dented from years of use, in the maps section, next to the picture window that's not so picturesque anymore with its Harry Potter lightning-bolt crack running down the side of it. The son—that's me, Aaron—slumps on a stool by the starving cash register, obsessively reading about dinosaurs. The shelves in the store, once so tidy and neat, spill over, the books like soldiers in a long-lost war. We have more volumes now than we did when we were a functioning bookstore because whenever Ira sees a book in the garbage or recycling bin, or on the side of the road, he rescues it and brings it home. We are a store full of left-behinds.

The morning this tale begins, Ira and I are sitting in our usual spots, reading our usual books, when an ungodly moan shudders through the store. It sounds like a foghorn except we are in the Cascade mountains of Washington State, a hundred miles from the ocean or ships or foghorns.

Ira jumps up from his seat, eyes wide and panicky. "What was that?"

"I don't—" I'm drowned out by an ice-sharp crack, followed by the pitiful sounds of books avalanching onto the floor. One of our largest shelves has split down the middle, like the chestnut tree in *Jane Eyre*. And anyone who's read *Jane Eyre* knows what that portends.

Ira races over, kneeling down, despondent as he hovers over the fallen soldiers, as if he's the general who led them to their deaths. He's not. This is not his fault. None of it.

"I got this," I tell him in the whispery voice I've learned to use when he gets agitated. I lead him back to his chair, extract the weighted blanket, and lay it over him. I turn on the kettle we keep downstairs and brew him some chamomile tea.

"But the books . . ." Ira's voice is heavy with mourning, as if the books were living, breathing things. Which to him they are.

Ira believes books are miracles. "Twenty-six letters," he used to tell me as I sat on his lap, looking at picture books about sibling badgers or hungry caterpillars while he read some biography of LBJ or a volume of poetry by Matthea Harvey. "Twenty-six letters and some punctuation marks and you have infinite words in infinite worlds." He'd gesture at my book, at his book, at all the books in the shop. "How is that not a miracle?"

"Don't worry," I tell Ira now, walking over to clear up the mess on the floor. "The books will be fine."

The books will not be fine. Even they seem to get that, splayed out, pages open, spines cracked, dust jackets hanging off, their fresh paper smell, their relevance, their dignity, gone. I flip through an old Tuscany travel guide from the floor, pausing on a listing for an Italian pensione that probably got killed by Airbnb. Then I pick up a cookbook, uncrease the almost pornographic picture of a cheese soufflé recipe no one will look at now that they can log onto Epicurious. The books are orphans, but they are our orphans, and so I stack them gently in a corner with the tenderness they deserve.

Unlike my brother Sandy, who never gave two shits about books but conquered his first early reader before he even started kindergarten, I, who desperately wanted the keys to Ira's castle, had a hard time learning to read. The words danced across the page and I could never remember the various rules about how an *E* at the end makes the vowel say its own name. The teachers would have meetings with Ira and Mom about delays and interventions. Mom was worried but Ira was not. "It'll happen when it happens." But every day that it didn't happen, I felt like I was being denied a miracle.

Toward the end of third grade, I picked up a book from the bins at school, not one of the annoying just-right baby books that got sent home in my backpack, but a hardcover novel with an illustration of a majestic and kindly lion that seemed to be beckoning to me. I opened the first page and read the line: *Once there were four children whose names were Peter, Susan, Edmund and Lucy.* And with that, my world changed.

Ira had been reading to me since before I was born, but that was not remotely comparable to reading on my own, the way that being a passenger in a car is nothing like being the driver. I've been driving ever since, from Narnia to Hogwarts to Middle-earth, from Nigeria to Tasmania to the northern lights of Norway. All those worlds, in twenty-six letters. If anything, I'd thought, Ira had undersold the miracle.

But no more. These days, the only book I can stomach is *The Rise and Fall of the Dinosaurs*. Other than that, I can't even look at a book without thinking about all that we've lost, and all we are still going to lose. Maybe this is why at night, in the quiet of my bedroom, I fantasize about the store going up in flames. I itch to hear that *foof* of the paper igniting. I imagine the heat of the blaze as our books, our clothes, our memories are incinerated. Sandy's records melt into a river of vinyl. When the fire is over, the vinyl will solidify, capturing in it bits and pieces of our lives. Fossils that future generations will study, trying to understand the people who lived here once, and how they went extinct.

"What about the shelf?" Ira asks now.

The shelf is ruined. Consider this a metaphor for the store. Our lives. But Ira's brow is furrowed in worry, as if the broken shelf physically pains him. Which it probably does. And when something pains Ira, it pains me too. Which I why I tell him we'll get a new shelf.

And so it begins.

///

The next morning, Ira wakes me with a series of gentle shakes. "Aaron," he says, a manic gleam in his hazel eyes, "you said we'd go buy a new shelf."

Did I? It's still dark outside. My head is full of cotton balls.

"C'mon!" Ira urges.

I blink until the digital clock comes into focus. It's 5:12. "Now?"

"Well, we have to drive to Seattle and back and if we leave at six, even if we hit traffic, we'll be there by eight when Coleman's opens and we can be done by eight thirty and there won't be traffic heading north, so we can be back by ten."

According to the laminated sign on the door Mom made a lifetime ago, Bluebird Books is open from ten to six, Monday through Saturday, closed Sundays. Ira insists on abiding by our posted times, even on snow days, even on sick days. It's part of what he calls the bookseller covenant. The fact that no one ever comes into the store before noon, if they come in at all, does not seem to play into his logic.

"Can't we get shelves in Bellingham?" I'm still not fully awake, which is why I add, "At the Home Depot?" even though I know Ira does not shop at Home Depot. Or Costco. Or Amazon. Ira remains committed to the small, independent store. A dinosaur who supports other dinosaurs.

"Absolutely not!" Ira says. "We have always shopped at Coleman's. Your mother and I bought our first bookshelf from Linda and Steve. Now come on!" He yanks away the covers. "Let's get moving."

Twenty minutes later, we are firing up the Volvo wagon and pulling out of the driveway. It's still midnight dark, dawn feeling very far away. At this hour, the businesses are all shuttered, so you can't tell which ones are kaput—like Dress You Up, which still has its dusty mannequins in the window—and which are just closed.

Ira slows to wave to Penny Macklemore as she unlocks the hardware store, one of many businesses in town she owns. "Good morning, Penny!" He unrolls his window, showering us both with a blast of Northwest air, whose dampness makes it feel far colder than it actually is. "You're up early."

"Oh, I'm always up this early," Penny replies. "That's why I catch all the worms."

"Well, we're off to buy some new shelves," Ira replies. "See you later."

We drive toward the interstate, down the winding road, past the mills that used to employ half our town and now stand empty, partially reclaimed by the forests they once transformed into paper.

"Your mom and I bought all our furniture from Coleman's," Ira says as he merges onto the interstate. "It's run by a husband and wife. Well, it was until Steve died. Now Linda runs it with her daughter." Ira pauses. "Kind of like you and me."

"Right," I say, wondering if Linda Coleman's daughter also has fantasies about her store going up in flames. Wood, after all, is as flammable as paper.

"No matter how long it's been," Ira continues, "Linda always remembers the last thing we bought. 'Ira,' she'll say. 'How's that display table working out?' Even if it's been years."

What Ira is talking about is the hand-sell. He is a big believer in the hand-sell. Once upon a time, he and Mom were very good at it. Before the asteroid came and ruined the business and frayed his brain, Ira had an almost photographic memory of what any given customer had read last, and therefore an uncanny ability to suggest what they should read next. So for instance, if Kayla Stoddard came in, stopping to chat with Mom about the brand-new coat (with tags on) Kayla had scored at the Goodwill, Ira would remember that the last two books Kayla had bought were *Murder on the Orient Express* and *Death on the Nile*, and would surmise, correctly, that she was on a Poirot kick and would quietly have *Appointment with Death* ready for her. He and Mom used to sell a lot of books this way.

"Linda will find us a good replacement for the broken shelf," Ira says as a gasoline tanker tears past the Volvo on the uphill. "And then we can organize a bit here and there and turn things around."

Ira often talks about *turning things around*. But what he really means is turning back time, to before the asteroid hit. And though I've read a fair number of books about the theoretical possibility of time travel, as far as I know, no one has invented a time machine yet. Still, I don't blame him for wishing.

When we pull into Coleman's, right at eight, the store is dark and locked. I run out to check the sign on the door. "It says it opens at nine," I call to Ira.

"That's odd." Ira scratches his beard. "I could've sworn it was open from eight to four. Linda arranged the schedule like that so they could be home with the kids in the evening. Though the daughter, Lisa is her name," Ira says, snapping his fingers at the synaptic connection, "she's grown now, so maybe they changed the hours. Now we're going to open late."

He frowns, as if there will be people waiting eagerly at our doorstep the way we are waiting at Coleman's.

"Well, since we have time to kill, do you want to get some breakfast?" I ask.

"Sure," Ira agrees.

We get back in the car and drive toward a shopping center. On one end of the parking lot is one of those giant health food emporiums. On the other side is a bookstore. Its windows are jammed with artful displays of new titles, smiling author photos advertising upcoming readings, a calendar of events. All signs of a bookshop thriving—in Amazon's backyard, no less—having survived algorithms, pandemics, TikTok. A reminder that not all species went extinct after the asteroid hit. Just the dinosaurs.

The sight of the store deflates Ira, who slumps in his seat and refuses to get out of the car. "Just go grab me something."

The health food store is decked out for Halloween: gourds and pumpkins and artisanal candy with "real sugar" because apparently that's a selling point. The prepared-food area is like a museum: fresh-cut fruit symmetrically laid out, a buffet of scrambled eggs and fluffy biscuits warming under a heat lamp. Ten dollars a pound. The egg breakfast at C.J.'s is five bucks, including juice and coffee.

I set off for something more affordable. And it's there, between kombucha scobies and shade-grown coffee, I see it: a table with records for sale. The cheapest one is twenty bucks. They go up, significantly, from there.

A tattooed hipster mans the table. He wears a fedora with a feather in it. I can't tell if it's a Halloween costume or just his "ironic" style.

"You collect vinyl?" he asks.

"Me? No!" I tell him. "I don't like records, or CDs, or music, for that matter."

The hipster rears back as if I just informed him that I mutilate kittens for fun. "What kind of person doesn't like music?"

My reply is automatic, an age-old distinction I don't even question: "A book person."

Around eight forty-five, bellies full of on-sale granola bars, we pull back into the Coleman's parking lot just as a guy wearing a red vest is unlocking the metal gate. "Hello," Ira calls, leaping out of the car. "Are you open?"

"We open at nine."

"Could we come in now?" Ira replies. "I'm an old friend of Linda's."

"Who's Linda?"

"Linda Coleman. Owner since nineteen seventy . . ." Ira points to the sign, the words dying in his mouth as he sees the placard beneath the Coleman's sign that reads UNDER NEW MANAGEMENT.

"Oh, yeah, they sold the store," the guy tells us.

"To your family?" Ira asks unsteadily.

"To Furniture Emporium," he replies.

"Does your family own that?" Ira asks.

"No, it's the chain. They kept the name, though, because people know this place. But it's really a Furniture Emporium now."

"Oh," Ira says. "I see."

The clerk is friendly enough. After he unlocks the door and flips on the lights, he says, "You can come in early." He opens the door. "Browse if you want."

Set loose, Ira is adrift. He jogs up and down the aisles, swiveling left and right like a lost child in the grocery store.

"How about this one?" I ask, pointing to an oak shelf that looks vaguely like the one that broke, in that it is large, wooden, and reddish.

"Okay, okay, good, good," Ira says, speaking in duplicate as he does when his anxiety spikes. "How much?"

I peer at the price sticker. "On sale for four hundred and forty-five dollars."

I have no idea if that's a lot for a shelf. Or if we can afford it. Though I technically own the bookstore, Ira still takes care of the business end of things.

"We'd like the red oak shelf," Ira calls to the clerk. "Delivered."

They start filling out the paperwork. When Ira gives our address, the clerk is not familiar with our town. I show him on my phone. "Oh, man, that's far."

"Linda always delivered for us. Steve used to drive the truck himself. Charged fifty dollars."

"Delivery that far is gonna be . . ." He types into the computer. "One fifty." He looks at Ira. "You'd be better off buying it online. Get free shipping."

GAYLE FORMAN

Online? You're better off telling Ira to sell his kidney. Which he wouldn't. Give it away? Yes, but not sell it.

"Ira," I try. "He has a point."

"I won't buy online. From a chain."

"But this *is* a chain."

"But this is where I've always bought my furniture." He nods to the clerk, who tallies up the total.

"Four forty-five, plus tax and delivery. That comes to six thirty-four."

"Six thirty-four," Ira repeats in a reedy voice.

"Maybe we should forget it," I begin.

"No," Ira says. "We need a shelf." With a shaking hand, Ira counts the bills in his wallet. "I have two hundred in cash. Charge the rest," he says, pulling out a credit card.

"Where'd you get that card?"

"Oh, I've had this one for years," he replies.

Before I can point out that he must know I know this is bull-shit, the card is declined. "Try this one," Ira says, forking over another one.

"How are you getting all these cards?" When Ira and Mom transferred ownership of the store to me on my eighteenth birth-day and then declared bankruptcy a few months later, it was sup-posed to wipe out the debt than had been sinking us. And it was also meant to wipe their credit clean. Ira's not meant to be eligible for new cards.

"They're in my name," Ira replies, his breath growing ragged as he hands over yet another card. "They won't hurt the store. They won't hurt you."

12

"*They?* How many cards do you have?"

"Just three."

"*Just* three?"

"It's not a big deal. Sometimes you have to borrow from Peter to pay Paul."

When the third is declined, Ira bows his head. "Linda used to let me pay on installments," he tells the clerk.

"Sure," the clerk says. "We can do that."

Ira looks up, a painful smile on his face. "Thank you. Is it okay if we pay two hundred now?"

"Yep," the clerk replies. "The balance is due before we deliver. We'll hold it for ninety days."

Ira blinks. His mouth goes into an O shape, like a fish gasping for air.

"Ira, he means layaway. Not credit. You have to pay before you get the shelf."

"O-oh," Ira stutters. His breathing picks up and his eyes bulge. I know what's coming next.

"Excuse us a moment." I lead Ira to a bench outside and help him to take deep, slow breaths. "Let's just forget the shelves."

"No!" Ira's voice is raspy, desperate. "We can't."

"Fine. Then let's order online."

"No!" Ira hands me his wallet. "Just go get something."

"But Ira . . ." I begin, the frustration twisting in my stomach. Because sometimes I just want to shake him. Why can't he see it? A shelf won't magically transform us into a bookstore like the one in this shopping center. It's over for us. Time to accept our extinction. Like Linda Coleman apparently has.

But then I look at him: this broken man, who has given me, all of us, all of him.

"Fine," I say, closing my fist around the wallet. I go back inside and slap two hundred dollars out on the counter. "What will this get us?"

What it will get us is metal shelves.

This turns out to be important.

Too Loud a Solitude

The next morning, Ira drops a stack of books on the counter beside me and announces, "First of November. Time to begin a new unit."

"Great," I say, forcing a smile. "What do we have this month?"

"Central Europeans. Communism and kinky sex."

"Sounds fascinating."

In case it's not been made abundantly clear, I was the nerdy book kid growing up, which in our town was like having leprosy. Luckily, there were a handful of other lepers in town, smart, brainy people who didn't regard reading a book as a sign of sexual impotence. They've all left, obviously. Off to college, like I was meant to be. But senior year, we were in the middle of a messy bankruptcy and property transfer, which made applying for financial aid impossible. So I figured I'd take a year, apply again when things were settled.

A lot can change in a year, though. Just ask the dinosaurs. By the time college applications came due again, Sandy was gone. Mom was gone. And Ira, though still physically here, was also gone. Leaving was an impossibility. And besides, by then I owned a bookstore. Job security for life, Ira told me without a speck of irony.

Ira, who had been halfway through a PhD program when he fell in love with Mom and dropped out, insisted I continue my education, college or not. So I now attend the University of Ira. It's an unaccredited school, and offers only one major, but you can't beat the tuition and the professor's so distracted most of the time, he barely notices that his student isn't reading all of the books. Or any of them.

"This is one of my favorites," Ira says, tapping a book on top of the pile called *Too Loud a Solitude* by Bohumil Hrabal.

"What's it about?"

"A garbage collector who rescues books from dumps."

"So, basically, your memoir."

"Ha, ha. It's slim but packs a punch. I think you'll like it."

"Can't wait."

Ira stands there, watching, so I open the book. *For thirty-five years now I've been in wastepaper, and it's my love story*, it begins. The font is tiny and the words skitter across the page the way they did when I was learning to read.

"Good, huh?" Ira is so genuinely excited to share another miracle with me that it makes me feel all the shittier when I reply with a completely insincere: "Tremendous."

Satisfied that I'm fully hooked, Ira returns to his corner and picks up his book. Once he's engrossed in his, I put mine down. I will never read it. I'll peruse some reviews and pull out some quotes and bullshit well enough to make Ira think I have. Two years ago, he would have seen right through me. But if a lot can change in one year, the world can end in two.

%//

Bluebird Books once had a small but devoted group of regulars. These days, we have two. Grover, our mail carrier, and Penny Macklemore, who stops in about once a week.

"Good afternoon," Penny drawls. "And how are we today?" She speaks in the cadence of a kindergarten teacher and wears a sweatshirt emblazoned with slogans like PROFESSIONAL GRAND-MOTHER. But don't be fooled. Penny is a shark with blue-tinted hair that she has set twice a week at the only salon in town, which she happens to own. She also owns the hardware store, the liquor store, the ValuMart, and the used car dealership, where her late husband worked for forty years.

"Doing well, Penny," Ira replies. "And how are you?"

"Fine, fine." Penny stumbles over the pile of fallen books teetering next to the split shelf. "Didn't you say you were getting a new shelf yesterday?"

Yesterday. It feels like ten years ago already. By the time we got home, Ira and I were both so dispirited it was all we could do to drag the flat-pack box to the basement. "Just need to set the shelf up," Ira says.

"Well, do it soon," Penny replies. "This place is a lawsuit waiting to happen."

"Who's going to sue me? You?" He laughs, like it's a joke, and Penny laughs along too. Though I wouldn't put it past her. Penny has made no secret of her desire to own a building on Main Street, a jewel in her small-town *Monopoly* crown. She's also made no secret that she'd like our store to be that jewel. We are smack-dab between C.J.'s Diner and Jimmy's Tavern, prime real estate Penny says is wasted on a bookstore. "I mean, does anybody read anymore?" she asks.

"Storytelling is as old as language, so presumably yes," Ira replies when she poses that question again today.

"Well, if it's stories you're after," Penny drawls, "Netflix has sixteen seasons of *Grey's Anatomy*."

Ira starts to lecture Penny about the primacy of the printed word. Of the particular transportive experience of ink on paper. How, when you watch, you are a spectator, but when you read, you're a participant. "Can *Grey's Anatomy* do that?" he asks, with the authority of someone who has never seen a single episode of that show.

"If you ask me," Penny says, "what people want . . . no, what they *deserve*"—she points out the window to a few such people: a grizzled group of out-of-work lumberjacks on their daily pilgrimage from C.J.'s, where they spend the first half of their day, to Jimmy's, where they spend the second half—"is something useful."

"Every town deserves a bookstore and nothing is more useful than reading." Ira gestures to a fading poster of Frederick Douglass that promises *Once you learn to read, you will be forever free.*

"People learn to read at school, Ira," Penny says. "And this is America. We're already free."

"So I'm told," Ira muses.

Penny gathers up her things. She's halfway out the door when she stops, turns around, and, in a voice that sounds almost sympathetic, says, "Ira, I know you think every town deserves a bookstore, but you ever consider that not every town actually wants one?"

Ira sighs. "Every day of my life."

Our second visitor comes in a couple hours later. Grover used to deliver us boxes of books, copies of *Publishers Weekly* Mom would pore over, thick catalogs full of the next season's offerings that I'd always crack before anyone else, inhaling the papery scent, tabbing books I thought looked good. Back then, Grover would linger, leaning against the porch swing with Mom, gossiping— between the two of them, they knew everything: who'd gotten engaged, who'd been arrested, who was pregnant. These days, he drops the mail like a hot potato, apologizes that he's late, and gets the hell out.

"Anything good?" I ask as Ira leafs through the mail.

"Just junk," he says, dropping everything into the recycling bin. "How's the Hrabal?"

"Great," I reply, even though I have not made it past page four.

After Ira settles back into his easy chair, I stealthily pull today's "junk," and all the rest of the junk beneath it, from the recycling bin and bring it back to the counter to take a look. There are several credit card statements. The first one is maxed-out, with a balance of more than $2,700. I open another one, also at its limit. Same with the third. All three are snowballing astronomical interest charges because Ira has only been making the minimum payments.

My throat closes and I taste them: strawberries, sweet and rotting and right on my tongue even though it's been years since I ate one. I used to gobble them up by the basket, but when I was twelve I popped one in my mouth and my throat went scratchy. I popped in another, and suddenly I couldn't breathe. I was rushed to the ER in anaphylactic shock. It turned out I'd developed what's called a latent allergy. "What a shame," Mom said. "He loves strawberries." To which the doctor had replied, "Unfortunately, sometimes the things we love can also kill us."

No fucking kidding.

I open an IRS notice next; it's in my name, threatening a penalty because apparently I have not filed a tax return. The bank statement brings more bad news: a balance decidedly low on digits. I look at Ira, calmly licking his finger as he turns the page, as if we were not at this very moment on the precipice of financial ruin.

How could he have let this happen? No, that's not fair. I know how Ira let it happen. The question is: How did I?

I gather the bills and shove them in my waistband. Only when the bell over the door rings does Ira look up. "Heading out?"

"Yeah. To see a friend."

Had Ira been paying a mote of attention, he would have known this was bullshit. I no longer have friends. The ones I once had are at college, and when they come back, if they come back, they don't call me. I can't really blame them. We'd always joked it was easy to separate the winners and losers in our town because there were no winners over the age of eighteen. By staying, I guess I joined team loser. The tragic irony of this is that to the people in our town, I've always been team loser.

I jog down Main Street, passing Jimmy's as the lumberjacks

spill out at five, which is when happy hour ends. I turn left on Alder, the only other commercial street downtown, which is where our accountant, Dexter Collings, has his office.

"Aaron," he says as I pound on the door. "I was just closing up."

I thrust the papers at Dexter, breathing hard.

"What's this?" he asks.

"More debt," I reply. "How? Wasn't the bankruptcy meant to wipe that out? And how did Ira get these credit cards?"

Dexter gestures for me to come into his office, which is a little like stepping into a Texas rodeo hall of fame, even though Dexter was born in Bellingham. There's a longhorn bracketed to the wall, a row of cowboy hats on hooks, a bronze statue of a rider with a lasso. He sits down into his big tufted leather chair and thumbs through the bills, humming as he goes.

"What?"

"The hospital bill appears to come from after the bankruptcy, so it was not included in the settlement."

"So we owe that money?"

He nods as he lays that bill down.

"And the tax return?"

"I told your father he had to file. I guess it got away from him." He flips through the credit card statements. "Hmm."

"What?"

"These appear to be recent. It's been a year, so your father was able to apply for new cards. They all have low maximums, at least." He squints at the fine print and whistles. "And high interest rates." He pulls out a bank statement. "How's your cash flow?"

"More like a cash puddle."

21

"Are you making enough each month to cover expenses?"

I shrug. "We don't sell much of anything in the store but Ira says he's been selling off his rare books collection." I try to remember the last time Ira had a shipment for Grover. I can't recall one.

"See this?" Dexter asks, pointing to a deposit on the bank statement for $800, and a charge on the credit card for the same amount. "It looks to me like Ira has been taking cash out of the cards to cover the business expenses."

Oh, Ira.

"This is not sustainable," Dexter adds, as if this is not abundantly obvious.

"What do I do?"

"Find a way to increase your income."

"Trust me, we're trying. Can I get another loan or something? To cover us? Borrow from Peter to pay Paul?"

"The property's pretty leveraged," Dexter says, leafing through the papers, "and because of that, and your age, you're going to have a hard time accessing credit even with the store as collateral."

"Speak English, Dex. I don't know what that means."

"It means you can't borrow from Peter to pay Paul when Peter's broke too. And even if you could . . ." He shuffles the papers together and hands them back. "You'd just be delaying." He trails off. Dex is a nice enough man. He doesn't want to tell me we are dinosaurs, post-asteroid. But I already know that.

"The inevitable?" I finish.

Dexter nods. "I'm sorry."

Sometimes a Great Notion

The store's closed when I get back from Dexter's, so I quietly let myself in. I wander over to the case where Ira's rare collection is housed. It's locked, but he keeps the key in one of the cubby drawers. When I open the door, the shelves are empty.

The starchy odor of pasta cooking upstairs wafts down, but instead of heading up to the apartment, I unlock the basement, flick on the fluorescent lights, and descend the splintering, rickety stairs.

The basement is split in two. The chaotic side of the room contains the messy Mom Jumble: a dozen haphazardly packed boxes of all the stuff she left behind. The sleeve of the rainbow bathrobe we used to call Joseph sticks out of one box. Her Mr. Coffee out of another. The collection of books on addiction she and Ira read together—maybe the one time when books failed him—sits in a crate in the corner next to Mom's ancient Schwinn.

Ira has offered to ship her some of her stuff, but she says she moves around too much. This is true, but I don't think that's the reason. When she left, it was like she needed to amputate herself from every shred of what had been our life. Her clothes, her books, her bike.

Ira.

Me.

The other side of the basement is neat and spartan. On the wall hang a dozen pine bins, locked. The one and only key is in my pocket.

Mom used to say that money problems are really math problems. Rehab stint number one: Sandy's college savings. Wilderness program: a second mortgage on the store. Rehab stint number two: my college savings.

I wonder if Sandy operated by a similar logic. Ten bags of heroin: Mom's SLR camera. Twenty tabs of oxy: my laptop computer. A handful of fentanyl patches: Ira's prized signed first edition of Ken Kesey's *Sometimes a Great Notion*.

I pull the key out of my pocket and open the first bin, which is alphabetically the last, *X–Z*: X, X Ambassadors, X-Ray Spex, XTC. And so on. According to the laminated index nailed to the inside of the door, there are 167 pieces of vinyl in this bin alone, a fraction of Sandy's collection.

I open the other eleven bins, one by one. I run my hand across the top of outer plastic sleeves, sharp, meticulously straight, like a military formation. This is his legacy, the one thing Sandy refused to destroy, the thing he loved more than any of us.

Find a way to increase your income, Dexter said.

There are 2,326 records down here.

Money problems are just math problems, Mom said. I lock the bins and shove the one and only key back in my pocket.

You gotta promise me, Sandy said.

The three voices clash in my head as I climb back to the ash heap of our store. This is my brother's true legacy.

///

But can I do it?

I ask myself this as I sit across from Ira, eating spaghetti from a box with sauce from a jar and parmesan cheese that tastes like sawdust. Can I sell of some Sandy's records to get out of the crater he created? After what he did. After what I did.

"How are your friends?" Ira asks.

It takes me a second to remember Ira thinks I was chilling with friends this afternoon as opposed to hanging out with a CPA.

"Good, good," I lie.

I'll find a music club, the kind full of people like Sandy. I won't sell all of them. Just enough to cover the mortgage payment for a few months, get us back on our feet. A few hundred. He'd barely notice.

(He would totally notice.)

"In fact," I tell Ira, the idea taking root because I guess I *can* do it, "I'm going out with them tonight. If it's okay to take the car."

"Oh, that's nice," he says, even though it's November 2 and even if I still had friends, none would be home on break now.

But that's what Ira does. Trusts people. It's his downfall.

///

The nearest musical venue is a club called the Outhouse, though it's a "club" like the coffee served at C.J.'s is "fine Italian roast." (It's Folgers. I've seen the cans.) It's basically a converted garage with a bare-bones bar and some fold-up plastic tables for merch sales.

I get there and case the joint, pay my cover, then come back to the Volvo, lift the hatch, pull out a crate, and set it on the curb. I can't bring it inside. It weighs a ton. But what am I supposed to do? Announce "Vinyl for sale" like the salesman in *Caps for Sale*, the first book Ira says he ever read to me (in utero, the day Mom's pregnancy test came back positive)? Do I flash my goods, like those guys in movies who hide a trove's worth of stolen jewels in their trench coats? Given it's mostly women hanging outside the club, I'm not sure how well that would go down. Do women even collect records, or is it more of a guy thing? Like serial killing.

If Sandy were here, he'd know exactly what to do. He had Ira's memory for things like printings and value. Not to mention his radar. We'd be driving and he'd shout to stop the car at a particular yard sale, even though it looked like the dozens of similar ones we'd just passed. But Sandy somehow knew that at this sale, behind the rusted lawnmower, would be a box of records, and in that box, amid the Andrea Bocellis and Barry Manilows, a rare ten-inch bootleg of the Who. From inside the club, I hear the feedbacky blare of guitar. My head starts to throb. What was I thinking? I *can't* do this. For so many reasons. I open the hatch, replace the crate, and lay the blanket on top of it.

"Hey, I know you."

I turn around but don't see anyone.

"Down here, dawg."

And that's when I see Chad Santos. Chad was a couple grades ahead of me in school, one of those beery, cheery snowboarder bros who went around high-fiving and saying things like, "Just living my best life." A few years ago, Chad flew off a cliff while snowboarding, broke his back, and wound up in a wheelchair. Not living his best life anymore, is he?

"You here to see Beethoven's Anvil?" Chad asks.

"The what now?"

"Beethoven's Anvil." Chad grins. "I've never seen any other guy from our town at one of their gigs."

"Oh, I'm not here to see them." I try to close the hatch, but Chad has angled himself in the way. "Sorry, do you mind?"

Chad peers into the Volvo. "What you got there?"

"Nothing."

Chad reaches in and pulls off the blanket. "Those records?"

"No."

"They look like records."

"I mean, they are. But they're not mine."

"Are they Sandy's?"

At the mention of my brother's name, my heart ricochets, as if someone has reached into my chest and yanked it.

"You are Sandy's brother, right?" Chad asks. "Sorry, I don't remember your name."

When I don't answer, Chad sticks out his hand. He's wearing high-tech fingerless gloves, fraying at the seams. "I'm Chad."

"I'm Aaron," I manage.

"Aaron, right. Man, I can't remember the last time I saw you."

I can. Junior year. I was walking home from school with Susanna Dyerson. We'd bonded over our mutual love of *The Sorrows of Young Werther* and our literary talks had progressed to makeout sessions in the woods, which was where we were headed when Chad and his bros drove by, pelting me with empty beer cans. It was, as things went back then, a minor humiliation. Except then Susanna suddenly remembered she had to go home and after that she just wanted us to be friends.

"Always a pleasure catching up with you, Chad." There's enough sarcasm in my voice to peel the enamel off my teeth, but Chad doesn't seem to notice. He just grins and bobs his head and refuses to get out of the way.

"So if you're not here for Beethoven's Anvil, tell me you're not here for the Silk Stranglers?" He shakes his head in profound disappointment. "They're trash."

"I'm not here to see Silk Strangers or the Beethoven's Hammer."

"Anvil," Chad corrects.

"Them either."

He cocks his head to the side. "Then what are you doing here?"

"Leaving." I close the hatch and pull my keys out from my pocket, maneuvering around Chad. "Good seeing you," I lie. "Take care."

"Hold up, dawg." Chad wheels after me. "Why don't you stick around? Beethoven's Anvil is high-key cool. And tell you what, if you don't like them, I'll pay you back your cover charge." I step to the right, unsure why Chad is being so insistent, except maybe to prank me. Chad angles his chair to his left, blocking my way. "You're gonna love them."

"What makes you say that?"

"Well, you're Sandy's brother, aren't you?"

I was. But not anymore. And never like that.

"See you around, Chad." I push past him, forcefully, and get into the car. When I drive away, he's still on the pavement. I watch him grow smaller in the rearview mirror.

When I get home, I can't bring myself to stop. When I was younger Sandy told me that the books came to life at night. He meant to frighten me, but I was enthralled by the idea. It's only now that I'm older, and know it's not true, that it *does* scare me.

I keep going, down Main Street, past Jimmy's, all the way to the other side of town, to the used car lot. The inflatable balloon that dances manically all day is now slumped in a corner. I loop back on Oak Ridge Boulevard, the main commercial drag outside of downtown, where the ValuMart is. It too is dark, the carts tucked in for the night. I keep driving, not realizing where I'm going until I see the hardware store, a small light on in the back.

I park on the empty street and walk through the misty night. It's almost ten when I tap on the locked door, but Penny Macklemore answers right away, smiling, as if she's been expecting me all along.

The Rules

My parents met because of books. I exist because of books. Really.

Ira had discovered the miracle of twenty-six letters so precociously that when in sixth grade all the students had to stand up and claim what they wanted to do when they grew up, Ira announced he wanted to read. His teacher told him that wasn't a job, unless he wanted to become a literature professor. Ira was halfway through a PhD program in comparative lit when he realized that a love of books did *not* equal a love of academia. He hated the politics in his department, the squabbling, the push to publish. He didn't want to publish. He wanted to read. Maybe his sixth-grade teacher had been right, and that wasn't a job.

Ira drove cross-country, hoping to figure out what he wanted to do. He stopped at every thrift store, every estate sale, every library sale he came across, collecting books all the way. By the time he'd reached the northwestern tip of Washington, he had about four hundred books—and no idea what to do with his life. He was on the verge of surrendering back to his program when he saw this woman hitchhiking by the side of the road.

By July, they were married. By September, they'd bought a

two-story building on the main street of a small mountain town, with an apartment upstairs and a retail space on the ground floor that they'd sell used books from—those four hundred volumes Ira had amassed would be the inaugural inventory. But right as they were about to open, Mom thought maybe they ought to know a bit more about what they were doing, so she went to what would be the first of many trade shows. That year, all anyone could talk about was a book called *The Rules*, a sort of retro dating guide that instructed single women how to land a man by essentially hiding all their less-desirable traits until there was a ring on the finger and it was presumably too late to turn back. Mom had a hunch and ordered twenty copies, which sold out almost immediately.

Mom used to joke that she pulled a Rules on Ira, luring him into opening a used bookstore full of dusty classics he could collect, only to make him sell contemporary hits like *The Rules* and *Twilight*. But as long as Mom handled all the new books and chatted up the customers, Ira was happy to continue collecting the rare editions and be the human algorithm.

"Yin and Yang," was how Mom put it.

"Eros and Thanatos," was how Ira put it.

See?

For some reason, I'm thinking about *The Rules* a few nights later when I return from the signing at Penny's office. Probably because it's pouring rain, as it will continue to pour rain for the next six to eight months. If anything, it was the Northwest weather that Rulesed Ira.

The year he met Mom had been one of those magical summers when the sun arrives early to the party in May and staggers home, the last to leave, halfway through October. By the time the weather showed its true colors—which is to say singular color, which is to say gray—it was November, and Bluebird Books was up and running. The ring was solidly on the finger.

Ira never loved the dark, gray winters, but after the asteroid, when Yin lost its Yang, when Thanatos went solo, they became unendurable. He's always cold now, even in summer. The wet gets into his bones. He complains of aching joints, suffers a constant hoarse cough. He sleeps in mittens and thick wool socks. And every night he soaks his feet in the bathtub, trying to get rid of the chill.

This is where I find him tonight, huddled on the ledge of the tub, wrapped in his old Pendleton blanket. When we get out of here, I will take us somewhere warm, where the sun hangs stubbornly in the sky no matter what the calendar dictates. I will reverse-Rules Ira. Trick him into moving somewhere where he will be warm, and if not happy, a little bit less sad.

"Ira, I need to tell you something," I say right as the landline starts to ring.

"Can you get that?" Ira calls. "It might be your mother."

Of course it's Mom. Who else calls on the landline anymore?

I decided not tell Ira what I was going to do before it was done.

I wanted it to be too late to turn back. Now it is. And I have to tell him. "I need to speak to you. Now."

"Can you get the phone first?" We disconnected the answering machine, so the phone continues to ring. She knows we're home.

"It's important."

"Your mother is important." He says this with all sincerity, no bitterness. He believes we're still a family. Just a different kind of family.

"Fine," I grouse. I grab the extension from the kitchen, pick up with a sigh. "Hey, Mom."

"Aaron, my love . . ."

I've read stories about how grief or trauma changes people overnight. Black hair goes gray. Smooth skin goes wrinkled. With Mom, it was her voice. Always strong and clear, if unapologetically off-key when she sang, which was often. The woman on the other end of the line, however, sounds like an old lady, even though Mom's not yet fifty.

I hear dogs barking in the background. The dogs are new. Which means she's moved again.

"Where are you now?"

"Silver City, New Mexico, taking care of two dogs, five parakeets, and a pair of cats. The cats are feral, so I just leave them food."

That's what she does now, bounces from place to place, petsitting. The last time I talked to her, she was minding an epaulette shark in a giant three-hundred-gallon home aquarium in Orlando, Florida.

"How are you feeling, my love?" she asks.

Penny had a fancy fountain pen for me to sign with, but I couldn't quite seem to get the angle right and there's a big ink spot on my thumb. I wipe it on my jeans, but it only smears. How I'm feeling is like Lady Macbeth.

"Good, good."

"And how are things in the store?"

"Same as always," I say, and though this is nearly always true—Ira's and my routine is unflaggingly, well, routine—tonight it's a blatant fiction.

There's an awkward pause. In the background, I can hear the birdsong.

"What are you reading these days?" Mom asks. In our family, this question is small talk, along the lines of *How's the weather?*

"Ira's reading West Indian authors and he has me on the Central Europeans."

"The writers with only consonants in their names?"

"Those are the ones. What's Silver City like?" I hear the glug of the tub draining, meaning Ira is almost done and I can get off the phone.

"The locals call it Silver. It's nice. A lot of sunshine."

Ira pads into the room, his feet bare, his toes long and finger-like, white with black hair. He gives me a kiss, his untamed beard tickling my neck. I hand him the phone without saying goodbye.

Her voice fills the air. She's still talking to me when Ira lifts the phone to his ear. "Hi, Annie. It's me now."

"When you get off, I need to speak to you," I tell Ira.

He nods. "Did you lock up downstairs?"

"Everything's taken care of."

He heads toward his bedroom, cradling the handset, tracking wet footprints on the wood. Before he goes into his room, he turns back to me and says, "Thanks for being you."

This is what he always says to me. And normally I reply, courtesy of Oscar Wilde, "Everyone else was taken." It's our long-standing schtick, but tonight, knowing what I just did, I can't bear to say it.

The Giving Tree

Ira winds up staying on the phone with Mom late into the night, so I don't have a chance to talk to him. The next morning, when he comes down to open the store, he's wrecked, his beard seems grayer, his posture more stooped, his thin frame even more depleted.

When I see him like this, I can't help thinking he's the human incarnation of *The Giving Tree*, not just because he's tall and lanky but because everyone keeps taking chunks out of him. For the life of me I never understood why we housed that book in the children's section. It belongs in self-help, along with all the other books about dysfunctional relationships. Or maybe in horror.

The steady soaking rain kept up all night, and this morning a new leak has sprung in the ceiling. I fetch another saucepan to catch the runoff, but as I go hunting for a tarp to cover the books, Ira trips over the pan, sending it flying into his shin. "Goddammit!" he yelps, hopping on one foot.

"Sorry," I say.

"Why are you sorry? You don't control the rain, do you?"

"If only," I reply. "Can I get you some tea?"

"I'll get it myself." But on the way to the kettle, he bangs into the pile of books that are still on the floor after the shelf collapsed. He yelps again. When he finally gets settled into his chair, he spills the tea all over his lap. "I seem to have woken up on the wrong side of the bed," he says, going upstairs to change. He comes back down with his sweater on backward, but I don't have the heart to tell him. Nor do I have the heart to tell him what I did last night. Better to wait until he's on more solid ground.

There are a lot of heavy sighs, a bit of mild groaning. Finally Ira says: "If you don't mind watching the store, I think I'll go for a walk to clear my head."

"Sure. Go for it." Ira often takes "walks"—which I'm pretty sure is a euphemism for smoking pot—when he gets agitated. He tries to keep it from me, maybe because he thinks I'd judge him for it. If it was anyone else, maybe I would. But Ira I begrudge nothing. And anyway, he's almost always calmer when he returns.

"When you get back, I want to talk to you," I add.

"Okay," he says, reaching for his rain jacket, a bright yellow slicker like the kind I had in elementary school.

Thirty seconds later, he's back. "What'd you forget?" Ira has always been a bit of the absentminded professor, but these days, he's constantly misplacing his keys, his glasses, his shoes.

"Some fellow down on the sidewalk asking for you."

"Send him in."

"Can't. He's in a wheelchair."

"Chad? What's he want?"

Ira shrugs. I follow him outside to the sidewalk, where Chad greets me with an elaborate high-five-fist-bump thing that I bungle.

"What are you doing here?" I ask when the handshake finally peters out.

"Is that how you greet your paying customers?"

Chad being a customer did not even occur to me. "Oh, sorry. Did you want a book?"

"Sure, what you got?"

"We're a bookstore, Chad. We have a vast variety of books."

"Even comic books?"

"Even those. Do you have a specific one in mind?"

Chad strokes the part of his chin where a beard would be if he had a beard. "Wonder Woman?"

"Any particular issue?"

"Whatever you got."

"Anything else? Aside from the Wonder Woman?"

"Well, I would like to come and peruse your vast variety of books, only how am I gonna get into your store?" He gestures to the stairs.

"Uh, right. Sorry about that."

Chad rolls himself forward and backward, leaning back as if to pop a wheelie. The wet leaves squish under his tires. Then, casual as can be, he says, "If you had a ramp, I could come check things out for myself."

"Yeah. We should probably have a ramp." I say this absently, politely, and insincerely.

But it's enough for Chad. "You know, I have a piece of plywood at my house that might work."

"Uh-huh," I say, watching Ira walk down Main Street.

"It used to be a skateboarding ramp and now it just sits there, because, you know, I can't skate anymore." Chad flutters his eyelashes, pitifully. "You know, because I'm paralyzed."

"Sorry about that."

"You could come take a look at it," Chad continues.

"Uh-huh," I say again as Ira grows smaller. Soon he will disappear. I should just run after him. Get it over with.

"Use it for a ramp."

"Uh-huh."

"Sa-weet," Chad says. "Let's go."

"Go? Go where?"

"To my place. To get the wood. For the ramp."

"What ramp?"

"The one you just said you'd put in."

"I don't think I said that."

"Sure you did. Just a second ago. Let's go."

"Now?"

"You got something else to do?"

I follow Ira's slicker as he turns onto Alder, out of sight. The weight of what I have set in motion thuds in my stomach. "Come on then," Chad says.

I look down Main Street. Back at the empty shop. "Let me lock up." I pause, wondering if I should leave a note because Ira never checks his phone. "How long will this take?"

"Only a few minutes." And because I don't yet know Chad, I believe him. So I lock the door and don't leave a note and follow Chad to his Dodge Ram. It's jacked so high off the ground that an able-bodied person would need a stepladder to get in, and I'm puzzling how he manages it when he says, "Wanna see something rad?"

"Uh, okay."

Chad opens the driver's-side door and pulls out a small box that looks like an old Xbox console. He presses a button, which lowers a platform that he wheels onto. He presses another button and is lifted to the cab. He scoots into the driver's seat and folds his wheelchair before pressing another button to maneuver a pulley that hooks the chair and lifts it to the truck bed. The entire operation takes about a minute.

"You coming or what?" Chad calls.

I clamber to the passenger side and haul myself into the seat with far less grace. As we head toward his house, he shows me how he controls everything—gas, brakes—from the steering wheel. "The town did a GoFundMe so I could retrofit my truck. Cost five grand. Pretty sweet, right?"

"Yeah, sweet," I say bitterly.

When we arrive at Chad's ranch-style house he points me toward the backyard, where, under a tarp, is his old skateboard ramp. He positions himself under the patio awning.

"Are you going to help?" I ask.

"I can't go over there. It's too muddy. My chair'll get stuck. I'll direct from here. It'll be a piece of cake."

It's not a piece of cake. It's a plate of barbed wire. Having not thought to bring gloves, I tear up my hands pulling nails out of the plywood plank. Having not thought to bring a jacket, I get soaked to the boxers. At one point, I'm yanking the plank toward the truck when I slide in a patch of mud, landing flat on my ass.

Chad cracks up, naturally. In the echo of his laugher, I hear Sandy's. And then I hear the whole damn town laughing at me.

Soon, I remind myself as I stand up. Soon I will never have to see any of these fuckers again.

⁂

When we get back to the store, Ira is in full meltdown mode because Chad's ten minutes multiplied, meaning I have left the store locked and unmanned during business hours and stranded Ira outside without his phone. He's pacing the porch with that wild-man manic energy, his beard sticking out at all angles like he stuck his finger in a socket. "I'm sorry," I shout, jumping out of the truck before Chad has pulled to a stop. "I'm sorry."

"Where did you go? I knocked and knocked and no one answered and I thought . . ." He trails off.

His entire body is trembling. I hold him tight, trying to approximate his weighted blanket. Dried mud cracks in the embrace. "I'm sorry."

"My bad, Mr. Stein," Chad calls as he lowers himself from his truck into his chair. "Aaron offered to build a ramp to your store!"

"You did?" Ira asks, solicitous even in his panic.

"We got the wood in the truck and everything," Chad says, gesturing to the sagging bit of plywood sticking out of the bed. "We just have to pull a bit of railing down. Then maybe bolster it with a few bricks, bracket it in place. Easy-peazy."

"You didn't mention the railing," I tell Chad. "Or the bolstering and bracketing."

41

"What'd you think we were gonna do? Just lean the plank against the stairs?"

I don't say anything because that's exactly what I thought we were going to do.

"And we'll need to take that down." Chad points to the blue-and-yellow porch swing where Mom used to sit no matter the weather, calling to people. Invariably, they'd come up to chat with her and wind up in the store. Ira used to call her the Siren. "He definitely didn't mention taking the porch swing down," I tell Ira. I turn to Chad. "I think we should forget the ramp."

"But we brought the wood over."

"So bring it back."

"Ah, dawg. My mom will kill me. That ramp's been sitting in our backyard, splintering, making her miserable. So when you suggested a ramp—"

"I didn't suggest a ramp," I interrupt.

"I thought how great to repurpose the wood, and make your store wheelchair accessible. Plus, you'd make my mom happy." He turns to Ira. "The sight of the wood just really bums her out, Mr. Stein. She says it's like a constant reminder of what I lost."

Sometimes the porch swing creaks, like Mom's still on it. But it's just the wind.

"I can understand that," Ira says, staring at the swing, tugging nervously at his beard.

"So by putting in a ramp, you'd be doing my mom a solid, repurposing this wood, *and* making your store welcoming and accessible. It would be, like, a triple mitzvah."

At this Ira and I gape at each other, neither one of us sure if we heard right. A mitzvah is a Jewish thing that literally means "blessing" but translates as "good deed." I'm not sure I've ever heard anyone here use that word, much less a Best-Life Bro like Chad. In case it has not been made abundantly clear, there are not a lot of Jewish people in our neck of the woods.

I don't trust Best-Life Bros like Chad, even if they're in wheelchairs, and down with a bit of Yiddish. I've lived in this town long enough to know better. But Ira, the Giving Tree, would never deny a mitzvah, and I will never deny Ira.

And this is how we get a ramp.

Peanuts

We are about two hours into our doomed construction project when the Lumberjacks arrive. In those two hours, I have managed to pry off some spindles, saw a section of railing, and angle the plank against the ledge of the porch. I've sent a shivering Ira inside to warm up and am just about to send Chad packing when a few of the guys, making their daily trek from C.J.'s to Jimmy's, decide to stop in front of our shop.

The oldest codger—his name, I will learn, is Ike Sturgis—approaches. He has a long brown beard that gives Ira's a run for its money, and is weathered in the way a lot of guys who worked on the mountain are, which makes it impossible to tell just how old he is. He could be forty. He could be ninety.

"What you got going on here?" he asks in a whiskey-barrel voice.

"We're putting in a ramp," Chad says.

"A ramp, you say?" He taps the corner of the wood with the edge of his boot. "With this?"

"Must be a temporary plank. For fit," says another of the Lumberjacks, who's ruddy-faced and appears to be about six months pregnant with beer. Minus the gut, he looks exactly like this asshole named Caleb who Sandy used to hang out with.

"That's what I'd assume, Garry," Ike replies before turning to Chad and me. "'Cause you boys wouldn't think of using *plywood* for a ramp, would you?"

"Well, yeah, I mean, we were, right, Aaron?"

Thanks for throwing me under the bus, Chad. "It was *his* idea."

"Richie, you wanna explain to these fellows why this plank won't work?" Ike says.

"Uhh, 'cause it's plywood," replies Richie, who can't be more than a few years older than me, which would make him too young to ever have worked on the mountain or in the mills.

"And rotting plywood at that." Ike steps hard on the ramp; it cracks. "Ain't gonna bear much weight."

"I used to skate on it," Chad says. "It worked out fine."

"Different uses," Ike explains. "You gotta wear-pattern problem. Skateboard's traveling all over that wood, back and forth. In a chair, wheels going up and down in the same track. More concentrated pressure. Basic physics."

"Well, I failed physics," Chad says.

"Me too," Richie says.

And then the two of them share a bonding high five to commemorate their mutual failure. Our town, ladies and gentlemen, in a nutshell.

Ike shoves a wad of tobacco into his lower lip and spits into an empty bottle of Diet Peach Snapple. "Garry, what happened to the extra pine we used for your loft?"

"Nothing," replies Garry. "Planks are just sitting in Joe Heath's place."

"You think there's enough for a ramp?"

There's the sudden *shzz* sound as Garry whips out his measuring tape. He crouches and squints as he sizes up the distance to the sidewalk. "Couple of twelve-by-twelves. Think so."

"That weathered old pine really stands the test of time," Ike says.

"Stained up real nice so you can see the grain," Garry replies.

"This plywood's got no business being anywhere but a scrap pile," Ike says.

Garry agrees.

They talk about the wood a bit longer among themselves, not saying another word to me, or to Chad, who by bringing in this inferior specimen of wood has been knocked down a peg or two. Not quite as far down as me, but nearly. After a few minutes of this, they zip up their measuring tapes and carry on down Main Street.

The substandard plank is still leaning precariously against the railing. And it's all so pathetic. Like anything that touches our store turns to rot. I was over it before we started on this project, but now I really am. And, soon enough, all this will be Penny's problem.

Chad clears his throat. I spin around and glare at him for inventing all this trouble today when I have more than enough without his help.

"We done?" I ask him.

He opens his mouth as if to say something, but before he can, I'm heading up the stairs, answering on his behalf. We're done.

///

Inside, Ira has fallen asleep in his chair. I cover him with a blanket and check my email. I have contacted a few bulk book buyers about purchasing the entire collection. A few have written back, asking for an inventory, which we don't have, but I can estimate. They don't pay much, dimes on the dollar, but it'll give us some income, as will the money from the sale of the building. Not a lot, but it'll be enough to get out of here, away from the rain and the rot, the Lumberjacks and Best-Life Bros. Away from it all.

///

Ira's still asleep when a pickup truck pulls up, its phlegmy engine rattling. I pay it no mind until I hear voices out front. Garry and Richie are hauling two giant planks of wood from the bed of a truck. They're trailed by Chad—who either left and came back, or never left—and Ike, who's gripping a toolbox that makes Chad's look like a jewelry box.

"What's going on?" I ask.

"What's going on," Richie says, as he and Garry start pulling down the plywood ramp that we just built, "is we're gonna build you a real ramp."

Real ramp. Chad winces.

"Hold up. We never discussed this," I say.

"What are you talking about?" Ike says. "We spent a good twenty minutes discussing it."

"No, *you* discussed it. With each other."

Ike taps his nose, which is crooked, like it's been busted on more than one occasion.

"You never asked me if it was okay," I tell him. "Or my father."

"You'd rather have a flimsy piece of plywood than these nice rough-cut boards?" Ike asks.

"I'd rather have none of it!"

"But how's your friend here gonna get in the store?"

"Chad," clarifies Chad right as I say, "I hardly know him."

"How's Chad, who you hardly know, gonna get in your store?" Ike asks.

The same way he's always gotten in. By not coming in.

"We got all the equipment here," Ike says, scraping his work boot against the pavement.

"But you never asked. And we can't pay for it."

"Who said anything about paying for anything?"

Does he think I'm an idiot? Does he think I don't recognize a Lucy when I see one? The joke's on you, bub, because I grew up with the worst Lucy of them all.

Lucy, by the way, is from *Peanuts*. When me and Sandy were kids, we loved those comics. Sandy got a particular thrill out of that running gag where Lucy holds the football for Charlie Brown and every time he runs to kick it, she yanks it away at the last minute and he winds up on his back. He thought it was just so funny that Charlie Brown fell for it, over and over again. This was a sign, I guess, but I was too young or too in awe of my older brother to heed it. Not even a few years later, when Sandy got cooler and then crueler and started doing things like inviting me to come into his room only to pants me while his friend Caleb snapped a picture. Or begging me to hang out with him and watch TV all day Saturday, only to spend Sunday pretending I didn't exist.

It took me a long time, much longer than it should have, to realize Sandy was Lucy. And I was Charlie Brown. But I'm not as stupid as I once was, so I tell Ike we won't be needing any of his ramp-building services.

And maybe that would have been the end of it. But then Ira shuffles barefoot onto the porch, blinking awake from his nap. "There you are," he says dopily before turning toward the sidewalk assemblage and nodding. "Hello, Ike."

"Ira," Ike replies tersely.

"What brings you here? Need a book?"

"If it's all right by you, we're gonna fix this ramp up proper."

Ira blinks, twice, still not fully awake. "Oh, sure." He goes back inside, without even thinking about it. Without even asking me.

Ike smirks, as if that settles it. But it settles nothing. Ira's not even the legal owner of the store. And in another month, neither will I be.

It hits me, belatedly, that Penny might not want a wheelchair ramp. But she definitely will not want the shoddy one we half built. And after years of being Lucied, maybe it's time for me to yank the football. So I tell Ike to fix the ramp. "Just don't expect me to pay for it."

For the next few hours, I listen to the sound of hammering, sawing, man sounds coming from outside while inside I stew. Because I know the other shoe is going to drop. They'll come in here in a few hours extorting large sums of money.

At five, Ira heads upstairs to make dinner, so it's just me in the store when Ike returns, just like I knew he would. And I'm ready for him. I've already put aside a twenty, enough for two happy-hour pitchers at Jimmy's. But that's *all* he's getting from me.

"We're outa dayli . . ." Ike begins, the rest of the sentence dying on his lips as he surveys the store: the teetering piles of books, the saucepans of water, the bruise-like stains on the ceiling.

When Ike sees the collapsed shelf, he gasps. He runs his hands down the crack, frowning so deeply the furrows in his face could collect water. "Is this mahogany?"

I shrug. "I guess so."

"Wood like that don't splinter without a reason."

"If you say so."

"You gonna fix it?"

"Replace it. We have metal shelves in the basement."

Ike literally shudders. "You can't replace that beauty with metal. Maybe we could—"

And here it is. The revised bid. The yanked football. "Thank you for your help," I cut him off, sliding the twenty across the counter, meeting his eye with my best tough-guy look.

Ike stares at the money, turns back toward the shelf. Then he shakes his head and, without touching the money, without saying another word, leaves.

Gone Girl

I'm closing up the following night when Chad rolls in.

"What are you doing here?" I ask.

"Wow. You really need to improve your customer-service experience." He looks around the store. "Thought I'd test out the ramp. It works." He makes jazz hands, his callused fingers poking out from his gloves.

"Good to know." I pause. "If that's all, we're closing."

"Uhh, what about that book?"

"What book?"

"*The Wonder Woman*?"

Right. The book. Yesterday turned into such a clusterfuck that I wound up not telling Ira about selling the store. I planned to tell him all day today but he was distracted and out of sorts, so now it's got to be tonight.

"Do you have it?" Chad asks.

Sighing, I dig under what used to be our well-organized graphic novel/media section to find a couple of Batgirl issues. "Will these do?"

Chad shrugs. "Why not?"

"You want both? They're two bucks each."

Chad nods, reaching into a satchel attached to his chair. It's black and covered in skater patches. He undoes one of the Velcro pockets and pulls out a five. "Keep the change."

"Thanks." I put the bill in the cash register, but Chad's still waiting. I open the door for him, figuring he might need help, but he just waits there.

"Least I could do for all the trouble you went through to put in that ramp," he says.

"Whatever. It's fine." I'm not mad anymore. I'm just tired. And nervous. I can hear Ira padding around upstairs. I can feel the weight of what I have to tell him.

"Umm . . ." Chad rolls back and forth, his version of pacing, I will learn. "I gotta confession to make."

"What?" I ask.

"See, the thing is . . . I didn't come here for a comic book."

"Did you want something else?" This happens, or used to happen, a surprising amount. Guys coming in making a lot of noise about political biographies they heard about but then quietly asking if we also happen to have that *Fifty Shades of Grey* book.

"I didn't come for any book," Chad says.

"What'd you come for?"

"So, this is gonna sound mad shady . . ."

I get that feeling, that midair, about-to-land-on-my-back, Charlie Brown dread.

"And like I'm hella sly," Chad continues, "which I am, but that's not what happened yesterday."

"What happened yesterday?"

"See, the reason I came over was not to buy a comic book or any book or even because I wanted a ramp." Chad inspects a stain on his pants with great interest. "I came over because after I saw you at the gig the other night I wanted to see if you wanted to go to another Beethoven's Anvil gig. I thought you could try to sell your brother's records again."

"I'm not selling his records."

"Oh. Well, either way, I thought you might want to come with me tomorrow night, which is now tonight. Right now in fact."

I let that settle for a moment, unsure if I heard right. "You conned me into building a ramp because you wanted me to go to a music show with you?"

"*Con* is a strong word, wouldn't you say?"

"Is it, Chad? Is it? I wrecked my hands." I hold out my swollen fists. "And we got all the Lumberjacks involved and I'm pretty sure they're going to shake me down for it."

Chad chuckles. "Yeah, things did kinda spin out of control, but it's cool you have a ramp because now I can come visit you and I'm sorry I didn't just ask you if you wanted to come to the gig, but I was worried you'd say no."

"*You* were scared *I'd* say no?"

Chad shrugs. "I don't have a lot of friends left in town, you know. And I've sure as shit never seen anyone I know at a Beethoven's Anvil show."

"I wasn't at the show! And Chad, you and I are not friends. We've never been friends."

"Harsh!"

"You want harsh? You threw a beer can at me! From a moving

53

car. I was walking with a girl I liked and who liked me back but after that she didn't."

"Oh, man, I cockblocked you . . . ?" I wait for Chad to laugh. To tell me to lighten up. Take a joke. That it's ancient history. That I should put it in perspective because he's in a wheelchair. But he just stares at his lap, shaking his head. "I used to be a real tool." He looks up at me. "I'm really sorry."

The apology catches me completely off guard. "It's okay. It was a long time ago."

"That it was," Chad says solemnly. "Anyhow, I won't bug you anymore. I'm sorry about the ramp. And your hands. And the beer can. And, you know, all of it."

He heads toward the door, shoulders slumped. He looks so pathetic. And Ira, well, I can tell him tomorrow.

"Hey, Chad," I call.

He turns around.

"Let me grab my jacket."

It's only when we're zipping down the interstate, forty miles out of town, that the rest of Chad's confession comes out. "So," he says casually. "The club we're going to, Maxwell's, it has some issues."

"What kind of issues?"

"Like a couple of stairs."

"A couple?"

"Maybe a flight."

"A *flight* of stairs?" I pause. "How are we supposed to get you up a flight of stairs?"

"Down, actually."

"How are we supposed to get you *down* a flight of stairs?"

"That part's easy," Chad says. "You ask Hannah."

"Who's Hannah?"

"Hannah Crew. She's the lead singer of Beethoven's Anvil. And she's awesome."

"Awesome as in so physically strong she's going to carry you down the stairs?"

Chad laughs at this. "Man, that would be sweet, but she's like five-two. Naw, but she'll find people who will. Trust me. She does it all the time. All you have to do is go into the club, find her, ask her, and the rest is gravy."

"Is *this* why you came by the store? Not to invite me to go to the show but to trick me into getting you carried into the club?"

Chad grins. "*Trick* is a strong word, wouldn't you say?"

"How about *bamboozle*? *Hoodwink*? *Dupe*?"

"You have an impressive vocabulary, dawg. I bet you aced your SATs."

I got 740 on the reading section, not that it did me any good.

"You're an unreliable narrator, you know that?" I tell him.

"Is that like the guy who narrates the telenovela on *Jane the Virgin*?"

"It's when the person telling you the story is maybe not telling you the entire truth. Sometimes it's because they can't see it themselves. But other times it's because they are trying to deceive you."

"Oh, you mean like Amy in *Gone Girl*?"

"You've read *Gone Girl*?" I ask, impressed, because Amy is exactly what I mean by unreliable narrator.

"It was a book? I thought it was a movie."

"It was a book *before* it was a movie."

"Oh. Didn't know that." Chad drums a little beat on the steering wheel. "Look, I get that recent evidence makes me seem like a grade-A douche, but I really did want to hang with you. I was bummed you didn't stick around the other night. And you'll dig the band."

"I doubt it. I don't really get into music like other people do."

"Well, you might not get into music, but you're gonna love Beethoven's Anvil."

Chad will turn out to be right. About this, and so much more.

///

Chad drops me off in front of the club, instructing me to find this Hannah and tell her that he's upstairs. He promises she'll take care of the rest. After I pay my cover and get my hand stamped I realize Chad has not told me *how* to find Hannah or even what she looks like. The club is dark, cavernous, and full of music hipsters. I could not feel more out of place if it were full of Elvis impersonators.

I try asking the bartender but I can't even get his attention. I try asking someone at the merch table but no matter how loud I yell, he can't hear me. The whole thing is making me nervous, which in turn is making me have to pee. I'm looking for the bathrooms when all of a sudden a door swings open and on the other side of it I see a girl quietly reading a book, as if this were a library, not a music club.

A strange little tingle shimmies up my spine.

And then I see *what* she's reading. *The Magician's Nephew.*

Officially this is the sixth volume in the Chronicles of Narnia, but it really is the first. Lewis wrote it as a prequel. Everyone's read *The Lion, the Witch and the Wardrobe*, but only the hardcore fans get to book six.

The tingle spreads out through my entire body.

When Ira stopped for Mom all those years ago, she nearly didn't get in the car. Ira had been on the road for four weeks, and looked it: unruly beard, haunted eyes, back seat full of books and food wrappers. "He was throwing off some serious Charles Manson vibes," Mom said. She almost bolted, but something stopped her. And that something was a song.

"As soon as I heard it, I got this whole-body feeling," Mom used to tell me. "I know it sounds crazy but it was like a message from future me to present me, telling me that in some way, this man and I, we weren't just *bound* to happen, that we had, in some sense, already happened. It felt . . . inevitable."

I stare at this girl, reading this book, my heart thundering so loud she must hear it. Because she looks up. She has dark brown eyes and a constellation of freckles across the bridge of her nose. "Can I help you?"

I remember why I'm there. "Sorry, I'm looking for Hannah. Hannah Crew."

She puts the book down. "Then you're looking for me."

My ears start to ring, the way they will after every Beethoven's Anvil show I ever go to.

Inevitable.

Oh, fuck!

※

For once, Chad has not exaggerated, and Hannah does exactly what he promised. She corrals a bunch of guys to carry him and his chair down the stairs and then personally pushes him through the crowd, situating us right next to the speaker.

"Can you make a buffer for these two?" she asks the people around us. "In case the pit gets too wild." They say yes. I will come to find that people always say yes to Hannah.

"Unless you wanna crowd-surf me," Chad says, grinning at the attention. "Wouldn't say no to that."

"No, I doubt you would," Hannah says. "Come find us back-stage when you're ready to go and we'll get you back out."

"Thanks, Hannah," Chad says, nudging me in the ribs. "Say thank you."

"Thank you," I repeat.

"Anytime," Hannah replies, and then she leaps, almost balleti-cally, like the cheerleader I will learn she once was, onto the stage.

Chad watches her go. "Amazing, right?"

My ears are ringing like mad. My heart is palpitating. I feel sick. There's no way this girl is my inevitable. No matter what she's reading. And anyway, even if she were, I don't want her to be. I've learned inevitable only ever bites you in the ass.

"Can I have your keys?" I ask Chad. "I'll wait in the truck."

"Why?"

"I really don't wanna be here. I mean, I'm happy to get you in and all but I'd rather not watch the show."

Chad stares at me. "What's your problem, dawg?"

"Nothing! I told you, music isn't my thing."

"How do you know something's not your thing if you've never experienced it?"

"I *have* experienced music."

"But not *this* music."

"I haven't experienced waterboarding, either, but I can confidently say that I wouldn't enjoy it."

Chad sulks. "I wouldn't have asked you to come just for the ride. I thought you wanted to hear the band."

"I didn't. I don't. I just did it as a favor to you."

"Next time, spare me your pity."

"Can I have the keys? I'll keep my phone on if you need anything."

Just as Chad reaches for his keys, though, the lights dim and the crowd surges forward.

"Too late now," Chad says. "You're gonna get anvilled whether you want to or not."

※

I spend most of the band's short, loud set trying to get away from the giant speaker, which is throbbing in time with my blooming headache. But there's a scrum of fans swirling around and every time I step away from the Chad Buffer Zone, I am attacked by elbows and feet, assaulted by shrieking. After a while, I surrender to it, slumping, fingers in my ears, looking at everything but the girl on the stage who I cannot stop looking at.

The set finally ends. "Can we go now?" I ask Chad as the band leaves the stage.

"You really hate joy, don't you?" Chad says.

"I told you I don't like music."

"Fine. Let's go say hi to the band."

"Can't we just leave?"

"You gonna carry me up the stairs?" Chad asks. "We need Hannah's help. And besides, I wanna say thanks."

We push though the throngs, Chad jubilantly calling, "Cripple coming through," which parts the crowds nearly as effectively as Hannah did.

In the greenroom, Chad introduces me to the rest of the band—Libby on drums, Claudia on bass, and Jax on lead guitar. I think those are their names. My ears are ringing for real now and I can't hear.

I look around for Hannah. When I don't see her, I'm relieved. And disappointed.

"You rocked so hard tonight," Chad gushes to Jax. "Legit fuego. Thought you were gonna blast me outa my seat."

"Thanks," Jax says. "I could see you from the stage."

"Who wants a beer?" Claudia asks, pulling cans off a six-pack.

I shake my head. "Not for me."

"I'll take his," Chad jokes, reaching for mine.

"You said we're leaving."

"Chill, dawg. It will take me precisely five minutes to suck down two beers." Chad grins at the band. "Don't mind him. He hates music."

"I do not!"

"Who hates music?"

And already, I know her voice.

"Aaron does!" Chad crows.

I swivel around to find Hannah Crew. She holds a club soda out to Jax and gives me an amused smirk.

"I never said I hated music," I explain.

"Dawg, you compared listening to the band to waterboarding!"

Hannah's left eyebrow arches. A tiny scar runs down the center of it. "Never heard that one before."

"I was being hyperbolic," I explain.

"Hyperbolic?" Hannah asks.

"He likes big words. He's book smart like that," Chad explains. "His family even owns a bookstore."

"Really?" Libby asks. "Which one?"

"Bluebird Books," I say.

"That used bookstore?" Libby asks, saying the name of our town.

"That's the one," I say.

"So . . ." Hannah drawls. "Owning a bookstore equals hating music?"

"I don't hate music!"

"Puh-leeze," Chad says. "An hour ago, he was begging to leave. And he still can't wait to get out of here." He turns to me, knocking his temple with his knuckles. "We haven't even tried to sell your records."

"You're selling records?" Claudia leans forward, suddenly interested.

I shoot a death glare at Chad. "I told you I'm not selling records."

"So you didn't have a crate of vinyl at the Outhouse the other night?" Chad asks me.

"I did, but . . ." I trail off.

"So let me get this straight," Hannah says, crushing her soda can in her tiny hands. "You're selling records *and* you've been to two of our shows in the past week but you hate music?"

I glare at Chad.

"Aww, cut him a break," Chad says. "He's cool and he knows everything about books. Like for instance, did you know *Gone Girl* was a book before it was a movie?"

"Everyone knows that," Libby says.

"Oh," Chad says, blushing.

"If it makes you feel better," Jax says, "I didn't know *Clueless* was based on *Emma* until like last year."

"Well, Aaron probably did. He knows all that stuff and more. He's read everything."

"Everything?" Hannah picks up *The Magician's Nephew*. "Have you read this?"

After I read *The Lion, the Witch and the Wardrobe* in third grade, I devoured the rest of the series in a ferocious gulp. When I got to the last page of *The Last Battle*, I picked up *The Lion, the Witch and the Wardrobe* and started again. I used to reread the entire series every year, starting on my birthday, like a pilgrimage back to myself. Mom used to call Narnia my first love.

What I think: *Yes, Hannah Crew, I have read* The Magician's Nephew. *And the fact that you're reading it means something. Even if I don't want it to.*

What I say: "Never heard of it."

A Wrinkle in Time

Ira wakes up the next day with a head cold. He blames it on the change in the weather, but I expect the combo of our disastrous trip to Coleman's and the ramp-building misadventure had something to do with it. He's flushed, and shivering under the Pendleton blanket.

I touch his forehead; it's clammy and warm. "You have a fever."

"I'm fine," he insists.

"Let me take your temperature." I head back into the apartment and root around for the first-aid kit, but all I find is a cluster of Band-Aids so old the glue no longer sticks.

"I'm going to the store," I call. "We need a thermometer. And some cold medicine. And some Band-Aids."

Ira nods. He looks so pathetic. "Maybe some chicken soup?"

Chicken soup was the one Jewishy thing Mom learned to cook. She'd make it whenever anyone was feeling bad with any ailment, whether it be a cold or a sprained wrist. She made it for Sandy when he detoxed at home, spending hours trying to coax a spoonful down. She and Ira both swore by its healing powers. I never bought it. Soup is soup, but right now, I'll take what I can get.

I decide to walk the mile to ValuMart, not because it's a particularly nice stroll—it's mostly a stretch of auto mechanics and gas stations—but because it's not raining and it will give me more time to figure out how I'm gonna tell Ira.

I've decided to sell the store.

No, that makes it sound like I'm still thinking about it. I *did* sell the store. It's been a week since I knocked on Penny's door and said, "If you want to buy our store, it's not Ira you need to convince; it's me."

Penny made me an offer I can't refuse.

Only she didn't. I asked her what she'd pay for the place. She wrote down a number on a piece of paper and slid it across her desk. It was so low, it would barely cover the mortgage, let alone our debt. "Forget it," I told her, getting up to leave. Penny chased me out into the night, a funny little smile on her lips. "Aaron, some free business advice: you don't walk away from an opening bid. Come inside. Let's negotiate." And so we did.

Don't you see, Ira? We are the dinosaurs and the asteroid's already hit.

Penny understood this. It took about an hour to come up with a price that would give me and Ira enough of a nest egg to make a fresh start. Another hour to negotiate the smaller details—like her letting us stay in the upstairs apartment, paying rent, until we find a new place, and agreeing not to tell anyone about the deal until I told Ira. "We both know you're making the right decision," she said after we'd finally come to terms. "Really, the only decision."

Ira, you can't fight the inevitable. The inevitable always wins.

After we agreed on the deal terms, Penny insisted I stay for a celebratory toast. Against my protests, she poured us each a shot of whiskey. "Did you know," Penny asked—after she'd downed hers and I pretended to sip mine—"that I almost bought your building a few years back when your family had all that trouble? The deal fell through." She smiled. "But I knew eventually I'd get it."

The aisles at ValuMart are narrow, the floors scuffed, the produce unappealingly wrapped in cellophane. I grab the cold medicine, a thermometer, and some off-brand bandages and head to the meat department for some chicken, but the only pieces are rubbery and yellow, and for a minute I just want to be back in that beautiful corporate health food emporium, with its buffed floors and grass-fed everything, even though I know Ira is right about places like that.

I put the chicken back, grabbing a few cans of soup instead. I put my groceries on the belt. The cashier is someone I know, a girl from my year named Stephanie Gates. She checks my groceries without a word, pretending not to know me like I am pretending not to know her.

On the way home, I pass C.J.'s. The round table up front where the Lumberjacks usually sit all morning is empty. I get a bad feeling.

I pick up the pace.

Our store comes into view, Ike's truck parked out front.

I start to run.

I arrive as Richie is lifting a ladder from the bed.

"What. Are. You. Doing. Here?" I ask, wheezing from the run.

"Good morning to you too," Garry says, pulling a tarp from the truck. "We're here to paint."

"Paint?" I pant. "What? Why?"

Now Ike appears, holding a five-gallon tub of paint in each hand. "Well, you see, me and the boys were going back and forth about whether to stain the ramp or paint it to match the facade, and that's when we noticed the facade was in bad shape." Ike uses his elbow to gesture to the front of the building, shingled and once painted a robin's-egg blue—Mom liked to keep things on brand— but which now has faded to a shade best described as overcast. "Anyhow. I took a splintered chip of the paint to Joe Heath. You know Joe?"

"No."

"He's got that old refurbished barn he used to run a scrap shop out of. He wants to retire, and is trying to offload all his surplus supplies, including several cans about the same color as your building. Have a look." Whipping a stir stick out of his coat like a sword, he opens the tub. "Now, it ain't an exact match." He gives the paint a stir and it emulsifies into a grayish blue that falls somewhere between the robin's-egg of yore and the gray of now. "But it's close. And we thought we best hurry if we want to get it all done while the weather holds."

"Should I start sanding?" Richie calls.

"Sure," Ike says. "Start with the three hundred."

"Wait!" I shout. "Stop."

"Why?" Richie asks. "You think we need two-hundred grit in-stead? Ike, the kid thinks we should use the two hundred."

"I never said that!"

"You want the one hundred?" Richie asks, scandalized.

"I don't want any of it."

"Why, you think we should power wash?" Garry asks. "I told you we should power wash."

"And I told you power wash is the fool's shortcut," Ike says. "It'll tear the wood clean apart."

"Everyone just stop!" I yell.

They stop.

"What is going on?"

"I told you," Ike says. "We're painting."

"No one told you that you could paint."

"Ira just did," Ike replies.

I breathe through my frustration, counting one, two, three, four, five so I don't lose my shit at Ira. But holy hell! I was gone for an hour.

"That's not Ira's call to make."

"Well." Ike pauses to load a wad of tobacco into his lip. "It better be someone's call. 'Cause it needs doing."

Just then Ira shambles onto the porch, looking like Jesus in a Pendleton blanket. "You're back." He sneezes. "Did you get the medicine? I think I do have a fever."

"Did you tell them they could paint?"

Ira pauses to consider, as if he doesn't remember, even though this conversation has to have taken place in the last hour.

"We got two days of relative sunshine," Ike says, "which in November is a gift."

"I can't argue with that," Ira says.

"I can. We don't need the building painted."

Ira follows Ike's gaze to the facade: the paint is patchy, some shingles are missing. "Respectfully disagree," Ike says. "In fact, I suspect a lot of your water damage inside is coming from leaks on the outside. I'll hazard that's what split that beautiful mahogany shelf. The one you're gonna replace with . . ." He trails off and shakes his head before spitting out the rest of the sentence. "*Metal.*"

"We couldn't afford to buy a new wood shelf," Ira tells Ike.

Oh, for Christ's sake.

"Why would you *buy* anything new when you could repair the old one?" Ike asks. "But if you don't find the source of your water damage, it's gonna start all over again. So before you even think about fixing the inside . . ."

"Hold up!" I yell. "No one's fixing the inside. Or the outside."

"Why not?" Ira asks. "I mean, we've wanted to for a while now. It just keeps getting away from us. And now these gentlemen want to help. For free."

"Ira," I say levelly. "There's no such thing as for free."

"Ike swore it wouldn't cost us anything."

I laugh, hard and caustic. "That's because he thinks we're stupid. They all do."

"Probably not half as stupid as you think we are," Garry shoots back.

A sharp whistle cuts through the morning. Ike pulls his fingers from his mouth. "Like I told your father, you don't need to worry about the money, but we're wasting clear skies, so can we stop all this bickering and get to work?"

"Telling someone not to worry about money is like the opening to every swindle ever perpetrated."

"Aaron!" Ira scolds. To Ike, he says, "I'm sorry. I don't know what's gotten into him."

"Nineteen years of living in this town is what's gotten into me. And I know that when people like you say something's free, it's not."

"People like us?" Garry asks. "You don't know us."

"You're Caleb's brother, right?"

His face hardens. "What's he got to do with it?"

"He was an asshole to me."

"Got news for you. He was an asshole to a lot of people. Doesn't make you special."

"Excuse me . . ." A middle-aged woman approaches the store. She's wearing turquoise nursing scrubs, bright-green Converse high-tops. Rainbow-framed glasses hang off a purple chain around her neck. Everyone stops to stare at her, and not just because of the outfit. The woman is Black and there are about as many Black families in our town as there are Jewish ones. "I was told this was a bookstore," she says, taking in the Lumberjacks and Jesus-Ira. "But perhaps I was misinformed."

"No. It's a bookstore!" Ira practically shouts. "Bluebird Books. It's our bookstore. Mine and my son's, Aaron's. I'm Ira."

"Hello, Ira. Aaron. I'm Bev." She taps herself on the chest. "I just moved to town to work in the clinic. I thought it would be nice to build a small library for our younger patients because sometimes the wait can be a while and I'd like to give the children something to look at that isn't a screen."

Oh, what sweet music to Ira's ears. He straightens up a bit. Smiles.

"I have a few requests." Bev pulls out a piece of paper. "And I'd love some recommendations."

What Bev is requesting is a hand-sell. The effect on Ira is dramatic. He stands up tall, shrugs off his blanket. "I can certainly help you with that." He opens the door for Bev. "Aaron, I'll leave you to sort this out with Ike." He nods at Ike and disappears inside.

Garry starts unfolding the tarp all over the porch.

"Stop it!" I snap.

"You don't want us to use a tarp?" Garry asks. "We'll get paint everywhere."

"I don't want you to use a tarp." I look at Richie. "I don't want you to use the one hundred or the two hundred or the thousand grit."

"Thousand grit's overkill," Richie says.

I look at Ike. "I don't want you to paint."

"Well, then, what do you want us to do?" Ike asks.

What do I want them to do? For starters, not kick a man when he's down. But that's what guys like these have always done. Whether it's Caleb picking on me in high school, or Ike trying to pull a fast one on Ira now.

"I don't want anything from you," I tell Ike.

I have no idea that this is the most hurtful thing I could've said to him.

※

After I get rid of the Lumberjacks, I come inside to find Ira failing at the hand-sell.

"We have it. We have it," he's saying, his voice high and reedy. "I know we used to have it."

"Have what?" I ask.

"Oh, Aaron." Ira is flushed and miserable. "I can't find anything on her list." He shakes his head. "I used to know where everything was."

"Maybe I can help." I turn to Bev. "What are you looking for?"

She puts on the rainbow glasses. "Anything Percy Jackson. Anything Dog Man. Something about a unicorn rescue society. A book called *Ways to Make Sunshine*. Oh, wouldn't that be nice around here. Any of the Wonder books. Anything by someone named Jason Reynolds. Anything from the Walter the Farting Dog series. A book about *A Wrinkle in Time* but not *A Wrinkle in Time*."

"I think we have *A Wrinkle in Time*," Ira says.

"Oh, I have that entire series," Bev says. "This one is about *A Wrinkle in Time*. It has a map on the cover."

"A map on the cover, you say?" Ira says. "Sounds familiar. Let me check." Ira heads to the corner that used to house travel, cookbooks, and parenting books, but that's the shelf that broke and the books are scattered on the floor.

"Wouldn't it be in the middle grade/career section?" I ask Ira.

He swivels around and heads to the back corner where that section is. Or was.

"Middle grade/career section?" Bev asks.

It was the particular way Mom cataloged our inventory, not by subject of the book but by behavior of the reader. She came up with this system not long after they opened and she began to notice that when moms (and in our town, it was always moms) came in looking for books on how to potty train, they wound up lingering in the travel section, looking at the glossy books of Icelandic geysers or French soufflés. She realized the new moms needed escapism and began shelving parenting with travel. And she shelved early-reader books with career guides because by the time the kids could read, a lot of those moms were trying to go back to work.

Her system, like so much about this place, made sense when she was here. But without her, and with Ira stashing orphan books in every nook and cranny, we can't find a thing.

Ira starts in on the picture books, sending an avalanche of them tumbling down.

Bev grimaces. "I didn't mean for you to go to all this trouble."

"No trouble. No trouble at all."

Ira flaps around a bit longer, lost now, in his own bookstore. Bev checks her watch. "I can just Google it. And order it online."

Ira stops dead in his tracks, face pained.

Et tu, Bev?

"No!" Ira insists. "Come back. I'll find the book. I know we must have it. We're just a little disorganized these days."

Poor Bev. She thought she was going to a real-life bookstore, not the fossil of one. And poor Ira, his first shot at a new customer and he's blowing it. All the starch has come out of him. "Can you come back?" he asks.

She must hear the raggedy edge of desperation in his voice. Because she promises she will. But as she leaves, Ira sinks into his chair, sick and dispirited. Like me, he knows that once things are gone, they never come back.

Just Kids

After the Bevacle, Ira falls into a funk. He sits in his chair all day, coughing and snorting and emitting a low level of contagious misery. So when Chad waltzes in, we are both in a mood.

"Hey, dawg," he says, holding his hand up for the high five. "How's it swinging?"

"It's not swinging," I say, limply slapping his palm but declining the elaborate handshake that follows.

"So check this out. I have a crazy idea."

"Does this one entail building you a ramp you don't need? Tricking me into getting you carried down a flight of stairs?"

Chad strokes his invisible goatee. "Are you pissed off about something?"

"Why would I be pissed? I mean, you make me build you a ramp and then disappear."

"Disappear?" Chad looks behind him. "Did I disappear? I don't think so. I'm here."

"Whatever."

"Dude, did we bone or something?" Chad asks.

"What?"

"I mean, I've never done that with a guy before, and it doesn't totally appeal, but, you know, a lifetime of heteronormative conditioning might have something to do with that. But if we did and I failed to call you or text you or send you heart-shaped emojis or do whatever's got you in such a snit . . ."

Suddenly, I'm not mad so much as tired. "What do you want, Chad?"

"I wanted to see if you wanted to take a trip to Seattle."

"Why? You need me to haul you down a flight of stairs or something?"

"Damn, shorty, are you always so paranoid?"

"Says the guy who conned me into building a ramp and getting him carried down the stairs at some club and then disappeared. And stop calling me shorty. I'm taller than you."

"Everyone's taller than me now. And I mean it as a term of endearment."

"Oh, do we have endearments?" I point back and forth between us. "I wouldn't know."

"So you *are* pissed!"

"I'm not pissed. I just don't appreciate being used. It's like you only come by when you need something."

"So you think I'm, like, booty-calling you?"

"If the booty-call fits."

Ira blows his nose loudly.

"The thing is, dawg, I thought you'd *want* to go with me to the big city. I have some business to take care of. And . . . Beethoven's Anvil might maybe be playing tonight. But we don't have to go to that. I know you don't like them."

"I don't *not* like them," I say, trying to play it cool, trying to pretend that I haven't been thinking about Hannah, Googling the band. "It was just really loud standing by the speakers. My ears rang for a whole day."

"This club has no stairs. We can stand wherever we want. But I get if you don't wanna go. We can skip the show. I really just need a wingman for my other thing."

Ira starts hacking.

"You okay there, Mr. Stein?" Chad calls.

"Ira," Ira rasps. "And I'm fine. Nothing a hot bath and a good night's sleep won't fix."

He's right. Might as well give him a day to recover. I turn to Chad. "Sure," I say. "I'll go."

※

"So what I am wingmanning you for?" I ask Chad on the drive to Seattle. "Some girl you like?"

Chad laughs. "Nah, dawg. We're gonna see a man about a dick."

"What?" I ask, panicked.

Chad laughs. "Relax, dawg. Nothing like that."

"So what is it like?"

"How much do you know about SCIs?"

"What's an SCI?"

"So nothing, basically. SCI is short for spinal cord injury. When I fell off that cliff, I severed my spinal cord at the thoracic vertebra four." He reaches over and touches me below my shoulder. "But not all the way through."

"So does that mean you'll, like, walk again?"

"Probably not. But, hey, I have total control of my hands." He lifts both off the steering wheel to sparkle his fingers. "And good trunk control, so I can sit up on my own and I can tell when I have to pee or shit, which is good." He pauses. "But there are . . . issues . . . in the performance department."

"So can you not . . . ?" I gesture toward my lap.

"Get it up?" Chad says. "I can. Sort of. But not reliably. Or the way I want to. Or used to."

"I don't understand."

"Not to toot my own horn, but before my accident, I was a boner machine. Ten seconds of porn. Boom, I was hard! The sight of Mrs. Newkirk's bra. Did you have her for ELA? She was hot!"

I nod.

"That would get me a rod. The wind blew and I'd pop a woody. Thinking about a boner I'd had would give me a new one." He sighs. "Ahh, the good old days."

"And now?"

He sighs again. "Like everything else, it's different."

"How?"

"For one, I can only get a boner if someone touches my junk."

"So?"

"Well, I get a boner *any*time someone touches my junk. A cat could walk across my lap. I once got a boner when a nurse probed my dick. Which is not hot. And neither was she. But I got hard because something was touching my junk."

"Like a reflex?"

"Exactly. It's even called a reflex boner. But the problem is that's the only boner I can get. And I wanna be able to get a psychogenic boner . . ."

"A what?"

"The kind of erection you get if you're watching porn, or making out with someone, or feeling lust, or love, I can't get hard from those. I need the manual stimulation." He grimaces a bit as he shakes his head. "And then there's orgasms."

"Can you not . . . come?" I trail off, realizing I've never talked like this to a friend. To anyone.

"Kind of. I get that tensed-up feeling before you shoot off, but then nothing comes out. It's frustrating as hell."

"But if you can get hard, and feel like you're coming . . . That's good, right?"

"I mean it's better than nothing. But it's not the same. I can't finish and even if I could, coming is like a physical thing, like sneezing. It's not connected to desire."

"Is that so bad?"

"Yeah, it is," Chad replies. "Think about it: You wanna fall in love with someone and have all the physical and emotional stuff, and I can't. It's bad enough wondering if anyone can fall in love with damaged goods like me. But if they did, could I fall in love with them? Like if I can't translate this." He taps his head. "To this." He taps his crotch. "Will it happen? I don't know which is the chicken, and which is the egg, but I know I want that all-consuming love. The one that makes all the other shit in life worth it." Chad looks at me. "I want that so much. Don't you?"

By all accounts, my parents had that. And look what it led to. So there's part of me that doesn't want anything to do with a love that can make or break you.

Except here I am, heading to Seattle to see Hannah Crew.

"Yeah, Chad," I say. "I think I do."

※

I assumed Chad's man with a dick would be a doctor but he turns out to be a super-handsome, white-toothed, hair-gelled guy in a wheelchair. He greets Chad with a hearty handshake. "So happy to meet you in person," he says in heavily accented English.

Chad introduces me to Frederic, who he's been corresponding with for nearly a year now but has only just met because Frederic lives in Budapest, Hungary.

"Oh, have you read any Magda Szabó?" I ask. "I think *The Door* is next on my reading list."

Frederic looks at me blankly.

"I only mention it because she's a Hungarian author."

"Never heard of her," Frederic says.

"Aaron's very smart," Chad says. "That's why I brought him along."

Frederic reaches for a leather attaché case and dials the combo, opening the lid with such a flourish I expect there to be a vial of some magical boner elixir inside. But what he pulls out is a glossy brochure with the words RESTORE YOUR ESSENTIAL SELF emblazoned on the cover.

Chad shows me the brochure. It's full of images of men in wheelchairs, some holding babies in their laps, others with gorgeous women draped over them, all looking very happy. Beneath the pictures are testimonials, the before-and-after language queasily familiar: *Changed my life. Restored my family. Gave me my future back.*

Frederic is featured on page three, with a blonde woman sitting on his lap.

"Who's that?" Chad asks.

"Lena. My wife."

Chad whistles. "Your wife's a stone-cold fox."

"Thank you. I think."

"Were you together before your accident?" Chad asks.

"Lena and I met after."

"And you can . . . you know?" Chad seems suddenly shy. "Perform."

"Lena has no complaints."

Chad stares longingly at the couples on the pages. "If a genie came to me tomorrow and said I could walk again or have sex like normal again, I'd choose sex."

Frederic smiles. "Consider Dr. Laszlo that genie."

"Who's Dr. Laszlo?" I ask.

"The doctor who restored my manhood," Frederic says. He taps the brochure. "The inventor of the Stim."

"Stim?"

"The Spinal Erectile Stimulator," Frederic clarifies.

"What is that?"

"It's a small device that is implanted in the spinal column, connecting the groin area to the non-damaged area of the spinal cord."

He turns to Chad. "I think of it as a man-made replacement for the neurological pathways SCI disrupts."

"How does it work?"

"It's in the brochure." Chad turns to Frederic. "Did you talk to Dr. Laszlo about me? Does he do T-4s?"

"He's had excellent success with T-4s, T-1s, even C-6s." Frederic pauses. "I'm a C-6, incomplete."

"Wow," Chad says.

"Wow?" I ask.

"It means his injury was higher, less chance of recovering boner function, and it worked for him." He turns to Frederic. "And how long until you noticed results?"

"Like most patients, I had improvements before I even left Bangkok."

"Bangkok?" I interrupt. "As in Thailand?"

"Yes," Frederic replies. "That is where the clinic is."

"Can't you have the procedure here?" I ask Chad.

"Naw, dawg. The FDA is slow as shit approving things like this and if I wait for them to get their act together, I'll be a sixty-year-old man and no longer in need of boners."

"But Thailand? Is it legal?"

"In Thailand it is," Frederic says.

"Is it safe?"

"I can assure you, the clinic is state of the art," Frederic says. "Most patients say it exceeds anything they've seen here in the US."

"I've been on the fence," Chad says, "but now that I've met you, I'm gonna do it!"

"I think you'll be very happy."

"So what happens next? Dr. Laszlo has all my records."

"Yes. You are approved. Once he receives the deposit, you will join the waiting list. Another third is due when the procedure is scheduled, usually three months prior. And the final third before travel is booked."

"How much does this thing cost?" I ask.

Chad ignores the question. "And how long's the waitlist?"

"Currently from nine to twelve months."

"Okay." Chad nods. "That'll give me time to come up with the rest of it, but once I pay the deposit, I get on the list?"

"Yes," Frederic replies.

"Will I lose my deposit if I can't get the money in time?"

Frederic smiles. "No. Dr. Laszlo is very understanding about financing. You only lose the deposit if you withdraw from the procedure."

"Oh, I won't do that," Chad promises. "And it really helped?" he asks Frederic. "And you can . . . ?" He gestures to his lap. "Like you did before? And live a normal life? Fall in love? Get married?"

"Your Lena is out there," Frederic promises. "And now you'll be able to find her."

///

We have a few hours to kill before the show, so Chad suggests we get some Thai food. "'Cause, you know, I'll be in Thailand soon." He Yelps a place nearby, which says it's accessible on the listing, but when we get there, the tables are so tightly shoved together Chad can't fit and the manager insists on rearranging things while apologizing profusely. I can tell the entire thing makes Chad uncomfortable and I'm relieved on his behalf when we finally get situated.

"What's the difference between spring rolls and summer rolls?" Chad asks, looking at the menu.

"Spring is fried."

"Let's do fried. Do you eat shrimp?"

"Why wouldn't I?"

"Isn't it, like, against your religion?"

"We're not religious like that, Chad. We don't even go to temple. Not that there's a temple to go to near us."

"Oh, cool. Wanna split the shrimp pad thai? It has the word *Thai* in it, so it must be a thing. And some spring rolls?"

"Sounds good."

Chad beckons over the waitress and we order. After she leaves, he adds, "Yelp says the portions are huge, so we can share and it'll be cheaper. 'Cause, you know, I'm in economy mode now."

"How much is the Stim?"

Chad unsnaps his chopsticks and rubs them together. "Not as much as you think," he says. "It's actually a total steal compared to how much things cost here."

"Total steal is maybe not what you should be looking for in a medical procedure."

"I only meant that it's not as inflated as healthcare here is."

"So how much is it?"

Chad hesitates. "Thirty grand."

"*Thirty thousand dollars?*"

"Keep it down, will you?" Chad says, gesturing around to the empty restaurant.

"Thirty thousand dollars is a lot of money," I whisper.

"It includes travel expenses, minus the flight," he adds.

"Isn't the flight the travel expense?"

"No, there's food. And your stay in the clinic and five weeks' rehab. You know how much rehab costs here? A thousand dollars a day."

"But isn't that covered by insurance?"

"Not all of it. We had a ton of debt when I got out, and had to spend nearly all the settlement money on it."

Yeah. We had a ton of medical debt too. And no settlement money. "Do you have thirty thousand dollars?"

"No," he admits. "I have enough to cover the deposit and some of the second payment. My dad—he gets why I want the procedure—says he'll take out a loan to pay for the rest. But my mom doesn't want to go further into debt for a surgery in another country."

"Your mom sounds wise."

"As opposed to who? Me?" Chad's mouth sets into a thin pursed line.

"I didn't say that. It's just . . . how much have you researched this procedure?"

"All I've done is research."

"So there are trials? Studies? Papers?"

Chad rolls his eyes. "Who needs that shit? I've gone to the source. Talked to guys who've had it."

"Like Frederic, you mean?"

"You got something against Frederic?"

"You met him online."

"News flash, Aaron. Online is how you meet people these days."

"But have you *met* any of them?" I pause. "It's pretty easy to scam people online. You know, like catfishing."

Chad guffaws. "You think Frederic is catfishing me?"

"Not like that. But, you know . . . what exactly is his role in all this?"

"What do you mean, what's his role? He's like me. Only he's had the procedure and he has Lena."

"And he just happens to be in Seattle?"

"So what? People come to Seattle all the time."

"And he doesn't work for the clinic?"

"I don't know. I don't think so."

"But the doctor's name is Laszlo, right?"

"Yeah."

"And he's Hungarian?"

"How should I know?"

"It's a Hungarian name. There's a famous author named László Krasznahorkai."

"Uh-huh." Chad looks bored.

"Well, don't you think it's a little fishy that some Hungarian guy just happens to be in the city and happens to have had the procedure and is meeting with you out of the goodness of his heart?" I pause. "Like, he obviously works for the clinic. Maybe he's not even paralyzed. Maybe Lena's not even his wife."

"You saw the brochure!"

"Anyone can make a brochure!"

"What are you saying?"

"I'm saying it seems shady and you should maybe do more research."

"I see," Chad says. "Because obviously I'm too stupid to figure this out on my own because I don't read books like you do or know authors like László Krapishinski."

"Krasznahorkai," I correct.

Chad glares at me. "I know you think you know everything about me, but if you'd known me longer than two weeks, you'd know I've actually been researching this since the day I woke up in the hospital."

"I just don't want to see you taken advantage of."

"Why do you assume I'm a moron? Just because I didn't know *Gone Girl* was a book you think I haven't done all the due diligence and come to the right decision? Your brother was right about you."

At the mention of Sandy, my blood goes cold. "What was my brother right about?"

"He said you were a condescending goody-two-shoes little shit."

"He said that?" My voice cracks, the hurt humiliatingly fresh, even after all this time. Fucking Sandy! He's the reason I know not to trust glossy brochures. We got so many of them over the years from places called New Horizons and Second Chances and Clean Futures, all of them brimming with heartfelt testimonials, promises of a fix. And in the beginning, I believed them. God, how I hoped one day Sandy could be one of those happy endings.

Here's what the brochures don't tell you: That the relapse rate for most addiction is more than fifty percent. That because of the particular way opioids remain in the system longer than other substances, they are even harder to kick. That just when you think you've reached the finish line, opioids pull a Lucy on you and yank up the football. And that there's no such thing as a miracle.

"I was only trying to help," I tell Chad.

"I don't need *your* help. I might never get my legs back, I might never get my boner back, I might never fall in love or have anyone fall in love with me, but I'd still rather be me than you."

"What's that supposed to mean?"

"It means you're a coward."

"How am I a coward?"

"You sit up there on your high horse, hating on everything, judging everyone else like you're better than us when really you're just a chickenshit."

"If I'm such a coward," I say, the blood thrumming in my veins, "why are you hanging out with me?"

"You know, that's an excellent question!" Chad shoves back against the table, cursing as he maneuvers around it. It takes a while, and by the time he's out, the waitress is back with our meal.

"What about your food?" she asks. "Not hungry?"

"No." Chad throws down a twenty and looks at me. "I lost my appetite."

I get the food to go and head back to the truck, where Chad is sulking in the driver's seat. I climb into the passenger side and he peels out of the parking lot, not saying a word. I assume we're going straight home. But he drives us to the club and, still not speaking to me, gets out. I scramble after him but he goes into the bar, which I'm not allowed in. So I sit in the empty club for an hour, then two hours, composing a treatise in my head on what a dickhead Chad is.

I'm a coward? Because I made some basic inquiries about a questionable procedure in a different country? No. Chad's an asshole. He always was an asshole. He's just using me. And I'm sorry, but who doesn't know that *Gone Girl* was a book first? An ignorant buffoon is who.

The opening band starts playing: they are loud and unpleasant, a groaning bass beat that sounds more like moving heavy furniture than music. I contemplate calling Ira and asking for a lift home, but Ira is sick, in bed, asleep. I'm stuck. As usual.

"Didn't expect to see you here."

It's testament to just how foul my mood is that the sight of Hannah Crew walking though the mist does nothing to make me feel better. She plops down next to me, her fishnetted legs inches away from mine, hoodie up, tight around her face. "You must a be a glutton for punishment."

"Yeah. That tracks."

"You here with Chad?"

"I don't know."

"You don't know?"

"I came with him. But he's in the bar. I think. I don't know. I can't go in there."

Hannah nods. "I get that." She touches my wrist. Her nails, painted gunmetal gray, are bitten down to the quick, and picturing Hannah gnawing on her fingers makes my heart twist.

"Want me to have someone get him?" she offers.

"Who? Chad? No. Chad can go to hell."

"You two have a falling out?"

"No! We're not even friends."

"You seemed pretty close."

"We've only known each other a few weeks."

"Time's not always a good measure of things like love, you know."

"Right. Feelings are not facts," I say pulling out some of Sandy's rehab lingo.

"Exactly," Hannah says, staring at me. After a bit, she stands to go.

"Well, if you want to be alone . . ."

I don't want to be alone. I'm so tired of being alone. "Stay. Please. I'm sorry. It's just been a day."

"They're all days," she replies. "You take 'em one at a time."

"I'm trying to."

She sits back down.

"You want to talk about it?"

I shake my head. "Not right now."

"Okay," she says. And we sit there, in silence, but it's not awkward. It's comforting, like Hannah is someone I've known for a long time. Like someone I was meant to know.

"I'm sorry I compared your band to waterboarding," I say.

"Please. I've heard worse. And at least you were telling the truth."

"But I wasn't. I hadn't even heard you when I said that."

"And now that you've heard us, did it change your mind?"

"Uh-huh." I pause. "Not waterboarding, more like garden-variety drip torture."

"So a lesser water torture?" Hannah asks, gripping her chest. "Be still, my heart."

Be still, mine.

"It really isn't personal," I tell her. "I'm just not a music person."

"Not a music person," Hannah repeats. "What does that even mean?"

I shrug. "Music doesn't do that thing to me it does to other people. Books do. But not music."

"So it's an either/or?"

In my family, yes. An age-old distinction. Years of defining myself in alliance with Ira, in opposition to Sandy. "Maybe?"

"Then explain Patti Smith."

"Patti Smith?"

"Musician. Poet. Author. Genius. She wrote one of the most incredible albums of all time, *Horses*, and she wrote some of the most incredible books too. Her memoir *Just Kids* is my bible."

I make a note to read *Just Kids*. Or try to.

"Music and books are not distant cousins," Hannah continues. "They're more like fraternal twins. Different ways of telling a story."

"People say that, but lyrics just don't do it for me."

"Lyrics are just one part of it, like dialogue is in a book. But songs have so much more. Texture and pacing and emotional build." Her excitement is so infectious I nearly believe her. "If they're done right, that is. It's hard to write a good song, much less a perfect one."

"What makes a perfect song?"

"That's totally subjective, but to me it's a song that uses all the elements, instrumentation, pacing, lyrics, to deliver an emotional experience. It's what I want our songs to do. But . . ." She grins at me. "It's impossible. Because what's perfect for me might be noise to someone else."

"I don't think any song will be perfect for me."

"Well, you've thrown down the gauntlet." Hannah kicks my ankle. "I'm gonna have to find you a perfect song."

"Now who's the glutton for punishment?"

Hannah laughs. "You gonna stay out here and mope or come inside? There's a cooler full of club sodas waiting in the green room." She stands up, dusting off her backside, and reaches a hand for me. I grab it and she hoists me up and we just stand there for a minute, hand in hand.

Neither one of us lets go as we walk toward the stage door right as Jax flings it open. "I've been looking everywhere for you!"

Hannah glances at her phone. "I thought we weren't up for another half hour."

"Not you," Jax says, staring at me. "You."

"Me?"

"You're Chad's friend, right?"

"Is he okay?" My throat tightens. If something happened to Chad . . . when we were in a fight . . .

"He's fine. Just come on . . ."

We follow Jax to the bar, pushing past the bouncer. There's a small scrum around Chad, who has fallen off the barstool. "Where's his chair?" I yell. The bartender points to the corner. I run and get the chair and help Hannah and Jax hoist Chad into it. He's like a rag doll, though, and falls forward. Jax catches him just in time.

"He needs fresh air," Hannah commands. "Let's get him outside."

"What about his tab?" the bartender asks.

"They'll handle it," Hannah says, pointing to Jax.

Hannah and I get Chad outside into the parking lot. Jax shows up a few seconds later with a bottle of water, which they prop against Chad's mouth. "Can you drink this?"

Chad takes a few sips, then sputters, coughs, and pukes.

"Oh, boy," Hannah says.

"Sorry," Chad mutters, and then he retches again.

"Get it all out," Jax says, patting his shoulder.

Chad shakes his head, miserable. "Sorry," he repeats.

"Nothing to be sorry about," Jax replies before turning to me. "Can you get him home?"

"I don't know how to drive his truck," I say. "I'll just wait for him to sober up."

"You could be here all night," Hannah says. "He's really plowed."

Jax looks back toward the stage door. "We gotta go on soon. Aaron, you stay with him out here. One of us will come back out to help you as soon as we're done."

"Okay," I agree.

Jax leaves. Hannah lingers. "You gonna be okay?"

I nod.

"You're a good egg, you know."

I swallow the lump in my throat. I'm not. Chad was right. I am a coward.

"I gotta go," she says. "We're almost on."

"Play extra loud so I can listen from here."

"Don't think I won't!" she says, disappearing into the side door.

Chad's mumbling something. I crouch before him. "What?"

"Betaable?" he says.

"What?"

"Behtanvil."

"Oh, Beethoven's Anvil. Don't worry. We'll see them another time."

He nods. Then drifts off. It's starting to rain, so I push him under the awning by the door. I can hear the band go on. Can hear Hannah sing "To Your Knees," the same song they opened with the other night. From out here, it doesn't sound so bad. I close my eyes and picture her boinging around the stage. My toe taps to the beat.

A while later Chad wakes up. Calls my name, then mumbles, "Ibuzsanedpus."

"I don't understand you."

"IthinkIneedapiss."

"You need to piss?" Chad nods. "Oh. Okay. How does that work? Do you need me to unzip your pants? Stand you up?"

He gestures to the satchel on the back of his chair. "Ziploc. Catheter."

I open the satchel, find the Ziploc. It contains a bunch of foil-wrapped catheters.

I hand it to Chad but he's so drunk he drops it.

I pick it up.

"You open it," he tells me.

I look for an opening.

"Hurry!"

"Stop yelling! You're making me nervous."

I fumble with the foil and get it open. It's a long tube with a suction cup at one end and a bag at the other.

"Now what? Do you need me to—"

"Fuck," Chad says.

"What? What happened?"

But then I hear the sound of water dripping. And it's not raining that hard. Chad hangs his head. "I pissed myself." He puts his head in his hands. "I suck." He shakes he his head. "I suck. I suck. I suck."

"You don't suck. It could happen to anyone."

"Has it happened to you?"

"Not specifically, but trust me, I'm no stranger to humiliation."

"Will you help me? Change? I keep a spare set of clothes in the truck."

"Yeah. Sure."

I fetch Chad's sweats from the cab. I unzip his pants, pull them down. I clean him off as best I can and get the sweats on, before throwing the soiled pants in the dumpster.

"I'm sorry," Chad says when it's over.

I'm not sure if he's talking about the piss, or what he said earlier, about me being a coward. But there comes a point when such distinctions cease to matter.

"I'm sorry too," I say.

When You Reach Me

Because Chad's still too drunk to drive when the set ends, Jax arranges for us to spend the night in a friend's elevator-accessible loft. After ferrying us over in the van and getting us situated, they return to the club to load out.

It takes a while the next day to rouse a hungover Chad and fetch his truck from the club, so it's past noon when we pull up to the store. Ike's battered pickup is parked out front.

"Those guys doing more work for you?" Chad asks.

"No. They are not." I jump out of the truck and bolt up the stairs. The collapsed bookshelf has been emptied of all its contents and pried off the wall, revealing a ghostly outline.

"What the hell's going on?" I shout at Ike. "What'd you do to the bookshelf?"

"We had to pull the shelf off to find the source of the leak," Ike explains. "As I suspected, you all got water in the walls."

"Where's Ira?" I demand. "What did you do with him?"

"Do with him?" Richie scoffs. "He went to C.J.'s to get coffee because you don't have any. What kind of bookstore doesn't sell coffee?"

"It's good we came when we did because any more water and

this fine old shelf might really have been beyond repair. And that would have been a tragedy." Ike strokes the wood. "She's a beaut."

"Sure is," Garry replies, fondling the other side of the case. This would be creepy even if Ike hadn't just deemed the shelf a *she*.

"Mahogany?" Richie asks.

"Yep. You don't see craftsmanship like that anymore, do you?"

"No, you do not."

"Same with these floors," Ike says. "Red oak."

"Tongue-and-groove, isn't it?" Richie asks.

Ike nods approvingly. It's like any second now, they're going to have a circle jerk about the wood.

The bell over the door chimes and I swivel around, expecting Ira. But it's Chad. "Just wanted to make sure everything's okay."

"It's definitely not okay. These guys have commandeered the store."

"Commandeered?" Richie asks.

"He likes to use big words," Chad explains.

"No one's commandeering anything," Ike says. "We're conversating."

"There's nothing to converse about! I already told you, we're not painting the building."

"You're absolutely right," Ike says. "We got bigger fish to fry."

"What? No! No fish. No frying!"

"The water in the walls needs attention and you got some rotting joists." Ike gestures to a section of floorboard that he's pried up.

I feel sick. I was gone less than twenty-four hours.

"With the weight of these books," Ike continues, "and the state of those joists, it's a miracle the shelf didn't fall clean through to the basement."

"That would not be good," Richie tells me.

"Yes, Richie. I am aware of that."

"Well, you don't seem aware, 'cause you didn't do anything about it," Richie replies.

"And this nice piece of mahogany," Ike continues, pulling out his bandana to polish the bookshelf. "You can't scrap it. Or replace it with metal shelves. Wood like this deserves a second chance."

"Fine. You take the bookshelf. Give it a second chance, a third even. But leave us out of it."

"But it's *your* shelf," Ike says. "We'd fix it for *you*."

"If you're talking repairs," Chad chimes in, "I'd widen the aisles." He looks bashful. "Just saying."

"Ain't a bad idea," Ike agrees. "Floor space isn't used as efficiently as it could be. You could sneak more shelves in here. Organize a bit better."

"Or organize it at all," Chad jokes.

"It *is* organized!"

"Yeah?" Garry points to the collapsed shelves. "Then why do you have cookbooks next to child psychology?"

I'm not explaining Mom's organizational system to Garry. He wouldn't understand. And it's none of his damn business.

"It does seem pretty disorganized," Chad says. "Do you even have an inventory system?"

"We do," I say. Even though we really don't. Mom used to keep track of everything on a spreadsheet but that hasn't been updated for ages.

"A *digitized* inventory system?" Chad asks.

"Not exactly."

"Not exactly?"

"No."

"No? How do you sell your stuff online?" Chad asks.

"They don't!" crows Richie. "I went to the website but just got an error message."

"I could build a database system," Chad says. "I'm taking a class."

"We don't need a database."

"What kind of bookstore doesn't have a digitized inventory?" Chad asks.

"The kind that doesn't serve coffee," Garry answers.

"Or have a website," Richie adds.

"We *have* a website!"

Chad looks it up on his phone. "Error message. Did you forget to renew the domain?"

I vaguely remember some emails a while back telling us we had to renew. But it was one of a thousand little fires I could never put out. And now the whole place is burning down.

The door rings again and in waltzes Ira, holding two coffees. Behind him is Bev, holding two more.

"Look who I bumped into," Ira bellows. "Hi, Aaron. Hi, Chad. Do you want some coffee?"

"I'm all good, Mr. Stein."

"Ira," says Ira.

"Nice to see you all again," Bev says. "I was telling Ira I got the title of the book that's about *A Wrinkle in Time* but not *A Wrinkle in Time*. It's called *When You Reach Me* by Rebecca Stead. I'm not sure if it's pronounced like *dead* or like *deed*."

"Aaron, can you look for *When You Reach Me*?" Ira asks.

"I need to talk to you."

"That's fine, but we help our customers first."

"It's important."

"So are our customers. Please find Bev her book."

"But, Ira!"

He stops me with a look.

"Fine," I say, folding my arms across my chest and malingering in the philosophy and puzzles-and-games section because I don't trust Ira, even hand-selling Ira, with these guys.

Ike starts talking to Ira. "So I checked the plans at the town clerk and you filed for plumbing permits a few years back. I wondered if you had plumbing in the wall?"

"Why are you checking our permits?" I demand.

"That's the first step in any renovation," Ike replies.

"Renovation? What renovation?"

"Aaron, I think you'll have more luck over there." Ira gestures to the middle grade/career section. He turns back to Ike. "There *is* plumbing in that wall," he says. "Annie put it in herself. She wanted us to add a café."

Sales had been declining, and customers dwindling. Mom had hoped a café would bring in revenue, and also people. We couldn't afford to hire anyone to do the work, so she ordered a bunch of DIY books and started to do it herself. She was halfway through when the asteroid hit.

"See," Richie crows. "Bookstores oughta have coffee."

"Shut up!" I tell him.

"Aaron!" Ira scolds. "Manners. And will you please find Bev her book?"

"I can come back another time," Bev says. "You seem busy."

"No!" Ira says forcefully. "Aaron will find you the book."

"How will I find her the book?" I yell. "We can't find anything in here."

"You would if you had an organizational system and a database," Chad pipes in.

"Shut up, Chad!"

"Aaron!" Ira gasps. "What's gotten into you? Talking to customers that way."

"It's all gravy, Mr. Stein. He had a long night."

"I think I'll go," Bev says.

"Don't!" Ira says. Then he adds, in a wavering voice, "Please."

"Nurse lady. What did you say the book you were looking for was called?" Garry calls.

"*When You Reach Me*," Bev replies. "And my name is Bev."

"This the book, Bev?" Garry trots to the front of the store, holding, miraculously, a copy of *When You Reach Me*. "Uh-oh," he says, flipping through the pages. "Looks like someone wrote in it."

I grab the book, check the title page. "The *author* wrote in it."

"Well, that was disrespectful."

"It was *signed* by the author."

"Signed?" Bev asks. "You have author visits? How wonderful!" She claps her hands together in delight. "Is there an events schedule? Or is it online?"

"They don't have a website," Richie says.

"We have a website!" I say. "It's just down."

"But we can get it back up," Ira says. "After the renovation. So check then."

"What renovation?" I cry.

"I will," Bev says, paying for her book. "The bookstore in my old town had so many events. Author readings and a book club knitting circle. They called it Knit and Lit." She plays with her glasses chain and smiles dreamily. "I miss that."

"Knit and Lit," Ike says. "Not a bad idea."

After Bev leaves, I pull Ira to the side. "Will you tell me what's going on?"

"I know. I'm sorry. I should've asked you. But after you left yesterday, Ike and the boys came back, and we got to talking about improvements."

"Ira," I object.

"I know! I know. But Ike says a lot of the material could be salvaged. And Joe Heath is retiring."

"So I've been told."

"He's getting rid of his inventory for cost, below cost. A lot will be free."

"Let's assume that's true, which I doubt it is—what about the labor?"

"Ike says we could pay them in coffee."

"*Coffee?*"

"And creamer," Ira adds. "Ike likes French vanilla and Garry's a hazelnut man."

"Ira." I reach for his hands. They're so thin and frail. He's only fifty-two years old. When did he become so old? "This can't be real. You see that, right?"

"But why can't it?" Ira asks, pulling his hands back to gesticulate around the store. "We aren't talking about major work. Just a few pieces of Sheetrock, a fresh coat of paint. To spiff up the place. Why couldn't we do author events again? Knit and Lits, even? Why can't this place get a second chance?"

Because there are no second chances after asteroids hit. Just ask the dinosaurs.

I need to tell him.

Why can't I tell him?

I can't tell him.

"What if it's too late?" I ask.

"It's not too late. Not if we work together. Remember that book I used to read to you? *Stone Soup*."

Stone Soup is another one of those feel-good classics for kids that, like *The Giving Tree*, is built on a dangerous lie. Three hungry soldiers get the stingy townspeople to give them food by pretending to make a soup out of stones. In the book it all ends happily. But think about real life: What would happen when the townspeople realized they'd been Lucied? They'd run after those soldiers with pitchforks and torches.

Ira can't see it but I do: He's being fed rocks and water by Ike and the Lumberjacks. He's being fed rocks and water by his own coward of a son.

"At least let them fix the shelf," Ira implores. "It was the first one we bought for the store. Your mother picked it out."

The look on Ira's face, so open, so hopeful—it guts me. It's like he believes that fixing a splintering shard of wood will change anything. But it won't. It won't bring the store back. It won't bring them back.

"Ira," I begin. "It's not gonna work . . ."

I watch my father's face crumple. There's only so many times you can break someone's heart. Unlike wood, it can't be fixed.

And it's one shelf. What harm can that do?

As it turns out, a lot.

The Scent of Desire

The olfactory bulb is a tiny bit of the brain deep in the amygdala that, according to a book I read a few years ago called *The Scent of Desire*, is why you can be walking down the street and smell something—perfume or drying pine needles or stale cigarette smoke—and *bam!* You're transported to some other place in time associated with that smell. It's not a memory. It's more powerful than that. It's as close as you can get to a time machine.

When I wake up the next morning to the aroma of coffee, I am transported to a different world, a different time: Mom is in the kitchen wearing Joseph, dancing around, using the robe's strap as a microphone that she sings into. Sandy is up early, sipping his coffee, teasing Mom for playing the same song every damn day. "Don't you ever want to switch it up?" Sandy asks. And Mom says, "No more than I want to switch you up." Ira is downstairs in the shop, getting ready for the new day. And for a minute, all is well.

But then I hear Ike's gravelly voice. And I realize Mom is not in the kitchen. Neither is Sandy. Just my olfactory bulb sending me to a world that no longer exists.

Even your own damn brain can Lucy you!

Downstairs, Ira is bustling around with Mom's old Mr. Coffee, refilling the Lumberjacks' mugs. Give him an apron and he could get a job at C.J.'s.

He's chatting with Ike while Richie and Garry box books from the broken shelf.

"We should probably box a few of the others while we're at it so we have more room to maneuver." Ike points to the teetering piles. "What do you think?" he asks me.

What I think is that these guys are playing us, even if I don't know how.

What I also think is that the books *will* need to be boxed up to ship to the bulk buyers.

"I dunno," I suggest, casually, kicking my leg back and forth. "Maybe we should box all the books."

"*All* the books?" Ira replies. "That seems unnecessary."

"It'll give Ike more room to maneuver, maybe widen the aisles like Chad said, and allow us to organize better." I sound so convincing, I almost persuade myself.

"No problem here," Ike says. "I got plenty of boxes in the truck and with three of us, it won't take long."

"Thanks, Ike," I say brightly before turning to Ira. "Hey, I was thinking, maybe we should go out for dinner tonight?"

"Why?" Ira asks, justifiably surprised. Eating out is not something we do. We eat because our bodies require us to. But asking Ira to dinner will signal an event. It will force me to tell him. Plus,

I've read how restaurants are good spots for breakups; being in public discourages a scene.

"Are we celebrating something?" he adds, ever hopeful that we might be.

Getting out of this damp, moldy, godforsaken crater, I think. But I don't tell him that. Instead I say, "Celebrating second chances."

Ira's tentative smile blossoms into a high beam and a piece of my heart dies. It's one thing to be cowardly, another thing to be cruel.

***

I settle in on the porch with the Brusatte, opening to a random page about the discovery of an allosaurus in Wyoming that the paleontologists nicknamed Big Al. Big Al was such a find, he got his own TV special. I wonder what he would think about that, not just dead but extinct too, and getting his fifteen minutes of fame. Not everyone gets that kind of second chance.

But not even Brusatte can hold my attention today. The residue of this morning's time travel still clings to me, and somehow I'm not totally in this world.

I pull out my phone and open a video of Beethoven's Anvil that I discovered last night. It's grainy, and the sound quality is terrible, which doesn't matter because the sound is not why I keep watching. It's her. It's Hannah. I watch the video a few times. Replay our conversation from the club the other night. Pick up the Brusatte, put it back down, watch the video again.

Every time I see her, I feel that thing: the inevitable.

The thing is: I don't trust the inevitable.

I mean, what has inevitable done for me?

Ruined my life is what.

I put away my phone and pick up the book again but wind up just kind of staring into the gloom. There's not a ton of foot traffic on Main Street on the best November day, but today it's particularly sparse, so when I see someone heading this way, someone looking remarkably like Hannah, I am pretty sure I am hallucinating.

She comes closer, high ponytail springing, wearing an oversized hoodie, HILLSDALE CHEER SQUAD emblazoned in peeling letters.

It can't be her.

I mean, why would she be here? In my town? Walking down my street? Waving?

This is not how life works. And definitely not how *my* life works.

I wave back.

Am I still sleeping? Has the olfactory bulb catapulted me not into the past but into someone else's future?

"What are you doing here?" I bark. She flinches because it comes out rude, like I'm questioning her *right* to be here when really I'm questioning the *reality* of her being here. I soften. "I just didn't expect you, is all."

"Sorry I didn't make an appointment. I can see you're very busy." She picks up the Brusatte. "Dinosaurs, huh?" She opens to the table of contents, running a finger down the listing. "Somehow I thought you'd be reading brooding literature. Dostoyevsky or Goethe or something."

She just name-checked two of my favorite authors. Who *is* this person?

"Any good?" she asks.

"Probably." I shrug. "I mean, I've read it like four times in a row."

"Four times?" She shakes her head, flicking the points of her ponytail. "It must be really good."

"It's really well written, but that's not why I keep reading it."

"Why do you keep reading it?"

"I don't know. I guess it's comforting."

"Dinosaurs are comforting?"

"Not them, but more like the reminder that everything ends. Dinosaurs. Families. People. The human race."

"Oh, yes, very comforting."

"You think I'm weird?"

"Contemplating extinction at eleven thirty on a Saturday morning is definitely weird." Hannah pauses. "But my kind of weird."

My heart pit-pats.

"So let's go see them books."

"Shit. I didn't know you were coming. They're pretty much boxed up."

"Why?"

"Minor construction work."

"Tragic. I came all this way," she says.

"Is there something specific you're looking for? I can try to find it." I know this is impossible. It's hard enough to find things when they're on the floor. But for her, I will tear the place apart.

"Nah." She glances at me, her dark eyes sparkling and full of mischief. "If the books are a no-go, I guess you'll have to show me the records instead."

%%

I lead Hannah through the store while Garry gapes, open-mouthed, as if I've brought in a centaur. Ike doffs an invisible hat. Richie makes a kissy sound.

"Don't mind them," I tell Hannah as I lead her down the stairs. "They were raised in a barn."

"Ahh, they're harmless," she says.

"Don't know about that." I flick on the lights. Hannah's curious eyes take in the Mom rubble. The bike. The robe. The addiction books. I see the questions forming on her lips. Quickly, I point in the opposite direction. "Behold, the vinyl." I shake my keys.

"Locked?" Hannah asks. "Is this a vinyl crime zone?"

A little on the nose, there, Hannah. "You'd be surprised."

I unlock the bins and she starts going through one. "Holy shit. Versus. Velvet Underground." She turns to me. "Is it all like this?"

"I guess so."

"Pretty impressive for a music hater."

For a second, I can see Sandy, stooped over the bins, obsessing over his beloveds.

And maybe Hannah can too. Or maybe it dawns on Hannah the dissonance of a professed music hater having such a collection. Or maybe she reads the look on my face. Because she gets it.

"These aren't yours?"

Sandy built the cabinets over a single weekend in a burst of manic energy, not stopping to eat or sleep until he'd finished installing them, lining them with special plastic to keep out warping moisture, putting each album in its right place.

"No," I say. "They're my brother's."

She is holding a Violent Femmes album, tight to her chest. She sets it down and in a quiet voice asks, "He died?"

There are so many reasons why Sandy could've given me his collection: Maybe he's in prison. Maybe he became a Hare Krishna. Maybe he grew out of his collecting obsession and got married, had kids, got old and boring. But Hannah is right.

"He died."

"That explains it," she says.

"Explains what?"

"I don't know. This vibe I got off you. Sadness. I felt it coming off you when you were watching me read."

"You knew I was there?"

"Yeah, stalker. I was gonna tell you to piss off but something stopped me."

"I didn't mean to creep. It's just you were reading *The Magician's Nephew.*"

"So?"

"That book means a lot to me."

"You said you'd never heard of it."

"I lied."

"Why'd you lie?"

"I don't know. I panicked. I've never seen anyone reading that before. And that book, the entire series, it's like really special to me. They were the first books I ever got into. When I was a kid, I read them obsessively. My mom used to say Narnia was my first love."

This makes her laugh but in a nice way. "Who's your second love? Harry Potter?"

YOU, I think. *You, you, you.*

"Let's make a deal," she says. "You don't lie to me and I won't lie to you."

She holds out her hand to shake and it's like she has one of those prank buzzers because as we do a jolt goes up my spine. A delicious jolt. "Deal," I say.

She turns back to the bins. "What was he like?" she asks, pulling out a Prince double album. "This brother of yours."

I see Sandy again, handing me the key. I blink him away. I don't want to see Sandy, here, now. "I don't really remember. It was a long time ago."

Technically, Sandy died fifteen months ago, but he'd been dying in pieces for years, so this feels true enough that I didn't just violate our pact.

I gesture to the Prince album. "You wanna listen to that or just fondle it?"

She scopes out the basement. "Is there a turntable?"

"Upstairs. I can bring it down. Give me a sec."

"Okay. I'll keep searching for a perfect song for you."

"You're gonna be looking for a long time."

"I love a challenge."

In the store, Garry and Richie are playing catch with the books. I intercept a copy of *The Heart Is a Lonely Hunter* that

Garry is tossing to Richie as if it were a Frisbee. "Show some respect!" I scold.

"It's a book, not the Bible," Richie replies.

I don't even bother to respond to that. "Where's Ira?" I say, looking around. No way would he stand for this kind of treatment of the books.

"On a walk," Ike replies.

"Be careful," I bark at the guys as I climb the narrow staircase up to the apartment.

The one turntable we still possess lives in Sandy's room, tangled in a Gordian knot of wires and cables, the remnants of his workshop. Sandy was fourteen when he started revamping old stereos out of component parts he nosed out from hidden corners of junk shops and the dump, with the same spidey sense that pinged when he was in the vicinity of rare vinyl. For a while, he did a pretty brisk business, shipping his stereos all over the country. He used the proceeds to buy records. "Funds his addiction," Mom joked, back when our family could joke about addiction.

I pause in front of Sandy's doorway, his *Milo Goes to College* poster barely hanging on to the door. I'd stopped going in here when Sandy became a dick, but even now that he's gone, I still avoid it. Every so often I catch a whiff of him and then that trickster olfactory bulb sends me time traveling, and I never know where it's gonna take me: Will it hurl me back ten years, me and Sandy "camping" in a pillow fort? Or will it fling me back to that morning, Mom's animalistic screams echoing through the house? Sometimes I don't know which memory is worse.

I hold my breath and burst into his room. The only turntable left is a shitty one with built-in speakers, too crappy to sell. I yank it out of the pile and carry it down the stairs, past the nosy Lumberjacks.

Hannah sits cross-legged on the cement floor, five albums fanned out in front of her. "My opening salvo." She points to the covers one by one: Prince, Versus, the Rural Alberta Advantage, Scrawl, Lorde. "Five of my perfect songs. Let's see if any of them stick."

We plug in the turntable and she puts on the Prince first. " 'Starfish and Coffee,' for all the weirdos in the house." It's a fine song. I appreciate it. I don't hate it. But I don't love it. And it doesn't do to me what it does to Hannah.

Because each time the needle scratches onto the vinyl, Hannah closes her eyes, fingers playing invisible chords, mouthing the words. I can see she goes somewhere and I wish I could join her, but I can't.

"So?" she asks after playing "Team" by Lorde, the fifth perfect-to-her song.

I shrug. "It was nice."

"*Nice?*"

"I mean, maybe perfect. I can't tell."

"Trust me, if it was a perfect song, you'd know."

"Can we keep trying?"

"I'd love to, but . . ." She checks the time on her phone. "I have to get to a meeting." She stands up, holding the pile of records to her chest, and steps toward me. I stand up to face her. We are so close, I can smell her, a little bit minty, a little bit smoky. I wonder if this is what she would taste like if I kissed her.

She holds out the records. I take them but she doesn't let go. "Oh for five," she tsks, shaking her head. "I'm off my game."

"I warned you I was a lost cause."

"Those are my favorite kind." She stands on her tippy-toes to kiss me, somewhere between the cheek and lip. "I'll put you on the list for our show tonight," she murmurs. "Come. And we'll keep trying."

Fight Club

As soon as Hannah leaves, I call Chad. "Guess what we're doing tonight?"

"Homework," he replies.

"Definitely not."

"I got this project on—"

"Forget your project," I interrupt. "We're seeing Beethoven's Anvil!"

Chad pauses. "Aren't they opening for the Sheaths?"

"Are they? I have no idea."

"They are. At a big theater, with expensive tickets. That sold out months ago."

"What if you're on the list?"

"Who's on the list?"

"We are."

"How are *we* on the list?"

"Hannah put us there."

"When?"

"Today." I pause. "She came by. We hung out."

"You hung out with Hannah Crew?"

"Not just that. She kissed me."

"No shit!"

"Well, it was sort of a kiss. Half on my mouth, half on my cheek."

"So more of a friend thing?"

"I don't think it was a friend thing." Was it? I remember how it felt when we shook hands. My palm still tingles. No, not a friend thing. "Pick me up at six?" I say.

"You got it."

It's only after I hang up that I remember I asked Ira to dinner tonight, to force myself to tell him. But that misery can wait until tomorrow.

※

Chad pulls up at five, idling at the curb. I appreciate his eagerness, but Ira frowns on leaving early, and after I bailed on our dinner I don't feel like I can push it. "I can't leave till six," I tell Chad.

"All gravy. I came for the boxes."

"What boxes?"

"Those boxes." He points to the steps, where Ike, Richie, and Garry are each carrying two boxes.

I run over to stop them. "Are those our books?"

"They ain't mine," Richie replies.

"What are you doing with them?"

"Giving them to Chad," Ike says innocently. "For his whatchamacallit."

"Database," Richie says.

"For that," Ike says.

"What database are they talking about?" I call to Chad.

"The one I'm building. For my class," Chad says. When I don't say anything, he adds, impatiently, "I told you I was taking a class on database systems. This is my project."

"I have no clue what you're talking about."

"We *talked* about it. Last week."

"No we didn't," I say.

"We did," Chad replies mildly. "You said you couldn't find anything in the store and I said you would if you had a database."

"And then you told him to shut up," Richie adds.

"There was that," Chad admits. "But you're always telling me to shut up, and anyway, the guys were boxing up the books, so Ike called me up and then I got my project approved. I even went to the library today. The librarian told me there's special software that's normally hella expensive but is free for students." Chad grins at me. "You're welcome!"

###

When Chad returns at six, my mood has soured.

"What's eating you?"

I climb into the truck and look back toward the store. The shelves are now emptied. Chad's building a database. The guys are "working for coffee." Ira thinks the store is getting a second chance. All because I'm too chickenshit to tell the truth.

I take a deep breath. I turn to Chad. "I have to tell you something."

He sighs dramatically. "You're not still hung up on the books, are you?" he says as we pass the middle school. A group of kids on lowrider BMX bikes are tracing circles around the muddy grass.

"I'm not hung up, but you should've asked me first."

"You want me to get down on one knee and ask to index your books? Sorry, dawg. No can do." We drive by the high school, where a group of older kids are passing a bottle back and forth. "I'm doing you a favor. Building you something you can use in your store," Chad continues, pushing through the light at the edge of town and gunning the truck toward the interstate. "It might even improve sales."

"I wouldn't count on it. In case you haven't noticed, our business is not exactly thriving."

"I'm paralyzed, not blind," he replies. "But I took a business class last semester and the prof made us write a business plan. Your dad says you don't have one. Which is nuts. You need a business plan to get things like loans from the Small Business Administration. Did you know you could get a loan?"

"We're already deep in debt. More loans won't solve that."

"They might. If you negotiate the debt down, and then consolidate it in a low-interest SBA loan, you can save thousands of dollars. Then you use the savings to diversify your revenue stream."

I look at him, agog. He's channeling CPA Dexter Collings.

"Yeah, I'm smarter than you think! And no offense, but you and your dad don't seem to know how to run a business."

Mom used to handle the business side of things, but after the asteroid, not even she could right the ship. "None taken. But Chad, even the best business plan won't save us."

"How do you know?"

"Because . . ."

Because I sold the business to Penny Macklemore.

"Because we're a used bookstore in a small town where the only people who read buy their new books online." I pause. "I'm thinking of selling the place. Get out while we can. Like the Colemans did."

I watch this trial balloon float up into the air and for a second I think Chad gets it because his jolly expression grows pensive.

"You know how long it takes to fall seventy-five feet?" he asks.

"No."

"About three seconds. Now, you probably think three seconds is nothing, but trust me, when you're plummeting off a cliff, it feels like a hella long time. Long enough for you to think, 'Well, I'm a goner.'"

"I'm sorry, Chad. That must have been terrifying."

"Once again, you're missing my point, dawg. I was *sure* I was dead too." He pulls onto the highway and zooms into the fast lane. "But look at me now, son. Just look at me now."

※

Bogart's Ballroom, the venue where Beethoven's Anvil is playing tonight, is one of those big theaters in Tacoma. In the 1950s it was a fancy cinema, in the 1970s it became a derelict shell, and it was nearly torn down in the 1990s until it was resurrected as a music club, picking up the spillover from the Seattle scene.

Outside a crowd lingers, some people holding up signs begging for extra tickets. I look at them smugly. We don't need a ticket. We are on the list. The Lumberjack-induced gloom begins to lift. Hannah put *me* on the list.

Chad parks while I fight my way through the throngs to the box office to collect our tickets, but the harried woman tells me to go around to the stage entrance for a wristband.

Stage entrance. Wristband. I feel, possibly for the first time in my life, cool.

The feeling lasts until Chad and I approach the refrigerator-sized human manning the stage door. "Hi," I say, my voice squeaky and uncool. "We're on the list for Beethoven's Anvil."

Without so much as glancing at his clipboard, the Refrigerator replies, "Nope."

"We are. Aaron Stein and Chad Santos. Or maybe it's Aaron Stein, plus one."

"You're not on the list."

"Do you mind checking?" I ask. "We would've been added today."

"Don't need to check," he replies. "Checked earlier."

"Can you look?" I tap his clipboard and he snarls at me like I just trespassed onto private property. Then he glances, for maybe a half second, at it before giving off a satisfied "Nope."

"You didn't even look!"

The Refrigerator glares at us.

"Maybe you misunderstood," Chad whispers to me.

"I definitely did not misunderstand."

"Maybe she forgot?" Chad says.

"It was eight hours ago."

"Well, maybe she changed her mind."

Of all the scenarios, that one is the most likely. But it doesn't seem like Hannah's style to pull something like that. If Hannah changed her mind, she'd have the guts to break my heart in person.

"Can you call her?" Chad asks.

"I don't have her number," I mumble, not wanting the Refrigerator to hear this, but of course, he does.

"Groupies," he scoffs as his walkie-talkie squawks.

"Can't you just walkie-talkie down? Tell Hannah Crew that Aaron Stein is here."

"Do I look like a secretary?"

"Just call down. Please."

"Sorry. I don't do groupies' bidding."

"Dude. Don't call us that," Chad says. "It's disrespectful to the band, and to us. We are fans."

"How's that work with chicks?" the Refrigerator continues. "Do you gotta munch the carpet? Or do you rub their feet and paint their nails?"

"That's really misogynist," Chad tells him. "You should examine your toxic masculinity."

"You got exactly thirty seconds before me and my toxic masculinity kick both your asses." He glances at Chad. "Don't think I won't because you're in that chair."

"Good to know you have a moral code," says Chad, totally unruffled. He starts to back up. "Come on, dawg. He's not worth it."

I'm shaking with adrenaline as we return to Chad's truck. I pound the door.

"Whoa. Don't take it out on the Dodge."

"I just hate guys like that."

"Who? Him? Forget him."

I bang my fist against my head.

"Whoa. It's okay, shorty. We can wait for the band. See Hannah when they load out."

"Then I'll really feel like a pathetic groupie."

"Don't let guys like that get into your head," Chad says.

"All I have is guys like that in my head." I open the door to the truck. "Let's just go."

"You sure you don't wanna stay?"

This is the fourth Beethoven's Anvil show I've been to, but so far I've only managed to see them once. If we're looking at the numbers, that's one for three. Maybe the universe is trying to tell me something.

"I'm sure."

Chad lowers the chair lift. "You know, guys like that are just flexing."

"Yeah, their muscles. Which are huge."

"Naw, they're flexing to hide how scared they are."

"Him? Scared?" I bark out a laugh as I climb into the passenger seat. "Of what? Us?"

"Yeah."

"Why would he be scared of us? No offense, Chad, but he could squash both of us with one hand."

"He's scared of becoming us."

"Why would he be scared of that?"

"Okay. How to explain this?" Chad asks, checking his rearview mirror as if the answer is there. "Have you ever seen the movie *Fight Club*?"

"No, but I've read the book."

"Seriously? It was also a book first?"

"Seriously."

"Are all movies books first?"

"Just the best ones."

"Then you know the story?"

"First rule of fight club is you don't talk about fight club."

Chad nods. "So I saw that movie a bunch of times in high school. Me and the guys used to get drunk and watch it. And the thing was, back then I thought—we all thought Tyler was fire. The badassest of the badasses. Everything we wanted to be. A hero who fucked and fought and took no shit from anyone.

"And maybe I would've kept on thinking that. But a few months after my accident, I'm watching the movie again, and it was like I'd been watching a different movie all along, because I suddenly saw Tyler wasn't meant to be the hero. He was a hot mess. How could I not see that before?"

I shrug. "I think a lot of guys want to be like Tyler."

"Not you though."

"No, not me. But then again, I read the book."

Chad chuckles. "I have a theory. That guys like the bouncer, guys like I was, they think they're supposed to be Tyler, and they go around fronting. But in reality, none of us really are. We're just stuck pretending. And when you pretend like that, you live in fear of being caught. So you double down on the act. That way no one can see past it."

"That's deep, Chad."

"Deep as the Mariana Trench." Chad winks. "I got hidden depths."

"I'm starting to see that."

"Look. I'm not saying I wanna be stuck in a chair, unsure if I'll ever have normal sex or fall in love. But being permanently freed from having to pretend to be a Tyler, man, that was a relief. Because in the end, those guys are so much worse off than me." He casts a sidelong smirk. "They're even worse off than you."

"Thank you?"

He claps a hand over mine. "You're welcome, son."

We fall into a friendly silence, the tire treads making a reassuring rhythm against the damp pavement. "Do you really believe all that?" I ask him after a while.

An oncoming truck passes us, high beams briefly illuminating the car. Maybe it's the intimacy of the dark, or the concentration of driving, but Chad's face has shed its usual clownish jauntiness and looks somehow achingly real. He cocks his head to the side, as if he means to lean on my shoulder. Then he straightens back up, and, staring ahead into the inky night, admits, "I don't know, dawg. But I'm trying to."

The Little Book of Hygge

Sundays the store is closed, and like God himself, Ira takes a day of rest. He doesn't usually get out of bed until noon. I wake up early no matter what, and back when I still could read about things other than extinct reptiles, I'd stay in bed, nose in book, until Ira and Mom roused me.

This Sunday morning I take advantage of the quiet to replay alternate scenarios of last night, imagining what would have happened if that asshole bouncer had let us in.

Before she kissed me, Hannah had said we'd *keep trying*. I beat off to the multiple ways we might've kept trying. As I wipe up the results with a towel, I suddenly think of Chad and get what he means about the connection between love and desire. And then I feel really weird thinking about Chad as I wipe up my jiz.

This is the rabbit hole I'm spiraling down when I hear keys in the shop door. Is Ira up? I check his bedroom; he's still out cold.

"Hello?" Ike calls up the stairs. "Anyone here?"

All three of them are in the shop, in their overalls, staring at the empty Mr. Coffee.

"Where's the coffee?" Richie whines.

"It's Sunday," I say.

"So? Jesus say something about not drinking coffee on Sunday?"

"I wouldn't know." I turn to Ike. "What are you doing here?"

But before he can answer, there's a loud crash. I swivel around. Garry has busted a hole in the back wall.

"What are you doing?" I shout.

"Opening the wall." Garry demonstrates by taking another swing.

"Stop it!" I lunge for the sledgehammer but it's too late. There's a gaping hole in the Sheetrock. "What the fuck!"

Garry kneels down, touching the exposed pipes. "This is some really good work."

"Did your mom really do the roughing?" Richie asks.

I'm caught off guard by the reference to Mom.

Ike shines his flashlight inside. "It's solid work. Café would practically build itself."

"Café? Have you been to talking to Chad?"

"I've been talking to Angela Silvestri," Ike says.

"Who's Angela Silvestri?"

"She was the secretary at the middle school. Just retired. Heckuva baker. She makes a mean crumb cake. It's got this cinnamon sugar topping, but with crunch. You know what gives it the crunch?" Before anyone can answer, Ike crows, "Life cereal. She puts it in the topping."

"Ike, I said you could fix the bookshelf. No one said anything about a café."

"We were talking with your dad," Garry says. "We think a café really would make the whole space more *hygge*."

"What's 'huggy'?" Richie asks.

"*Hygge*," Garry corrects, pronouncing the word like he's swallowing it. "It's some Danish thing about how to make spaces more cozy. My girlfriend got a book called *The Little Book of Hygge*. Went around trying to make the whole house *hygge*. We got lots of throw pillows and sheepskin rugs, and she painted stencils all over the walls. It's nice."

"A café will make it more *hygge*?" Richie asks.

"Yep," Ike answers. "Especially a café with crumb cake."

"Will you shut up about crumb cake and *hygge*!" I shout.

"Yeesh," Garry says. "We're just trying to help."

"Help? Is that what you call it?" I look at Ike. "I've lived in this town long enough to recognize a Lucy when I see one."

"Who's Lucy?" Richie asks.

"From *Peanuts*!"

They stare at me blank-faced.

"You know. Charlie Brown? Lucy?"

"Oh, Lucy van Pelt," Richie says. "What about her?"

"She always pretends to hold the football for Charlie Brown and at the last minute she yanks it up and he winds up flat on his back. Well, I'm not falling for it."

"You're upset about Charlie Brown?" Richie asks.

"I think he's mad about Lucy," Garry says.

"I'm mad about you!" I shout.

"Which you?" Garry asks.

"All of you, but especially you, *you*!" I jab a finger toward Ike. "We agreed you'd fix the shelf. That's it."

"See, the thing is, the shelf's been keeping me up at night," Ike says. "It's been neglected. This whole place has been neglected." He gestures at the broken bookshelf, the water-stained ceiling, the warped floorboards. "Ain't no one taking proper care of it. If they were, it wouldn't have come to this."

"You cannot be serious," I say, the rush of anger from last night outside of Bogart's Ballroom returning tenfold. I am so fucking tired of guys like this.

"Serious as a heart attack. Someone needs to see to this place."

"Don't you dare!" I begin, my voice shaking. "Don't you dare lecture *me* about neglect."

"Not lecturing anyone," Ike says. "Just stating a fact."

"Oh, you like facts. How about this one? For the past few years none of you, not a single one, gave two shits about us. I mean, where were you when we needed you with your GoFundMes? Or even a casserole. Or just a kind word, a condolence. So you don't have any right to talk to *me* about neglect."

"Well, that's got nothing to do with this fine wood."

"Shut up! Just shut up about the shelf! The shelf can burn for all I care."

Ike recoils at this threat of harm to his precious. "You're not thinking straight."

"You don't get to tell me what I'm thinking. And you don't get to put ideas into Ira's head. If you don't get your asses out of here right now, I'll . . ."

"You'll what?" Richie asks, scoffing the way the Refrigerator did.

"I'll . . ." And before I know what I'll do, I'm doing it. I'm swinging my fist at Ike.

I miss. Of course.

Before I can regain my footing, I'm up against a bookshelf, arms pinned behind my back. "Now just wait a gosh-darn minute," Ike says.

"Did you just try to punch Ike?" Garry asks.

"Go to hell!" I shout.

"*You* go to hell," Garry shoots back.

"Now everyone just calm down," Ike says, still squeezing me tight. "Seems we are having ourselves a little misunderstanding."

"No misunderstanding," I say, pulling away, fruitlessly, because Ike's grip is granite.

"Yes, a misunderstanding. And we're gonna brew that pot of coffee and we're gonna sit down like civilized men and straighten it out."

I yank myself away at the exact moment that Ike releases me. I stumble backward, my elbow rearing up and colliding with Richie's nose.

"Oww!" Richie cries. "He hit me."

"I didn't hit you." I spin around to see Richie's nose geysering blood. "Oh, shit!"

"You clocked Richie," Garry yells. "You little bastard!"

"I *elbowed* him. By accident," I begin, but it's too late. Garry is already charging me. But once again, Ike's faster. He jumps in front of him.

"Now everyone just cool your jets!" he roars, holding Garry back with one hand, while drop-kicking me to the floor, and also somehow handing Richie a bandana to staunch his blood-spurting nose.

It's at this precise moment that Ira makes his way down the stairs to the store. He takes one look at me, on the floor, the pool of blood, turns an unnatural shade of green, and passes out cold.

※

Ike insists on driving me, Richie, and Ira to the clinic. Garry stays behind to clean up the blood before it seeps into the wood. Because according to Ike, once blood penetrates the grain, it's impossible to get out.

Bev's working and she takes Ira, now conscious, and Richie, barely bleeding, back at the same time, leaving me and Ike to awkwardly leaf through old issues of *Family Circle*.

When I finish reading an article about how to make the perfect confetti cake, I look up at Ike. "I'm sorry I punched you."

"You didn't punch me."

"I'm sorry I *tried* to punch you."

"Why'd you try to punch me?"

"I don't know. The thing you said, about the neglect. It made me feel like shit."

"Why?"

"Well, because the neglect is my fault, obviously."

Ike is silent a spell before he says, "Do you know my wife, Binatta?" I shake my head. "Her friends call her Beana."

"*Beana's* your wife?" Beana used to be one of our best customers, the kind who came in once a week and bought a frontlist hardcover. But she hasn't been in the store in ages. I figured she'd started getting her books online. Like everyone else.

130

"Married forty years and counting," Ike says.

"I didn't know that. I haven't seen her in a while."

"Not for about six years, I'd guess." Ike pulls out his can of tobacco and then looks around the waiting room, seems to realize he shouldn't dip in a medical office, and puts it away. "That was when her fibromyalgia got real bad. Her joints got so swollen, it was just too painful to go anywhere. But she loved to read." Ike whistles. "Always did, but after her condition got worse and she had to quit her job, it was all she did. Sometimes two books a day. An expensive habit, especially after the mill closed. When your dad stopped seeing her so often, he called her up on the telephone and asked if she might read some of those free books the publishers send you ahead of time."

"The galleys?"

"That's right. He set aside the galleys for her. And it tickled her so because she felt like she got to read things before everyone else. She used to tell your dad which ones she liked, which ones she didn't. Though even when she didn't care for a book, she always finished. And your dad never charged us because he said she was doing him a service and he wasn't allowed to. Showed me where it said right there printed on the books: *Not for sale*."

Ike clears his throat. "But then a few years on, I started to notice that the books he was dropping off for Beana weren't paperbacks no more but hardcovers, like she used to buy. And they didn't have that 'not for sale' thing on them. I figured out he was now giving Beana actual books, not the free ones."

I nod. "When we stopped buying new books, we stopped getting the advance copies."

"I didn't know that. But I knew we'd gone from doing favors to getting them." Ike tugs on his beard. "I've always provided for my family. It don't feel great to need charity.

"Around that time, our daughter sent Beana one of them tablet readers. She didn't like it at first. No pages to turn. But she got used to it and now she loves it because it's easier to hold, easier to see, and she can get a dozen library books on there at once."

"That makes sense."

"'Course with that tablet, there wasn't much cause to come into the store, so I didn't. Even when I knew I ought to have. Not just to buy books. But to offer condolences, on account of what happened with your brother." Ike stares at his gnarled hands. "Don't know why I didn't. Knew it was wrong. But sometimes too much time passes and there don't seem a way back. I hadn't set foot in the store in years when we built that ramp. And when I saw what happened to it, to your father, I just felt downright ashamed."

"Ike," I say, my heart feeling somehow larger and smaller at the same time. "You didn't wreck our store. It's not *your* fault."

He searches his pockets for his bandana, not finding it because it's up Richie's nose. I hand him a box of tissues and he honks out a few trumpety blows before he looks up. "You know what's the biggest threat to wood? Not fire. Not water. But termites. They get into a perfectly healthy house and gnaw away until there ain't nothing left. I might not have been the only one, but I was one of the termites that weakened your foundations, and I'll be darned if I'm gonna let it fall down on my account."

"But Ike . . ." I say. "What if it's too late? What if the termites have eaten away so much of the wood that there's nothing left to save?"

Ike dabs his eyes as he contemplates this, but before he answers, the door swings open and Bev emerges, Ira and Richie trailing behind her like wayward children.

"They're both fine. No broken bones." She points to Richie, who glares at me, like he's even more pissed off that I didn't give him a legit injury. "And no strokes." She gestures to Ira.

"I had a panic attack," he announces cheerily.

"Are you sure?" I ask Bev. "He's never passed out before."

"If you'd seen your only son covered in blood, you'd have passed out too," Ira says with a dopey smile on his face.

"Panic attacks can manifest in all sorts of ways," Bev says. "Scary but not life-threatening, unless you're driving."

"She gets them when she's driving. And you'll never guess what she does to calm herself down." When no one guesses, Ira says, "She sings!"

"What can I say?" Bev shrugs. "Singing calms me down."

"She's going to help me get a handle on my depression and anxiety!" Ira chirps gaily.

"Seems like she already has," Richie mutters.

"She gave me Ativan!"

"I did," she says. "And we discussed other options."

"Support groups!" Ira says. "Bev's going to take me to one. Her husband died."

"Condolences," Ike says.

"Thank you," Bev replies. "And yes, support groups can be very helpful."

"You gonna put him on them drugs?" Ike asks.

There's an awkward moment. Bev smiles mildly and says, "Like I said, all options are on the table."

"Because Beana tried Zoloft but it gave her headaches," Ike says. "We switched her to Wellbutrin. Works like a charm."

"My dad takes Zoloft, no problem," Richie announces, then remembers he's mad at me and glares anew.

"I'm really sorry, Richie," I tell him.

"We're all sorry," Ike adds. "And we're all friends now."

"Oh good!" Ira beams. "Now we can go back to work. I told Bev all about how we're fixing up the store and I promised her we'd have Lit and Knits."

"Knit and Lits," Ike corrects.

"Those too," Ira adds. He looks at me. "See, Aaron, I told you, it's not too late."

"That's what I've been trying to tell him," Ike says, swinging an arm around my shoulder.

The average dinosaur supposedly lived between seventy and eighty years, which is basically the average life span for a human. I think back to those thirty-three thousand years after the asteroid hit and before the last dinosaur disappeared. Some of them must've carried on, right? Chewing plants, eating turtles, having sex, playing with their hatchlings. Some of them must have been the dinosaur equivalent of happy.

And so when I tell Ike and Ira, "Maybe it's not too late," I kind of even almost believe it.

The Art of the Deal

Penny Macklemore keeps a couple offices in town—one in the back of the hardware store, another in the car dealership—but the place you can reliably find her is at C.J.'s Diner, where she eats lunch every day. Cindy Jean won't let anyone else sit in the corner booth between the hours of eleven and three.

"Aaron, what a pleasant surprise," Penny says as I approach her booth.

"Mind if I sit down?"

"Please do."

I slide opposite her.

"You look pale, like you could use a bit of iron. Cindy Jean, let's get this boy a burger."

"It's fine. I just came to talk to you."

"Have a fry, at least." She dips a limp spear in ketchup and holds it up to my lips. I have no choice but to accept it. "Good. Would you like an order of fries?"

"No, thanks. I'm really not hungry."

"Suit yourself." She dabs her lips with a napkin and then bares her teeth at me. "Do I have lettuce stuck anywhere?"

"What?"

"When you age, your gumlines recede and food gets stuck. Gerald used to point out if I had anything in my teeth, but he's passed on now so there's no one to warn me." She bares her teeth at me again. "Do I have any gunk?"

"Nothing that I can see."

Not quite trusting my response, she takes a knife and holds it up to her mouth like a mirror. When she's reasonably assured there is no loose vegetation there, she puts down the knife. "I take it you've come to talk to me about the work going on at your store."

"You know about that?" I let go of the breath I have been holding since I decided to back out of the deal. If Penny knows, Ira will never have to. Everything might turn out okay after all.

"I make it my business to know everything that happens in this town. How do you feel about pie?" Before I answer she calls, "Cindy Jean, what kind of pie do you have?"

"Cherry and apple, same as always," Cindy Jean replies. "And pumpkin for the holiday."

"Do you have a preference?" Penny asks me. "Aside from pumpkin, which I never cared for."

"I don't really want pie."

"Oh, share a slice of pie with me. Otherwise I'll eat the whole thing. Which do you like better? Cherry or apple?"

"Cherry, I guess."

"Cindy Jean," she calls. "We'll have the cherry." She turns to me. "Now what is it you need, dear? You want to back out of the sale?" She says it so breezily, like she expected it, that my limbs go rubbery with relief.

"I do."

"Why's that?"

"Our circumstances have changed."

"How so?"

"I think I might have been wrong. Maybe people here *do* want a bookstore."

"Interesting." She turns toward the kitchen. "Are you warming the pie?"

"Always do," Cindy Jean replies.

"Not too hot, or the ice cream melts." She turns back to me. "Don't you love pie à la mode?"

"I guess so."

"Me too!" She takes a bite of her pickle. "Oh, nice and dill. So you were saying people here want a bookstore?"

"I think so."

"Well, you know me. I'm more of a TV person. I'm a big fan of that show *Survivor*. Have you ever seen it?"

"No."

"Gerald used to love that show. We used to watch it together every Wednesday."

"Uh-huh." The pleasant rubbery feeling in my limbs starts to harden into unease.

"Cindy Jean," Penny calls. "Are you getting me my Sanka?"

"Do I ever not?" Cindy Jean replies.

"Just making sure. Do you want any Sanka?" she asks me.

"No. I don't want any Sanka."

"Okay. Now where was I?"

"*Survivor*."

"Right. So you see, on *Survivor*, when they don't want you, they vote you off the island. This town voted you off the island years ago. A fresh coat of paint won't change that."

"It's not just paint. It's also . . . other things." I scramble to remember how Chad put it. "We'd diversify our revenue streams."

Cindy Jean drops off the pie and Sanka. "Now look what you did," Penny scolds. "The ice cream's already a puddle."

"'Cause the pie's hot. You wanted it heated," Cindy Jean says.

"Warmed, not piping." Penny sighs as she takes a forkful of the hot, melty pie. She chews, swallows, and says, "So what's in it for me?"

"For you?"

"If I let you out of the deal, what's in it for me?"

"I dunno. You'd be doing the right thing. A mitzvah."

"A whatzvah?"

"A good deed."

"Oh, you sound like Gerald, God rest his soul. He didn't understand business at all. And I didn't either until after he passed, without a dollar in the bank. And then, oh you'll like this, I read a book."

"A book?"

"Yes! It changed my life." She forks a piece of pie and holds it up to my face. "Would you like a bite?"

"No, thanks."

"Oh, go on." She holds the fork there until I have no choice but to accept. The filling is cherry, but all I taste is strawberries.

"The book was called *The Art of the Deal* and it taught me how in business, nothing is personal. There are no good deeds. So I'd want to know what's my incentive to let you back out of this deal, especially given I've already spent a fair amount of energy, not to mention money."

"How much?"

"Oh, about three thousand dollars in legal bills and bank fees."

I gulp. "What if I pay that back?"

"Do you have three thousand dollars lying around?"

We both know I don't. But I could probably scrounge it up. Ask Chad for a loan. Maybe Mom. Maybe get a credit card of my own. "I can figure it out."

"It's a start, but that just gets me back to even." She takes a loud slurp of her Sanka. "But say you were to *buy* out my option . . ." She taps her bubblegum-pink nails against the table. "With an additional ten thousand dollars, I might reconsider."

"Ten thousand dollars?"

"Well, thirteen, total. By December first."

"That's in two weeks."

"December first is the day we agreed to close by."

"I'll just pull out of the deal. I can do that."

"You most certainly can. Of course, you'll still have to reimburse my expenses, which will most certainly grow. And pay a penalty. It's all in the contract."

"It is?"

"If you'd had a lawyer read yours, you'd know all this."

"You didn't say anything about lawyers! It was just you and me signing the contract."

"Who do you think executed the contract? My lawyer. You should always have a lawyer read your terms. Even though lawyers can be very expensive. Though not thirteen-thousand-dollars expensive. Sometimes you can be penny-wise but pound-foolish. Penny-wise. Ha!" She laughs at her own joke before stabbing another piece of pie.

I feel sick. "I can't believe you're holding my store hostage for thirteen grand."

"Oh, pish. I'm just looking to leverage my assets. You see, winners take advantage of opportunities when they present themselves." She scrapes up the last bits of cherry from the plate, the knife sending a nail-against-chalkboard shudder through me. "Though I suspect that's one lesson you already know."

"What's that supposed to mean?"

"Cindy Jean, check," she calls before turning back to me. "Well, for one, you sold the building to me without consulting your father. Now, I don't pretend to know the ins and outs of your relationship, but I suspect you did that because you wanted to sell the store and you knew he didn't. Which leads me to believe you have your own agenda."

"But . . ." I sputter.

"Oh, I'm not judging you. If anything, I admire it. Though for the life of me I'm not sure why you let Ike and those gentlemen do any work, knowing it is for naught. That I don't understand."

"I'm trying to help my father."

"Everyone always says they're trying to help someone." She dabs her lips with the napkin, which between the burger and pie now looks like a crime scene. "But really, Aaron, if we're honest, we're all just trying to help ourselves."

Goldmine Record Album Price Guide

I get back to the store that afternoon to find Ira waiting for me, his slicker on.

"I have to talk to you," I tell him. "Now."

"I'm meeting Bev for support group." He smiles. "My first one."

"This is important."

"So's this," he replies. "We can't have me fainting all over town, now can we?"

"But . . ."

"It'll keep."

///

When Ira's not back by six, I'm now on the verge of a panic attack myself. This morning I woke up feeling hopeful. I thought I'd found a way to make it work. Make Ira happy. And Chad. And the Lumberjacks.

I should've known better.

I lock up the store and go upstairs to make some pasta for dinner. I'm so distracted and distraught that when the phone rings, I pick it up without thinking.

"Aaron," Mom says. "I'm so glad you answered."

"Oh, hey, Mom. Ira's out."

"That's okay. I called to talk to you."

"Oh."

A silence falls over the line.

"How's the weather?" we both ask at the same time.

"Sunny and cold," Mom answers.

"Rainy and cold," I answer.

"Jinx," Mom says.

"Haven't we had enough of those?" I say.

The line goes silent again.

"What'd you want to talk to me about?"

"I was thinking maybe you might want to come for a visit," she begins in a halting voice. "Silver's not that far from you. You could drive."

"Maybe in a few months," I say. "Things are really busy right now."

"Of course, my love." I can tell she's trying to hide her disappointment and it makes me feel like shit. "Your father mentioned you're having some work done on the store."

Knowing the work is for naught, I hear Penny say.

What have I done? Now, not only am I going to let Ira down, but Ike and the guys too. Chad was right. I'm the biggest coward.

"Did you say something?" Mom asks.

"Uh, just muttering to myself."

"Something bothering you?"

"Just money stuff."

She chuckles. "Money problems are just math problems."

"Insanely hard math problems," I reply. "Like calculus level."

"You boil down your priorities," she says. "The rest sorts itself out."

In my experience, nothing sorts itself out, and at first, I write this off as Mom New Age gobbledygook. But then I think about what she said. Priorities. Maybe she's right. Maybe it's not calculus level at all. Maybe it's basic arithmetic: Betraying Sandy < Saving Ira.

Suddenly, I know how to dig myself out of my hole. Dig Ira out of his. The truth is, I've known it all along.

"Thanks, Mom. That was helpful."

"It was?"

"Yeah, but now I gotta go."

"Oh, okay." The hurt in her voice bleeds across the miles.

"I'm sorry. It's important. Can I call you back later?"

There's another heavy pause on the line because Mom knows I won't call her back, even if she doesn't know why. "Anytime, my love."

After I hang up with Mom I immediately call the Corporate Health Food Emporium. It takes twenty minutes of bad hold music, three transfers, and two minor lies to get the name and number of Lou, the guy who I saw selling records there.

I get his voicemail. I leave a message: "Hey, my name's Aaron. I have some good vinyl to sell," and hang up.

He calls back thirty seconds later. "How many albums?" he asks. "What genre? What condition? How are they stored?"

When I tell him, his breath goes kind of ragged. "Can I come now?"

Ira's due back any minute. "How about tomorrow, around lunchtime?" I'll figure out some errand to send Ira on.

"You won't sell them before then?"

"I won't."

"You promise?"

If Lou only knew. "I promise I won't."

Lou says he'll be there. I instruct him to text before he comes in. He agrees. I'm pretty sure if I'd asked him to cut off his pinkie before coming, he'd have agreed to that too.

※

The next morning, the Lumberjacks are taking the morning off for what they're calling a "scouting mission." I have no idea what this is but I persuade Ira to go with them.

"But who will watch the store?"

"I will."

"But you already did that yesterday."

"It'll give me a chance to catch up on my reading." I pick up Karel Čapek's *War with the Newts*, one of my neglected Central European novels. "I've fallen behind," I add, which is the understatement of the year.

"If you're sure," Ira asks.

"Positive," I say. "Do you need money?" I pull a few twenties out of the till. "Have fun. And take your time."

※

Here's the thing: Sandy never should've asked me to do it. Made me, of all people, the guardian of his vinyl. I refuse to feel bad about selling it. It's his fault we're in this predicament as much as it is mine.

But Ira . . . I do feel bad about lying to him, so as penance, I pick up the Čapek and try to actually read it. The first sentence alone takes up an entire page and while part of my brain can register all the hallmarks of good writing—a strong voice, a weird setup, humor—my attention keeps getting snagged on words like *island* and *equator*, which makes me think of traveling, which makes me think of Thailand, which makes me think of Chad, which makes me think of Hannah, who I have not heard from.

I'm still struggling to get past page six of the Čapek when my phone buzzes with a text. From Lou. I'm here. Sorry I'm so early. I got excited. LMK when I can come.

It's ok. Come now, I text back.

When I see the dented Subaru wagon rumble down Main Street, I know it's Lou even before he parks. People who collect lots of shit that can't get wet, like books, like records, tend to drive old, battered wagons.

As I lead him into the basement, he has that look in his eye, the one Sandy would get when he'd see a junk shop or a yard sale and yell "Stop" because his vinyl radar had pinged. When I open the first bin, Lou's breath judders.

I show him the laminated index. "It's all itemized. If you want to know what's in each bin."

"If it's all the same to you, I'd rather just go through them blind," he says in a reverent whisper. "Treasures like this don't come around all that often."

"Have at it." I take a seat on the edge of the stairs.

He starts pawing through the albums, one at a time, gasping now and then. I can see it's going to be a while.

"I'll be upstairs. If you find anything you like, just put it in a pile and holler when you're ready."

Lou does not question this, nor the cloak-and-dagger secrecy of the endeavor. He's already in the zone.

Back upstairs, I try again with the Čapek and manage another four pages.

"Holy shit!" I hear Lou scream.

"You okay?" I call down to the basement.

"You have Nico's *Chelsea Girl*," he replies. "I think I've died and gone to heaven."

I give up on the Čapek and return to my trusty Brusatte, opening to a random page the way I used to shake a Magic 8-Ball for guidance. I wind up reading about the discovery of a mass grave of metoposaurs—car-sized salamanders from the Triassic period, which Brusatte and his pals discovered in Portugal. It makes me feel better to know that something that lived fifty million years ago can still be here now.

When I hear Ike's truck coughing down Main Street, I check on Lou again. "I'm going to close the door," I call down. "When you're done, don't come up. Text me."

"Roger, boss," he says.

I close the door and lock it, just in case.

Ira comes skipping up the porch stairs. "You wouldn't believe what we found!" he says, vibrating with excitement. "Tell him, Ike!"

"A whole mess of oak floorboards to replace the rotting ones," Ike says. "A couple of lamps that'll need to be rewired. And best of all . . ." He peers out the door. "Hurry up, will ya?"

"It weighs a ton!" Richie complains. "Can't we use a dolly?"

"Just lift from your knees," Ike says.

Richie and Garry struggle up the stairs holding some large, bulky, and clearly heavy object covered in a tarp.

"Oh, for cryin' out loud," Ike says, grabbing hold of it on his hip. "Aaron, put a cloth down, will ya. I don't want it to get scratched."

I quickly look around and see Lou's left his jacket upstairs. I throw it on top of a sawhorse and Ike gently sets down his prize before whipping off the tarp with a jubilant "Ta-da!"

It's a large cylinder with many knobs coming out of it, covered in a layer of rust and grit.

"Ain't it a beaut?" Ike asks.

"It's a something," I reply.

"Do you know what it is?" he asks.

"A robot?"

"Guess again."

"One of those old diving bells?"

"It's . . ." Ike trails off with dramatic flourish.

"An espresso machine," Richie shouts.

"Why didn't you let me tell him?" Ike fumes.

"*That's* an espresso machine?" I ask.

"Vintage Italian," Ike says. "What they would use to make espresso and cappuccinos and all those fancy drinks in Italy. What's the name of the company?"

"Something like Lady Gaga?" Richie says.

"*Gaggia*," Garry corrects, with perfect Italian pronunciation.

"They don't make things like this anymore. Fixed up, these babies sell for a thousand dollars," Ike says. "We got this for two fifty."

"But I only gave you forty dollars," I tell Ira.

"Oh," Ira says. "Chad fronted us the rest."

"Chad? Why'd he give you money?"

"'Cause we knew you'd kick up a fuss," Ike asks. "Now, should we put it in the basement?"

"No!" I shout. "I mean, it's a mess down there. Just leave it here."

"Okay," Ike says.

"That was fun, lads," Ira says, settling into his chairs. "Thanks for bringing me."

"Why don't you go get some espresso at ValuMart to test out the machine?" I ask Ira.

"Oh, first I have to take it apart and clean it and reassemble it," Ike says, looking delighted at the prospect.

"Also, ValuMart doesn't sell espresso," Garry adds.

"Well, you could drive to Bellingham to get some. So we're prepared." I pull another two twenties out of the till, leaving it empty.

"I'm gonna stay here and work on Gaga," Ike says. "And I'll probably have to replumb the line to make sure the pressure's adequate. Gonna take a few days." He looks utterly thrilled at this prospect.

"Then you three go!" I push Ira, Richie, and Garry toward the door.

"We don't have to go all the way to Bellingham," Ira says.

"You might as well get the good stuff."

"You're sure excited about coffee all of a sudden," Riche says suspiciously.

"Well, a good idea is a good idea."

I get them out the door. "Be right back," I tell Ike, who's already started in on the machine.

Lou sits cross-legged on the floor, like Hannah did a few days ago. Only he has several rows of records around him, and a large paperback book open in his lap. "I didn't even get through a quarter of the bins, but this is already more than I can afford." He taps on the smaller row. "These are worth easily worth two hundred. And these"—he taps on the larger row—"double that. I can only afford these." He taps on the two-hundred-dollar selection. "But I'll get an advance on my paycheck and come back for the rest."

I do the math: two hundred dollars today plus four hundred later. It's six hundred dollars. A lot of money. But about one-thirtieth of what I need.

Lou misreads my frown. "You can check if you don't believe me." He hands me his book. "*Goldmine Record Album Price Guide.* My bible. I wouldn't rip you off. It would dishonor the records."

"I don't think you're trying to rip me off," I say. "It's just I kind of wanted to offload all of them, quickly, and I thought since you had that business . . ."

"Oh, you mean the table at the health food place?" Lou shakes his head. "That's not mine. That's owned by someone else. I just shill for him. Mostly to get any good stuff before he does. But his shit is nothing like what you've got."

"Would he buy these records?"

149

"Probably, but he'd rip you off." He glances upstairs. "You have a space. Why not sell them yourself?"

"I can't."

Shrugging, Lou opens his wallet, counting out ten crisp twenties. "Let me ask around. I know some people who would go apeshit for this. Would pay you what it's worth. And would honor the vinyl."

"Okay," I tell Lou. "So long as they honor it by December first."

I empty one of Mom's boxes and load Lou's records inside, throwing one of her sweaters on top for camouflage. "Gotta keep the records cushioned," I tell Lou.

"Who's this?" Ike asks as we emerge from the basement.

"Lou," says Lou.

"What's he doing down there?"

"Looking at the gas meter," I lie.

"You work at Cascadia?" Ike asks, giving Lou the side-eye. "Where's your uniform?"

"He works in the corporate department." I lead Lou to the front door.

"My jacket," he whispers.

"I'll give it back next time."

When we get to Lou's car, he hesitates. "Are these stolen? Because I can't accept stolen vinyl. It wouldn't honor the records."

"They're not stolen," I tell Lou. At least not in the way he thinks.

He belts the crates into the back seat, like an overprotective father. I hand him the *Goldmine* book but he tells me to keep it. "I think you're gonna need it."

Beethoven's Anvil

When Chad calls to ask if I want to take a road trip to catch Beethoven's Anvil in Vancouver, it's been nearly a week since I heard from Hannah. I'm assuming I blew it.

"Son, you weren't far enough along to blow it," Chad says. "She probably hasn't called you because they've been on the road."

"They have?"

"Vancouver's the last stop on their tour, so we can surprise her. See if we can't get you a real kiss."

"Sure," I say, playing it casual, though the mere mention of kissing Hannah gives me the stirrings of what I now know is a psychogenic boner. "And maybe I can try to sell some records."

"So you *are* selling them?"

"I am."

"You're gonna bring them with?"

"I thought I'd start with some flyers. Then I can sell them by private appointment."

"Private appointment. Fancy."

"That's me. Fancy."

"Okay, Mr. Fancy. I'll see you tomorrow."

The next night, Chad comes by the store to check out Gaga. Ike has taken it completely apart, oiled the bits, and scrubbed the rust off. The brass is so gleaming, Penny Macklemore could check her gums in it.

"Looking good," Chad tells Ike.

"Missing some parts, but she'll be up and working in no time."

Chad turns to me. "You ready?"

I nod, heart galloping at the thought of seeing Hannah again even though she is five hours away.

"You got your papers?"

"In here." I tap the backpack full of flyers.

I climb into Chad's truck. "Hey, about Gaga, thanks for fronting the money."

"I thought you'd be pissed. Like you were about the inventory."

"I'm not. It's just, don't spend any more money on the shop, okay?"

"How come?"

"For one, you're saving for the Stim. And also, I have no idea when I'll be able to pay you back."

"Who said anything about paying me back?" When I don't answer, Chad continues. "There's more than one way to skin a cat."

"There is?"

"Sure. I mean you could reimburse me, with interest." He waggles his eyebrows exaggeratedly. "Or you could make me partner and let my investment be my equity stake."

"You want to be a partner? In our store?"

"What's so crazy about that?"

"It's like wanting to book a berth on the *Titanic*, after it hit the iceberg."

"Was that movie a book first too?" Chad asks.

"Not that one," I reply.

"Just checking. Anyhow, I know the store's not thriving, but once we open new revenue streams with the café, the records . . ."

"Chad, we *cannot* sell the records in the store."

"You just said you were selling them."

"But Ira can't know that."

"Why?" Chad asks.

"He'd be devastated."

"Why?"

"Because I promised Sandy . . ."

"Promised him what?"

You gotta promise me . . .

"That I wouldn't."

"But Sandy's dead," Chad points out.

"I'm aware of that."

"Aren't promises, like, null and void when someone dies?"

I shut my eyes against the memory.

"Not this one," I tell Chad.

"Fine. We'll diversify in other ways. And if you make me a partner, you wouldn't have to pay me back. Or even pay me, until we turn a profit."

"I hate to break it to you but we haven't turned a profit in years, and the chances of doing so, even if we diversify, are small."

"Like how small?"

"I don't know."

"Gimme a number. Thirty percent? Twenty?"

"Maybe ten."

"Ten, huh?" Chad grins, as if he's won the point. "Do you know the survival rate for seventy-five-foot falls?" Before I can answer, he crows, "Ten percent!" He breaks into his most shit-eating grin. "So don't come at me with long odds, son. I eat long odds for breakfast!"

Not long after, I start seeing billboards in French. They don't have French signs in southern Washington. They do, however, have them near the Canadian border.

"Shit! Chad, you went the wrong way."

"No, I didn't."

"We're going north."

"Obviously."

"The show's in Vancouver, *Canada*?"

"Did you think it was in Vancouver, *Washington*?"

I don't answer. That's exactly what I thought.

"Who plays in Vancouver, Washington," Chad scoffs, "except for bands too shitty to get shows across the river in Portland?"

"I dunno. Bands who live in Washington, not Canada."

"We live closer to Vancouver, Canada, than Vancouver, Washington. What's the big deal? I go there all the time . . . Wait, did you not bring your passport?"

"I don't even *have* a passport."

"How do you go to Canada without a passport?"

"I don't go to Canada. I thought we were going to Vancouver, Washington."

"But I told you to bring your papers!"

"I thought you meant *flyers*!"

"Why would I tell you to bring flyers to sell records in a city five hours away?" Chad shouts.

"I don't know!" I shout back. "Why would you tell me to bring flyers to sell records in another country?"

"I didn't! I told you to bring your passport."

"You said papers . . ." I cry. Because this means I'm not going to see Hannah. And I didn't see her at Bogart's. And maybe there is no such thing as the good kind of inevitable. I smack my head against the window. "Fuuuuck!" I scream. "I'm such an idiot."

"You're not. It's hella confusing with two Vancouvers."

"I meant thinking it was gonna happen with Hannah. It's never gonna happen."

"I wouldn't say *never*," Chad says. "She did half kiss you."

"Well, I'm never gonna full kiss her if I don't see her."

"Who says you're not gonna see her?" Chad says, veering from the fast lane toward an oncoming exit without dipping below seventy.

"I don't have a passport, remember?"

"So?"

"Kind of a deal breaker."

"That depends," Chad says, pulling off the highway.

"On what?"

He looks like the cat who swallowed the canary. "If you like Hannah enough to commit an international felony."

About ten miles from the Canadian border, Chad pulls the truck over. "This is your stop."

We've traveled forty miles east out of our way to go to a quieter border crossing where Chad swears he will be able to drive through without even stopping. He apparently comes up to Canada all the time for cheaper prescription meds and has some kind of special pass. "At Peace Arch they sometimes stop you, but at this crossing, you basically roll right through."

I get out of the cab and climb into the bed of the truck. Chad instructs me to pull the cover over me.

"You okay?" he calls.

"I think I'm gonna puke."

"Well, do it quietly."

"What if we get caught?"

"They never stopped me before."

"You never went across with me before. I have bad luck."

"Son, there's no such thing as bad luck. And before you argue with me, remember a para just said that."

"It's different with me."

"So do you wanna bail?"

There's part of me that does want to turn around. The doomsday worrywart that is always searching the sky for flaming asteroids. That part of me knows that if I get caught, it'll mean arrests and lawyers and more agita for Ira and spending more money we don't have.

But I am so tired of that part of me. I want to eat long odds for breakfast too. I want to be more like Chad. And I really want to see Hannah.

"Fuck it," I say. "Let's break some laws."

"Aaron Stein, OG for love." Chad laughs. "If we ever start a band, can we call it that?"

The doomsday worrywart recognizes that us starting a band is about as likely as me and Hannah getting together. Or me getting over the border successfully. But for now, I've banished that motherfucker. And so I tell Chad, "You bet your ass we can."

///

The moment I become an international felon is so unremarkable I barely register it. I feel the truck slow, then accelerate. Then a few minutes later Chad hits the horn, *beep, bippety beep-beep*. We didn't come up with a code but I know what this means. A few miles later, he pulls over at a Tim Hortons and I hop out.

Because we had to detour so far to the other border crossing, it's nearly ten when we get to the club. Chad's worried we've missed the set but I don't care about *hearing* Hannah so long as I get to *see* Hannah. The friendly bouncer tells us they're up next, before checking our IDs and telling Chad about the access ramp.

"Wow," I say after we're let in. "Bouncers are so much nicer in Canada."

"Everything's nicer in Canada."

I get Chad situated next to the stage and head off to buy him one of the two beers he has promised to limit himself to, plotting how I'm going to find Hannah. I'm trying to get the bartender's attention when there's a touch on my wrist. I swivel around, unable to hide my smile.

"You're here?" Hannah looks surprised.

"Why? You think a thing like a border would keep me away?"

"Not the border, but your deep hatred of music . . ." she teases. "I'm glad you came. When you didn't show up at Bogart's, I sort of figured you weren't into it."

"I did show up. We weren't on the list."

"I left two tickets for you at the box office myself."

"Are you serious? The box office sent us to the stage door and the bouncer was such a prick. He said we weren't on the list and refused to check with you. And then it was sold out so we couldn't buy tickets. And I would've called you but I don't have your number."

"We should probably remedy that." She grins, whipping out her phone.

"We should." I grin back.

After we exchange digits, she flags the bartender and orders a bunch of beers and two club sodas. "One for you too?" She holds up a bunch of raffle-type tickets. "On the house."

"I have to make a confession. I don't actually like club soda."

Hannah laughs. "You should've told me." The nice Canadian bartender clears his throat, waiting. "How about a ginger beer?" Hannah asks me. "It's nonalcoholic."

"Sure."

"And a ginger beer," she tells the bartender. The bartender gets to work and Hannah turns back to me. "I'm glad about the bouncer. I mean, not glad, but happy that's the reason you didn't come." She nibbles on her thumbnail.

"We tried. I swear we tried. I tried so hard I almost got my ass kicked by the bouncer on your behalf. And he was big. Like refrigerator big. It would've hurt."

"I'm flattered."

"You should be. And Chad lectured him on toxic masculinity."

"I'd have loved to see that." The bartender returns with the tray and Hannah hands over the drink tickets and a Canadian ten-dollar bill for a tip. "I gotta go. But come backstage after the show. I have something for you."

"Really? What?"

"I'll show you after the set. So no rushing off."

"I committed an international felony to see you tonight. I'm not going anywhere."

I return to Chad, who's now deep in conversation with two Canadian superfans.

"I was just telling them how we know the band," Chad brags.

"You're so lucky!" Canadian Fan One replies. And for that minute I do feel that way. Me, Aaron Stein. Lucky. Who'da thunk it?

"We're huge fans," Chad says. "Snuck him over the border without a passport and everything."

"Wow," the fans enthuse.

"I just saw Hannah at the bar." I can't stop grinning. "She wants us to come backstage after."

"That's my boy," Chad says. "OG for love."

"OG for Love: Is that your band?" one of the fans asks politely.

Chad and I just crack up.

Officially speaking, this is my fourth Beethoven's Anvil show—but it's only the second time I've actually seen them play. And it's the first time since I started to get to know Hannah.

Maybe that's why I notice things. Like how the band comes on stage, one member at a time: first Claudia, then Libby, then Jax, the pitch amping up as each one picks up their instrument, culminating in this wave of energy that erupts the minute Hannah bounces onto the stage, already singing, already dancing, barely stopping to take a breath for the entire set.

Like how the set is paced: for the first few songs the temperature and intensity are dialed up until the crowd is screaming along to the anthemic "To Your Knees," but then it's brought back down again, with the moodier and more melodic "Negative Numbers." As the crowd sways together as one, I realize none of this is accidental. Hannah is the author, plotting us through an emotional experience, but with music.

I didn't buy it before, when she said books and songs were different ways of telling a story. I'm starting to believe it now.

///

After the set ends, Chad invites the Canadian Superfans to meet the band.

They squeal, loudly, and squeal again when we enter the greenroom, swarming around Hannah, Jax, Claudia, and Libby, fangirling, taking selfies, finding scraps of paper to get autographs. Hannah keeps glancing at me, then looking away. Like maybe she's as happy to see me as I am to see her.

Finally, the Superfans leave. "Thank you so much!" gushes Canadian Fan Two to Chad.

"We'll keep an ear out for your band," says Canadian Fan One.

"And good luck sneaking back over the border," Canadian Fan Two says to me.

"Thanks," I say.

The door shuts behind them and I finally get a moment with Hannah.

"Your band?" she asks, eyebrow going up.

"Long story . . ."

"And one I have to hear," she says, with a slow smile.

"So you see, when I heard you were playing in Vancou—"

"Hey," Claudia interrupts. "What did they mean about you sneaking over the border?"

"That's the thing," I tell Hannah. "I didn't have a passport, so Chad smuggled me across."

"Hid him in the bed of my truck," Chad brags.

"Then you were serious before?" Hannah asks. "About the international-felon thing?"

"I mean, yeah. It's no big deal, right? It's just Canada."

"Illegally crossing an international border is pretty serious," Libby says.

"We used the NEXUS lanes," Chad says.

"The NEXUS lanes close at midnight," Claudia adds. "Which is now."

"And going home, it's the American border agents," adds Libby. "Not nice like the Canadians."

"Maybe they won't search the truck," Chad says.

"You better hope not," Libby says. "Otherwise Aaron might be headed straight to Gitmo."

"At least it'll be a Canadian Gitmo," Jax says. "It's probably nicer."

"Everything's nicer in Canada," Chad agrees.

I sink into a chair, my scalp pinpricking with perspiration as the doomsday worrywart returns to his rightful place. What was I thinking? My breath speeds up but I can't seem to get enough air in my lungs. Black spots dance across my vision.

"Hey." Hannah's voice sounds far away. "It's gonna be okay."

"How? How is anything gonna be okay?"

She is quiet for a minute as she thinks, and then her voice takes on that clear, calm authoritative tone I heard the night she corralled people to carry Chad into Maxwell's. "Like this. Everyone, listen up: Change in plans. We're going to leave now, and Aaron's going to come with in the van, hidden with the equipment. Chad, you okay to drive back alone?"

"Sure. No problem."

"I can drive with you," Jax volunteers. "If that's cool."

"Totally cool," Chad says.

"Okay, Jax will drive with Chad. We'll hide Aaron under the equipment and Claudia will exploit her magnetic sexuality to flirt with the customs agents. Then we're going to drive over the border without any kind of problem." She takes my hand. "I'll get you home." She squeezes. "I promise."

Jax and Chad agree to stick around to get paid while I help the band load out. In the back of the van, Hannah makes a cubby for me amid the amps, the guitar cases, the drum kit. If it weren't for the possibility of high crimes, it would be cozy.

When it's time for me to get in, she holds up a blanket. "I'll leave this off until the border so you don't get claustrophobic. And I'll stay back here with you until then to make sure you don't get crushed to death in an avalanche of musical equipment. The irony of it would be too much."

"Ha, ha," I say meekly.

It's quiet as we wind through the streets. Every time we take a turn, Hannah leans against the cases to keep them from shifting. When we get on the highway she asks Claudia how long till the border.

"About forty-five minutes," Claudia replies.

"Perfect timing."

"For what?" I ask.

"My surprise." She slips a pair of earbuds through the crack in the gear. "Put these in."

"Is this a playlist of your perfect songs?"

"No, it's my attempt at a playlist of *your* perfect songs."

"I don't have any perfect songs."

"Yet. Hence the list. My attempt to find your perfect song."

"How'd you do that?"

"I guess I thought about you, tried to channel you, and here's what I came up with."

The thought of Hannah spending all this time to find me a song gives me a lump in my throat. "Thank you," I croak.

"Don't thank me yet. You ready?"

I nod.

"Okay, the first song is 'Papa Was a Rodeo' by the Magnetic Fields. I chose it because it tells a story, and you being a books guy, I thought you'd appreciate it." She presses play.

The song is as slow as rising bread. Against a melancholy guitar riff, a guy with an earth-deep voice begins to sing. It's a love song. But the saddest kind. About loving someone, and not being able to love them at the same time.

"Well?" she asks when it's over.

A dozen butterflies flutter around my stomach, though I can't tell if it's the song or the fact that Hannah chose it for me. Maybe there's no daylight between the two. "What's next?"

"I went out on a limb on this one. 'Clair de Lune.' "

"Classical?"

"Yeah. But that's not why I chose it. The song comes from a poem by Paul Verlaine; in it, he describes the soul as somewhere full of music, in a minor key." She puts her hand over her heart. "So that seemed, I don't know, right somehow. The poetry. The minor key."

"Why minor key?"

"Minor keys are beautiful. And melancholy." She takes a breath. "Made me think of you."

"Because I'm beautiful or melancholy?"

"Stop fishing." She plays the song. The melody must seep out of the earbuds because as the music fills my head, Hannah dances her fingers through the air, as if she's tracing the invisible arc of the notes.

When the track ends, she says, "That might be one of my perfect songs too."

"How do you know when a song is perfect?"

"When it Beethoven's Anvils you."

"What's Beethoven's Anvil? Aside from your band's name."

"It's the title of a book."

"You named your band after a book?"

"Not the book so much as the phenomenon the book describes."

"Which is?"

"Well, the book is written by a jazz musician. And it's his attempt to understand why the brain reacts to music so powerfully, so primally. And it all boils down to how when we play or listen to music, we enter a communal experience. We vacate our ego and become, I dunno, part of the music. It sounds hokey, but to me, when I hear a perfect song, that's exactly what happens. Everything else just disappears, all there is in the world is just me and the music."

In the moment that follows, everything I hear—the slap of the tire treads against the pavement, the squeak of the speaker casters against the metal truck floor, the beat of my swelling heart—has a beat to it. I can't find to a way to explain how I feel but words can't contain it. Maybe only music can.

"Hannah," Claudia calls. "We're nearing the border. Better come up front."

"Okay. I'll leave you with this," Hannah says, handing me her phone. "The songs will get you home."

There must be a queue to cross the border because the van slows to a near stop. I listen to the next song, and the one after that. I can't tell if they're perfect or not. But they do help me quiet my doomsday worrywart.

The van lurches forward just as I hear a familiar fluty riff, the opening notes to a song I know so well. "This Must Be the Place," by Talking Heads. The song Mom started every morning listening to. The song that was playing on Ira's radio when Mom almost ran away from him. The song that made her stop and turn around.

It wasn't just that Talking Heads were, still are, Mom's favorite band. It wasn't just that she was in fact hitching home from a musical festival they'd played at. It was the song itself. As David Byrne sang, *Home is where I want to be, but I guess I'm already there*, Mom felt like he was talking to her. Telling her this man would bring her home.

Hannah put this song on my perfect-song list. This is the song that's playing as we cross the border. This is the song that brings me home.

///

After we are safely back in the United States, Hannah rushes back to me, pushing away the bass amp. Her face is flushed and hopeful and beautiful, and when I see her, it's like my insides are turned out, like if she touches me, I will hemorrhage feelings.

I pull her toward me. The moment our lips touch, everything goes quiet, everything recedes. All there is in the world is just me and Hannah.

It is the Beethoven's Anvil of kisses.

The Complete Idiot's Guide
to Starting and Running
a Coffee Bar

I'm dreaming of Sandy. I'm in his room, amid his peeling band posters, his cork wall of ticket stubs from every show he went to, his corner workshop of turntables. His bed is unmade, as it was that morning. His boxer shorts are half in, half out of the hamper, as they were that morning. His face is blue, like it was that morning. Only unlike that morning, Sandy is alive. He's playing records for me, in a way that he never did in real life. One track after the other. He's bouncing to the beat, talking to me. But I can't hear the music. No matter how hard I listen. And I can't hear what Sandy is saying to me. No matter how I hard I listen.

※

I wake, utterly disoriented. In a short time I've become used to the whine of the table saw, the rifle pow of the nail gun, the Lumberjacks' low-fi bickering. But today there's none of that. It's like the quiet of the dream has trailed me to the waking world.

Downstairs in the shop, Ira sips his tea while Chad quietly

works on his laptop. They aren't talking but there's something about them, a warmth, as if they've known each other for years, not weeks.

"Good morning, sunshine!" Chad says when he sees me.

"Good morning," I say.

"Afternoon is more accurate," Ira notes. "It's past noon."

"It is?" I ask, rubbing my eyes. "Why didn't you wake me?"

"Chad said you had a big night." Ira closes the book in his lap. It's not one of his West Indian novels but one of those Idiot's Guides we used to sell so many copies of. This one is called *The Complete Idiot's Guide to Starting and Running a Coffee Bar.* "Did you have fun?"

"I did," I say, warming at the memory. I look around. "Where are the guys?"

"Off scavenging for parts for Lady Gaga," Ira says.

"What are you two up to?" I ask.

"Chad's working on the inventory," Ira says. "And I'm getting ready to meet Bev for support group."

"Tai chi," Chad reminds him. "Support group is tomorrow."

"Right. Tai chi." Ira reaches for his coat.

"Did you take your Lexapro?" Chad asks.

Ira knuckles himself on the forehead. "I did not. Thanks for reminding me. Now, where did I leave the bottle?"

"In your pocket," Chad says.

"Right," Ira says. "Thank you, Chad."

"Anytime, Mr. Stein."

"Please call me Ira."

"Sure thing, Mr. Stein."

After Ira leaves, Chad turns to me. "Are your dad and Bev boning? Or whatever the old person version of boning is?"

"Thanks for the image, Chad." I watch Ira skip down the stairs. He has seemed happier of late, though I'm not sure whether it's the store renovation or the meds he began taking or Bev cheering him up. Maybe all three.

"Speaking of boning, how'd it go with Hannah last night?"

"Good," I say. "We kissed. For real."

I expect this news to have an impact, but Chad's attention has been diverted to his phone, which is vibrating with incoming texts. "How was it?" he asks absently as he taps a message back.

How to describe that kiss? Or the one that followed when she dropped me off? Those two kisses kept me awake most of the night.

"I mean, I've kissed people before, obviously, but it's never felt like that."

"Uh-huh," Chad says, cracking up at his phone.

"It was like, I don't know, we were inhabiting each other."

"Cool, cool," he replies, still texting.

"If you'd like to be alone with your phone, I can leave."

"Sorry, dawg." Chad puts down his phone. "I'm happy for you. Bring it in for a hug."

"Uh, okay." As I awkwardly hug Chad, I feel his phone vibrate with more incoming texts.

"Who keeps texting you?"

"Jax."

"Oh, right. You drove back together. Was it weird?"

"Why would it be weird?"

"Because you don't know each other very well."

"It wasn't weird. It was the opposite of weird. Like we just started talking and didn't stop."

"What'd you talk about?"

"Everything. Music. Love. Bathrooms. Sex." Chad's cheeks now go pink as his phone buzzes with yet another text. He reads it and literally laughs out loud. "Anyhow, we kinda went there right away. Like, I talk a lot with other paras about, you know, the sex thing, when the big head's outa sync with the little head. Jax has had different experiences, and they had an interesting take about not trying too hard to connect one to the other. You know, letting yourself be turned on up here, or down there, and maybe it's okay if it doesn't happen at the same time."

"You packed a lot into a two-hour drive."

"So did you from the sounds of it." Chad grins. "You and Hannah. It's for real?"

"Yeah. Crazy as it seems, I think we're inevitable. Like the good kind of inevitable."

"There's a bad kind?" Chad asks.

"Most inevitable things are bad. Death. Extinction."

"Taxes," Chad adds.

"Exactly."

"Jax said Hannah hasn't really been involved with anyone since she got sober. So she must be really into you."

I'm so chuffed by the "involved with" and "really into you" parts that it takes a second for me to process the rest of what he said.

"Sober?"

"Oh, shit. Jax told me not to tell. They already goofed by telling me. Because it's meant to be anonymous. It just came up because they were in rehab together."

My ears start to ring. No. Chad must've got it wrong. I must have heard it wrong.

"Rehab?"

"Yeah. That's how they met."

The club sodas. Hannah and her Saturday meeting. The twelve-step lingo. Suddenly it all clicks into place.

Hannah is an addict.

I've fallen in love with an addict.

"Excuse me," I say to Chad. I run upstairs, without thinking, straight into Sandy's room. As if he's going to be there. As if he's going to tell me what to do. I take a deep breath but all I get is more silence.

Tuesdays with Morrie

"Fudge a duck on a hot sidewalk!" Ike yells as he wipes a spray of espresso grounds off his face. "Pardon my French."

"Not sure that's French," Garry says.

"Gaga three, Ike nil," Richie says.

"Gaga *four*," Chad says, peering into a box of books. "Aaron, *Eat, Pray, Love* . . . Don't tell me. Fiction."

"Memoir," I reply absently, checking out the window for Lou, who is supposed to be bringing by a couple of big spenders today.

"But it was a movie," Chad complains.

"And before that it was a memoir," I snap. "They're not mutually exclusive."

"Yeesh," Richie says. "What's eating you?"

"He's obsessing about his girlfriend," Chad replies.

"I'm not obsessing, and she's not my girlfriend," I say. "I mean, I don't know what we are yet."

"Yesterday you said you were inevitable," Chad says.

That was before I found out she was an addict. Now I need more information. For instance, what kind of addict is she? Is she the Sandy kind, which is to say cruel, manipulative, destructive? No. She can't be. I never would have fallen in love with a Lucy.

"Dagnabbit!" Ike yells as a blast of steam hisses from the wand. He lifts his wrist, covered in angry welts, to his mouth. "This darn thing makes no sense."

"You sure it's not the plumbing?" Garry asks.

"The plumbing's perfect," Ike replies with a snarl. "It's the darn-tootin' machine. It's like everything's the reverse of where you think it should be, like how they drive on the wrong side of the road in other places."

"Pretty sure in Italy they drive on the right side, same as us," Garry says.

"Now how do you know that?" Ike demands.

"From *The Italian Job*."

"I don't know why you won't watch a YouTube tutorial," Richie says.

Ike's look is withering. "I don't need a *computer* to teach me how to work a machine."

Chad pulls more books out of the box. "Hey, Aaron, what's the deal with these?"

And how am I supposed to get this information? Just casually ask, *Hey, Hannah, did you ruin your family's life? Did you pull the football out from under your little brother time and time again?*

"Aaron," Chad asks. "What's the deal with all these copies?"

And why didn't she tell me? We made a deal not to lie to each other. Isn't this a whopper?

"Aaron," Chad repeats. "Why do you have so many copies of the same book?"

"Huh?"

Chad holds up a stack of *Tuesdays with Morrie*.

"Oh, that must be left over from when Mitch Albom did an author visit."

"Mitch Albom was here?" Garry asks. "When?"

"Ages ago. I was a kid but apparently it was my mom's greatest triumph. He was huge by then, and she met him at a trade show, and she just asked him if he'd come to our store. And he did."

"Whole town showed up," Ike says, grinding more beans. "Line went down the block. Beana waited hours to get her book signed."

"Man," Garry says, shaking his head. "Wish I'd been there. I love *Tuesdays with Morrie*. Ain't too proud to say I cried my eyes out when I read it."

"Me too." Chad says. "I mean when I saw the movie. But it must have the same ending. When they say goodbye and you know Morrie's about to die . . ."

"Hey!" Richie objects. "No spoilers."

"You're not gonna read the book, so what do you care?" Garry asks.

"Maybe I will read it," Richie shoots back.

"If you do, I'll read it too," Chad says.

"If you two read it, I'll reread it," Garry says. "And we can talk about it."

"Like the Knit and Lit?" Richie asks.

"Yeah. But we can drink beer instead of knitting. Lit and . . ." Chad taps his temple. "Getting lit?"

"Books and Brews?" Richie suggests.

"I like that," Garry says. "Can we borrow some copies, Aaron?"

I stare at my phone. Should I just call her? Say, *Hey, why didn't you tell me you were an addict? I mean, it's cool and all but you should know that my brother . . .*

"Aaron?" Garry asks again. "Can we borrow some of the Morries?"

"Yeah, sure. Take as many as you want."

"For real. Maybe I can send a few to Caleb," Garry adds. "He says the prison library is shit."

This gets my attention. "I didn't know Caleb was locked up."

"Serving three years for breaking and entering. Idiot broke into a cop's house."

"I'm sorry."

"Don't be. If he hadn't gotten locked up, he probably would've wound up like your brother."

"Why?" I say, but then I realize what Garry means. Caleb's an addict. Hannah's an addict. Is everyone but me an addict?

The bell rings over the door. "We're closed," Richie shouts without looking up. "For renovations."

"Uhhh . . . I'm here for my jacket?" Lou says. Behind him is a guy in a porkpie hat and a woman with a buzz cut and sleeve tats.

"Right, your jacket," I say, jumping up. "It's in the basement."

I lead them down the stairs. "*These* are your big spenders?" I whisper to Lou.

"Don't be deceived. These guys are total vinyl junkies."

Maybe everyone *is* addicted to something. Maybe it's not a big deal.

I grab my phone and text Hannah: Hey, can we talk?

"And they brought beaucoup bucks," Lou adds.

"Good. I have till the end of the month to sell a shit ton of these records."

"We'll get you there."

I unlock the bins. "Remember, don't come up. Just text me when you're done."

"Got it, boss."

Ike is waiting for me at the top of the basement stairs, arms folded across his broad chest. "What's going on down there?"

"Nothing," I say.

"I know nothing when I see it and this ain't nothing." He pushes past me down the stairs and sees the Lous.

"Aha!" Ike exclaims. "I knew that fellow wasn't from Cascadia. No uniform."

"I'm selling records," I admit.

Ike sighs noisily. "Now we gotta change the blueprint."

"What blueprint?"

"Of the store."

"Why?"

"To sell the records."

"I'm not selling the records."

"You just said you were."

"Not on the store floor."

"Why not?"

When I don't answer, Ike asks, "What do you know about Viagra?"

What I know about Viagra is that I don't want to hear Ike say the word *Viagra*.

"It was originally developed for blood pressure," Ike says. "And when they discovered the side effect, they switched it up. And now it's like the bestselling drug of all time. Maybe records are gonna be your Viagra." He turns to Lou. "Hey, Mr. Not Cascadia. Can I ask you a question?"

"Sure," Lou says.

"If you were gonna install record bins in a bookstore, where would you want 'em?"

"We aren't installing bins," I say right as my phone buzzes with a text. It's from Hannah.

Ruh-roh.

Quickly I text back: No ruh-roh here. Just wanna see you. I add a heart emoji.

"But just say we were gonna put in bins," Ike continues. "Would you want 'em up front by the register? Or in the back by the café?"

"Up front is good for impulse buys," Porkpie Lou says.

"No. Back of the store would be better," Sleeve Tat Lou says.

"Why's that?" Ike asks.

I'm only half listening, distracted by the three dots on my phone. Hannah's typing. But then it stops and there's no reply. Fuck. Did I just mess this up too?

Sleeve Tat Lou is telling Ike why she thinks the back of the store is best. "You know how when you go to a department store to buy a hat, but while you're riding the escalators up, you have to walk all the way across the floor to get to the next escalator and so by the time you get to the hat section, you've also bought boots and a sweater?"

Ike nods, as if he frequently impulse-buys while browsing at department stores.

"Same idea. Record collectors will drive hours for vinyl like this. You might as well make them wade through the books. They might buy them too."

I'll come by tomorrow, Hannah finally texts. But no emoji.

"And what about cappuccinos?" Ike is asking the Lous. "Would record buyers also like cappuccinos?"

"Are the Flamin' Groovies overrated?" Porkpie Lou asks.

"I don't know, are they?" Ike says.

"Decidedly," Sleeve Tat Lou says. "Coffee would be dope. Maybe beer too."

"Beer, Books, Coffee, and Records," Lou says. "That's a store I could live in."

"Diversify your ass!" calls Chad from the top of the stairs, where he's been eavesdropping. "Told you so!"

"We can't sell the records in the store!" I shout.

"Why not?" Ike asks.

"Because Ira can't know I'm selling them."

"Why not?" Ike asks.

Because when Sandy built the bins and handed me the key, he made me promise not to sell them. By then, our relationship was on life support, so I couldn't understand why he was trusting me with his records. Still, I promised. And now I'm breaking the promise.

"Ira just can't know," I tell Ike.

"Don't you think he'll find out?" Ike asks me in a quiet voice.

About the records? Maybe. But what I did to Sandy?

No, that my father can never know.

Moby-Dick

The three Lous have spent close to a thousand dollars. Not bad for a week's worth of sales, and if I had thirteen more weeks, maybe it would work. But I don't have thirteen weeks; I don't even have two.

I've asked Lou for his boss's number but he has suddenly stopped returning my texts.

Meanwhile, in the store, Ike continues to battle Gaga. He has taken her apart and put her back together twice, and still she explodes every time he tries to pull an espresso. All other work on the shop has slowed because Ike is too distracted by Gaga to boss Garry and Richie around.

I pace the store, running the numbers in my head. If I can't sell the records to Lou and his friends fast enough, maybe I can borrow the remaining money from Chad. Pay him back once I sell more records, before he has to pay his second Stim installment.

"Son of a monkey!" Ike yells at Gaga. "I give up!"

"He's never gonna give up," Garry whispers. "Gaga's his Great White Whale."

I do a double take, which Garry clocks with a wry smile. "What, you think I've never read *Moby-Dick*?"

"I barely got through it myself."

"I read it junior year with Mr. Smithers. You have him, or had he kicked it by the time you were in school?"

"I think he died."

"Well, he was a gnarly old coot. Before he became a teacher, he worked on fishing boats in Alaska, so he was always telling us gruesome tales of people losing hands and shit. He mixed his stories in with *Moby-Dick*, so it made the book kinda relatable, I guess. Anyhow, I remember everything from that book. Like Ahab had a monomania."

"What's a monomania?" Richie asks.

"That is," Garry says, pointing to Ike as Gaga explodes once more, sending a metal bit flying through the air where it nearly hits the door. "Fiddlesticks!" he shouts.

"Somebody lose this?" Hannah asks, picking up the metal bit as she walks through the door.

"Take it," Ike says. "I give up!"

"Sure you do, Ahab," Garry mutters.

"What is it you give up on?" Hannah asks.

"This hunk of junk," Ike says. He pulls out his bandana and lovingly polishes the hunk of junk.

Hannah steps closer, skirting a quick glance at me before focusing on Gaga. "Is that vintage?"

"Vintage eye-talian," Ike says.

"Mind if I take a look?" Hannah asks.

"Have at it, but you need an engineering degree to work this thing."

"Let me see what I can do." She inspects the machine with a

practiced eye, making humming sounds. "See this projectile here." She holds up the metal bit. "That's your portafilter. Your espresso goes in it." Hannah demonstrates, tamping the powder gently. "You have to be careful not to press it too tight or the water can't get through."

"Told you that you pressed it too tight," Garry says.

"Shut up," Ike says. To Hannah: "Go on."

"The portafilter goes in the grouphead." Hannah twists it into the spouty thing.

"Grouphead," Garry repeats. "Ike, maybe we should be writing this down."

"Richie, write this down," Ike orders.

Richie grabs a pen and paper as Hannah fits the portafilter into the grouphead. "I think you pull down on the lever here." She pulls down one of Gaga's robot arms. The seal sounds like a kiss.

"Is there water in the canister?" She peeks inside. "Yep, and it's heated up. Now, where's the brew button?"

"Right there," Ike says, tapping it gingerly like it might launch a missile. "If you want my advice, you better take cover. She has a tendency to blow."

"I'll bear that in mind," Hannah says with a bemused smile. She places a cup under the drip tray and hits the button. Instead of making that terrible knocking sound, the machine gives out a long hiss and then a low hum, releasing a shot full of rich brown espresso.

"Look at the foam on it," Richie says. "It looks like a teeny-tiny coffee beer."

"It's called crema," Ike says admiringly. "You made crema on your first try."

"Hardly my first try," Hannah replies. "I spent six months working as a barista."

"I didn't know that," I say.

"Yep. After I dropped out of college and moved up here from Arizona."

"I didn't know that either."

"So many mysteries yet to be revealed . . ." she says as we lock eyes. And I feel it. The tingling. The knowing. The inevitable. It's still there. Even if she's an addict.

"Now let's make some foam," Hannah continues. "You want cold milk, right out of the fridge. It froths better and you get more aeration." She flips the wand, and suddenly it sounds like an actual coffee bar in here. "You don't want to overdo it, or you'll scald the milk and alter the flavor. You should be able to drink it without waiting for it to cool." She taps a metal canister lightly against the counter. "Now you let the foam settle." She pours the milk over the espresso, topping it with a dollop of foam. "*Voilà.*" She holds the drink out for Ike.

He stares at the cup. I wonder if his pride is wounded. After all, he's been wrestling this machine for days and Hannah figured it out in two minutes. But then he whips out his bandana and cleans a spot of milk off Gaga before accepting the cup from Hannah. He takes a sip, closes his eyes, and sighs. Then he opens his eyes again and looks at Hannah. "You think you can show me how to do it?"

Hannah spends the next hour teaching Ike how to make various espresso drinks. Each time I think she's done, Ike has a new request. I watch, tapping my foot, clearing my throat. It's not that I'm excited to have this conversation with Hannah but recent experience has shown the more I put something off, the more impossible it becomes.

"You think I can figure out how to make those designs? Hearts and trees and the like?" Ike asks after he's mastered macchiatos.

"Maybe a bluebird," Richie suggests.

"Bird's gonna be hard," Garry says. "Maybe a feather. Or a book. Book's just a rectangle. That could be the signature foam swirl."

"Great, can we master foam designs later?" I ask, gesturing toward Hannah.

"Aaron wants to be alone with his girlfriend," Richie clarifies.

"She's not my girlfriend," I say. Hannah frowns. "I mean, she's not *not* . . . It's just . . . We just . . ."

"We can do swirls next time," Ike interrupts, saving me.

Thank you, I mouth to Ike, and then Hannah and I retreat to the relative privacy of the porch, where she pulls out a small pouch and starts rolling a cigarette. "Don't judge," she says as she lights it, the flame illuminating her freckles. "It's cliché, I know. But I usually only smoke one a day. Unless I'm at a meeting. You know how that goes."

"I do?"

"Don't you?" She looks confused, which makes me confused,

but before I can process any of it, I spot a janky wood-paneled station wagon crawling down Main Street as if the driver's lost. A car like that, it's gotta be a collector.

"Hang on," I tell Hannah, leaping off the porch stairs and waving down the car. "You a friend of Lou's?"

"Yep. I'm Bart. Here to see the vinyl."

"Park out front. I'll show you in."

I turn back to Hannah. "I gotta deal with this. Give me five."

"Yeah, no problem," she says.

I take Bart to the store, stopping to look over my shoulder back at Hannah. "You won't leave?"

"I won't leave."

I lead him to the basement, ignoring Ike's look. When I open the bins, his breath catches, his jaw drops. "Whoa," he says. "This is like the Shangri-la of records."

"Your own personal *Lost Horizon*."

"Huh?" he says, not getting the book reference.

"Never mind. I'm gonna give you my number. When you're ready, text me. We'll settle up down here."

"Lou already told me the deal," Bart says absently, pulling out AC/DC's *Back in Black* from the first bin.

When I get back to Hannah, she's stubbing out her cigarette. "So," she says. "Are you breaking up with me?"

"What? No! I mean the girlfriend thing, I just didn't wanna . . ."

She gives me a look. "I'm kidding, Aaron."

"You are?"

"Hard to break up if we're not together yet."

Yet. I cling at that *yet* like a drowning man clings to a life preserver.

"So, I don't know how to broach this . . . the . . ." I point to the cigarette stub. "Whole meeting thing?"

She exhales, visibly relieved. "I'm *so* glad you brought it up."

"You are?"

She nods. "It's not like it's a secret. But I haven't really dated since I got sober, and a year out of the game, I'm rusty. I kept waiting for it to come up naturally, as it usually does with people in the program. Or I thought maybe we'd bump into each other at a meeting . . ."

My mind digests this in chunks:

1. Hannah has been sober for a year.
2. Hannah thinks we are dating.
3. Bump into me at a meeting? Why would she bump into me at a meeting unless . . . ?

Oh, fuck.

"Hullo! You must be Hannah," Ira calls, clomping up the stairs with Bev. "So nice to meet you. I'm Ira. This is Bev. And, Aaron, look who we found!" Ira smiles broadly as he gestures to Penny Macklemore. "I wanted to show off what we're doing with the store."

My brain tries to process all of this: Hannah thinks I'm an addict. And Penny's at our store. But my brain cannot process it. My brain has short-circuited.

"Can you give me like five more minutes?" I ask Hannah.

She cocks her head to the side, a little less chill this time. "Okaaay?"

I race into the store after Penny. Is she going to tell? No. She can't tell. That was one of my conditions. But I didn't have a lawyer or anything, as she reminded me. I didn't put it in writing.

I try to read Penny. But she's a closed book.

"Guess what?" Ike bellows at Ira. "Gaga's working."

"Mazel tov!" Ira calls.

"Who's Gaga?" Penny asks.

"The espresso machine," Bev replies.

"Would you like one?" Ira asks Penny. "On the house."

"That's very kind, but I don't go in for those fancy coffee drinks."

Ike offers espressos to Bev and Ira too, who both decline. "I wanna keep practicing," Ike says.

"What about that guy in the basement?" Richie suggests.

"What guy in the basement?" Ira asks.

"Uhhh . . ." My mind is reeling to what of Mom's stuff we might be selling. "Some guy wanting to buy the porch swing."

"We're selling the porch swing?" Ira asks.

"Yeah. I mean, the ramp is where the swing hung." I glance at Penny to see if she has any opinions on the ramp, and then at Hannah to make sure she's still on the porch. None evident, and yes. "There's not really room for it anymore."

"Oh, okay," Ira says. "It's just that Annie used to sit in that all day long."

Bev pats Ira on the shoulder. "It'll be good for someone to get use out of it," she says. "A second life."

Ira nods.

"I'll go see if the porch-swing guy wants an espresso," I say. I run to the basement, where Bart is in the zone. "Can you do me a huge favor?" I ask him. "Can you take that when you leave?" I point to the swing.

"What is it?"

"A porch swing. You can have it for free."

Bart's brow furrows. "But I don't have a porch."

"Can you take it anyway?" Bart stares blankly. "You have room in your car. You can sell it. Or dump it as soon as you get out of town. I don't care."

Bart shakes his head. "Seems like a hassle."

I look around. "I'll throw in a couple extra records for free."

Bart licks his lips. "A couple?"

"Three."

"Guess I got me a porch swing."

Back upstairs, the shitstorm has turned into a shit tsunami. Because Angela Silvestri, she of the crumb cake with Life cereal topping, has arrived with a Tupperware full of samples.

"We were thinking of having baked goods in the café," Ira is telling Penny. "And Angela volunteered to make a few test batches."

"It's not written in stone," I interject. "I mean, none of it is. We might not even do a café."

"Of course we're gonna do a café," Ike says. "By the way, did the *porch-swing guy* want an espresso?"

"Uhh, maybe later."

"Doesn't *anyone* want one?" Ike asks.

"I wouldn't say no to a latte, one shot," Angela says. "The cake pairs very nicely with coffee."

"I didn't know you baked professionally," Penny tells Angela.

"Oh, it's always been a hobby," Angela replies. "But I recently retired and I'm so bored I could cry. And then Ike called and asked me about supplying the café's baked goods and at first I said I couldn't do it, but then I thought about you, Penny."

"About me?"

"Yes, if you could go into business at your age, why couldn't I? Maybe this is the beginning and one day I'll have a chain of bakeries." She beams at Penny, who grimaces back. "Now, who wants a slice?"

"I do!" I jump to the front of the line, wedging myself next to Penny, grabbing a piece. "Penny, come talk to me before you leave about that, uh, paint thinner."

"Paint thinner?" Ike asks.

"Penny had a deal on some paint thinner at the hardware shop."

"Didn't see anything about it," Ike says.

"It's not advertised," I say.

"Hmm," Ike considers. "We're at least two weeks away from painting."

"Two weeks?" Penny asks. "That puts you into December?" She says this mildly, without even looking at me.

"She's right," Ira says. "We should be open by Black Friday."

"Finishing up by then's gonna be a stretch," Ike says. "Particularly because I won't get much work done next week when I'll be in

Walla Walla visiting my daughter. Though we could push to open before Christmas."

"Catch the holiday rush," Garry says.

We haven't had a holiday rush in years, but that doesn't stop Ira from nodding.

"None of this is set in stone," I repeat to Penny. "Why don't we talk about it outside?"

"Have your cake first," Angela says, thrusting a slice at Penny and one at me.

"I think I will," Penny says, accepting the famous crumb cake. "Aaron, I'll be with you in a minute."

Back on the porch, Hannah's looking a bit peeved. "Everything okay in there?"

"I'm not an addict!" I blurt out, as I thrust the cake toward Hannah.

"What?"

The cake sits there in midair. "I'm not in the program. I'm not an addict."

Hannah's face bunches up in confusion. It would be adorable were it not for the source of the confusion. "But you don't drink. You said you can't go into bars."

"I can't go into bars because I'm underage. And I don't drink because I don't. I've never had a drink or smoked pot or anything."

"But you had all those recovery books in your basement."

"Because of my brother . . ." I trail off. "*He* was the addict."

"The brother who died?" Hannah asks.

"Yeah," I say, the taste of rotting strawberries making me want to gag.

189

"I am so sorry," Hannah says.

"It's okay. It was just a misunderstanding."

"Why didn't you tell me about your brother?"

"It's not my favorite topic of conversation." I look at her. "Why didn't you tell me about your addiction?"

"My sponsor's been asking me the same question. I don't really know." She shakes her head. "It's not like it's a secret, but I think I was just enjoying myself, enjoying you; it felt easy, almost like we already knew each other and could skip over all the processing and just *be*." She knocks herself on the head. "Stupid, Hannah."

"No! Not stupid." I grab her hands. "I mean, I'm not an addict but I also felt that connection. From the moment I saw you reading. Like I knew you. Like this was gonna happen." I zig my hand back and forth between us. "Like it had already happened."

Hannah is nodding, like she felt it too, and for a second I feel hope. It will be okay. It doesn't matter that she's an addict. I mean, she said she's been sober a year. Sandy never made it past his three-month chip. A year means you're practically one of the brochure success stories. She's nothing like Sandy. I never could fall in love with someone like my brother.

"None of this matters," I tell her. "I don't care if you're an addict. What matters is who you are, not who you were."

"Who I was is part of who I am, Aaron."

"I'm not saying it right . . ." But before I can say it right, Penny walks out.

"Aaron," she calls. "Shall we discuss that . . . paint thinner?"

"Paint thinner?" Hannah asks.

I stand up. "Last time. I swear." I follow Penny to the bottom of the porch and beckon her around the corner. "You didn't tell Ira, did you?"

"Now, why would I do that? We had an agreement." She stares at me hard. "We *still* have an agreement."

"And I have until the end of the month to get you thirteen thousand dollars. You don't need to come in and check on me."

"I'm not here to check in on you. I'm fine however this goes. If you raise the cash, I'll have a nice dividend. And if you don't, I'll have a renovated space. It's a win-win for me." She pauses to consider. "Maybe I'll start a coffee bar of my own. I don't much care for those drinks, but other people seem to. I bet I could put quite a dent into Cindy Jean's business."

"Why would you want to do that? You eat at C.J.'s every day."

"But I don't *own* C.J.'s." She narrows her eyes at me. "Don't look at me like that. It's just business." She turns back to the store. "Anyhow, from what I hear, you might get your way after all."

"What did you hear?"

"That your friend in the wheelchair emptied out his savings account."

"Where'd you hear that?"

"From Rita Fitzgibbons."

"Who?"

"She's the bank manager. She said your friend made a substantial withdrawal and I assumed it's for all that." She gestures into the store. "Wouldn't be how *I'd* invest my money, but if it weren't for other people's foolish business decisions, I'd be out of a job."

"No, Chad didn't pull that money for the store; it's for the deposit on his proced—" I stop myself. This is none of Penny's damn business. "So you didn't come to check in on us?"

"Oh, Aaron, I know every move every person makes in this town, whether or not I stop into your store." She smiles. "I stopped in for cake. I love all sweet things. Cake. Pie. Real estate acquisitions." She gives her fingers a dainty lick. "I'll see you December first."

Once Penny leaves, I bound back to Hannah. "Look, Aaron, I can see this isn't a good time."

"It is. I swear. You have my full attention. Now, where were we?"

"You were saying you don't care that I'm an addict and I was saying you *should* care."

"I didn't mean it like that. What I meant is . . ." I stop to gather my thoughts so I don't mess this up again. In the silence, my phone starts ringing. It's Bart. Shit.

"Do you need to get that?" she asks coolly.

"I'm sorry. I really should." I pick up. Bart says he's ready.

"This will take five minutes. Less than five," I promise her. "Then we can get out of here, go somewhere a little less hectic."

"Maybe we should do this later."

"No!" My voice pitches up. I will not lose Hannah. "Everything's fine! Just give me five more minutes."

I race down to Bart. I charge him a flat twenty dollars apiece, even though some must be more valuable. We hide the records under the porch swing and carry them up the stairs, through the store.

"Goodbye, old friend," Ira says to the swing in a raspy voice.

I open the door for Bart and call out to Hannah, "I'm all yours now."

A slice of Angela Silvestri's crumb cake sits on the railing. But Hannah? She's gone.

Moneyball

A few hours later, Chad shows up, his mood as ebullient as mine is morose. "Oh, man. I had the best afternoon. Jax found this hiking trail that's wheelchair accessible. I haven't been hiking in years, and damn, my arms ache. Then we had lunch. They bake bread. And it was still warm, and we had that with some venison jerky and marionberry jam. Best meal I ever had. One of the best afternoons I've ever had." He finally notices me. "And how was your day?"

"How was my day?" Where to begin. Ike mastered Gaga and now the Lumberjacks are full steam ahead on café plans, even though I have ten days to raise eleven thousand dollars and my best option is Lou's boss, but Lou won't answer my texts. Oh, and I probably blew it with Hannah. "My day was shit."

"I thought you were seeing Hannah today."

"I was. I did."

"Did something happen?"

"She thought I was in the program."

"What program?"

"*The program.*" I lower my voice to a whisper though I'm not sure why. "For addicts."

"Oh, you mean Narcotics Anonymous."

NA? I was hoping she was more garden-variety AA-type addict.

"Does it matter?" Chad asks.

"*Sandy* was in NA."

"Yeah. And so is Jax. And about a hundred other people I know. I mean, it's a good thing."

No. A good thing would be if they never started using in the first place. Everyone talks about how it's not addicts' fault, it's a sickness, hereditary, like diabetes. But this is such a crock. Your eye color, your height, *those* are hereditary. Addiction is a choice, a choice Sandy made over and over again. Hey, here's an easy way not to become an addict. Don't take drugs!

"And being in recovery means they're getting better," Chad adds. "If you're in NA, you're not using."

I think of Sandy. Not always the case. In fact, almost never the case.

"Aaron, the fact that Hannah Crew is even slightly into you is like a miracle. Don't blow it on a technicality."

As usual, Chad's right. "I think I already blew it."

"So unblow it."

"How? What do I do?"

He opens his arms wide, as if greeting the world. "Whatever it takes."

What it takes, Hannah tells me when I call her up to apologize, is for me to go with her. To an NA meeting.

"A meeting?" I ask, trying to sound open-minded.

"I'm the lead speaker." Her voice is steely and unreadable. "It seems like an opportune time to put all our cards on the table."

"Aren't NA meetings typically more of a second-date-type thing?" I joke to mask how little I want to do this. When Sandy was sober, he'd go to two, sometimes three meetings a day, spewing quotes from the Big Book like a zealot, which would have been obnoxious enough if he didn't keep relapsing. Or if after he relapsed a few times he had the humility to at least stop proselytizing. But he didn't.

"I don't think anything about us so far is typical," Hannah says, her voice warming. "And if this is gonna be my first sober relationship, I wanna do it right."

"So we're gonna be in a relationship, are we?"

"Slow your roll, boy," she says, but I can hear the smile in her voice. "We can decide what we are after the meeting."

///

The next morning, I do a sneak attack on Lou, calling him early, from the landline.

"Hello," he says in a sleepy voice.

"Lou, it's Aaron."

"Hey." I hear him yawn. "Didn't recognize the number."

"Calling on our landline."

"People still have those?"

"You worship vinyl, so don't judge."

"Fair point." He pauses. "How'd it go with Bart?"

"Good, but not good enough."

"Okay, how short are you? I'll send some other guys."

"I don't want other guys. I want one guy. Your boss."

The line goes so quiet I think the call dropped. But then Lou whimpers a no.

"What do you have against him?"

"He's the worst kind of vulture, swooping in to buy whatever he's heard is cool, thereby sucking all the cool out of it. He got rich turning artists' lofts in South Seattle into condos. Then he got richer corporatizing the weed dispensaries. And now he's into vinyl. He'll ruin it."

"How can he ruin vinyl?"

"Trust me. He can." Lou pauses. "You ever read that book *Moneyball*?"

In this case, I only saw the movie, not that I'll cop to that. "Refresh my memory."

"It's about these guys who learn to use stats to build a perfect baseball team. And they do. They assemble a team with way less money. It sounds all great and underdoggy, but then everyone starts playing moneyball. And in doing so, they took what was an art and turned it into a formula. And they ruined it. Baseball's so much more tedious now, like watching robots play. There's no magic to it." Lou sighs. "Daryl's a moneyballer. He doesn't sell stuff, he *monetizes* it." Lou's voice breaks a little. "He doesn't even *like* music."

"Neither do I."

"So you keep saying," he shoots back. "But you've kept those records pristine, man. You've honored them."

"But that wasn't me. That was my brother."

"Well, then you've honored *him*."

If Lou only knew. "I'm sorry, but this is how it has to be. I'm out of options and out of time."

The line goes silent so long I think Lou hung up on me. But then he says: "You know what I don't get?"

"What don't you get?"

"Why is it that guys like Daryl always seem to win and guys like us always seem to lose?"

I've spent the past few years asking myself that. "I don't know, Lou," I say. "I honestly don't know."

///

I call Daryl Feldman's office at nine o'clock. The assistant says he's booked until after the holiday. I call every hour until finally she relents. "He just had a cancellation," she tells me. "Can you get here by five?"

His office is in Seattle, a two-hour drive with no traffic, and there's always traffic. I'm meeting Hannah—an hour's drive from Seattle—at seven. It's now three. If I leave now and everything goes right, I can make it work.

Of course, being me, everything does not go right. The Volvo refuses to budge past sixty even on the downhill, and it needs gas, and I can't find a parking spot and wind up pulling into one of those garages that charge by the second. I sprint to Daryl's office, pushing open the door at ten past five.

"Am I too late?" I gasp to the assistant.

"He's just wrapping up a call."

Twenty minutes later, he's still wrapping up a call. "Do you know how long he'll be?" I ask.

"Any minute now."

"It's just I have to be somewhere at seven."

"We can reschedule if you want." She peers at her computer. "He's out most of next week for the holiday, but we can do the following Monday—no, scratch that, Tuesday."

The following Tuesday is too late. "I'll wait." I text Hannah that I'm running behind.

I had built Daryl Feldman into a slick Wall Street mogul, Gordon Gekko with a soul patch, but when, at 5:46, I'm ushered into his office, I'm greeted by a short, dumpy guy, the kind of person Ira would call a schlub.

"So sorry to keep you waiting," he says, gesturing for me to sit down. "You want a coffee? Or beer? It's almost six."

"Uh, maybe a water."

"Sure! Ella, bring us some waters, the LaCroix Pamplemousses." He says *LaCroix* with a French pronunciation. Ella brings in the waters. Before she pours his, he plucks out an ice cube. "Two cubes, Ella."

"Sorry. Sometimes they stick."

She leaves and Daryl's eyes follow her. "She can't figure out how to separate the ice cubes, but that ass." He takes a gulp of his water. "I hear from Lou that you have some primo vinyl to sell."

"I do. Two thousand two hundred and sixteen pieces." I pull out the laminated indexes and slide them over. "They're listed by genre, pressing, condition. Some are boxed sets. A few imports.

Some very rare bootlegs. Some sell for hundreds of dollars. I looked up the Iggy Pop and it's—"

"How many again?"

"Two thousand two hundred and sixteen."

He pulls out an adding machine and does some calculations. As the tape whirs I imagine what number will spit out. Maybe it'll be more than thirteen thousand dollars. Maybe it'll get me out from the Penny deal and leave us a cushion to spend on the store. Pay Ike and the guys with more than coffee.

He rips off the tape and hands it to me. I blink. $4,432. "This is your offer?"

"I do two bucks a pop."

Never mind the fact that he needed an adding machine to multiply 2 times 2,216, but four grand? "You can't be serious."

"I'm never not serious about business," he says.

"You must know from Lou that they're worth way more than this."

He sighs. "Hell, it's Thanksgiving, so I'll round up to forty-five hundred."

"But you don't even know what I'm selling."

He shrugs. "I pay per piece."

"But some of these records are really valuable."

"And some will be worthless. I've found it all evens out in the end."

"Trust me." I push the index toward him. "Nothing in this collection is worthless. If you just look at the inventory. Lou practically hyperventilated when he saw it."

"Bet he did. Asked for an advance on his paycheck to buy more. But that's why Lou's Lou and I'm me." He takes a long, self-satisfied slurp of water. "Look, I've been doing this for a while now. I have overhead and shipping costs and I have to hire guys to do fulfillment for online orders. And do you have any idea how much of a pain it is to ship records? You need these special mailers, and special cardboard inserts. And if a record's at all warped, the buyers want a refund."

"If a record warps, the sound is off!"

He shrugs. "So they say. Whatever. Who needs records when you can play any song you want on your phone for free?"

"It's not the same! Just because there's Netflix doesn't mean you can't read books. And four thousand five hundred dollars, are you kidding me? That's not remotely enough. Even wholesale they're worth triple that. Four thousand five hundred dollars dishonors the records!" I shout.

"Jesus. Calm down. It's just business."

That's exactly what Penny said when I accused her of holding the store hostage for ransom. It was just business.

"What do you think businesses are?" I stand to leave. "They're not machines. Or widgets. Or bar codes. They're people! People just trying to get by. Because what else can they do?"

Daryl looks at me like I'm speaking Latin or some other dead language, and I suddenly know the answer to Lou's question.

Why do guys like this always win? Because that's how the world works. Some species is always going extinct. Some other species is always waiting in the wings to emerge. We are the dinosaurs. And the Pennys, the Daryls—they're what comes next.

The Big Book

Hannah's meeting is at a school gymnasium outside of Bellingham. As soon as I pull into the parking lot and see the smattering of cars, some bearing peeling bumper stickers with slogans like FRIEND OF BILL W, my stomach bottoms out.

I do not want to be here. I do not want to listen to the serenity prayer or applaud people for doing something some of us have always done.

But I do want to see Hannah. I want to be with Hannah. And I'll be damned if I'm going to let Sandy ruin the one good thing in my life.

I follow the trickle of latecomers inside. Hannah's standing underneath the basketball hoop, deep in conversation with Jax and a large, muscular woman with two long braids coiling along her otherwise-shaved head.

Even though I only ever went to a couple meetings with Sandy, it all feels too familiar: the urns full of burnt coffee, the trays of stale donuts, people huddling in clumps, peeling away the rims of their Styrofoam cups. It was just like this at the last meeting I went to. When Sandy was the lead speaker.

I tap Hannah on the shoulder. She spins around, her expression unreadable. "You made it." She introduces me to Fran, her sponsor, who grips my hand in a finger-crushing shake.

"We were taking bets on whether you'd show," Fran says.

"Of course I'd come! Wouldn't miss it." My voice clangs like an out-of-tune piano. "Just ran into some traffic."

Jax nods in sympathy. "I-5's a parking lot."

The crowd starts to sit in the folding metal chairs. Hannah chews on her nail.

"You okay?" Jax asks her.

"Mildly terrified," Hannah admits.

"Just speak your truth," Fran says. "And then nothing can go wrong."

"I'm glad you're here." Hannah reaches for my hand and squeezes.

"Me too," I lie. And I squeeze back.

"Hi, my name is Hannah and I'm an addict."

Hi, my name is Sandy and I'm an addict.

"Hi, Hannah," the crowd responds, already charmed.

Hi, Sandy. The crowd loved Sandy too. He was charismatic. It's why he was got away with so much for so long.

Hannah wipes her palms on her jeans. "I'm already sweating bullets. Usually that doesn't happen at the start of a show but I guess this isn't a show. It's the opposite of that."

She takes a deep breath and scans the group, landing on me.

"Three years ago, I got into a car accident and got addicted to painkillers."

I was in ninth grade the first time I snorted oxy. I didn't do it because I was unhappy or lonely or abused. I did it because it was there.

"That's the official story, anyhow. Because, you know, I come from a 'good' family, a 'happy' family. The kind of family where this 'sort of thing' doesn't happen."

I didn't know that I'd woken a sleeping monster in me. And even if someone warned me, I'm not sure it would have changed a thing.

"That's the story we tell in my family—if we tell any story at all, because we'd rather not discuss this unpleasantness. 'Hannah became addicted to painkillers after a car accident.' This is true, but that doesn't make it the truth. Here's the truth: In seventh grade I started slipping bourbon into my morning thermos of coffee because that little bit of numb made the day more bearable. In eighth grade I learned to sneak laxative pills to keep my tummy flat. A year before the accident that turned me into an official addict, I crashed my dad's car because I'd snorted three tablets of Adderall. The car was repaired with no further discussion. Mine was a truth happening in plain sight that no one cared to talk about. Least of all me."

In the beginning, it's all fun, right? It's chasing the next high, not really thinking about how you get it, or who you hurt. I mean, sure, maybe you lift a few twenties from a cash register, steal a rare book your father treasures, but those are just things, right? And it's all under control.

"And even after I was officially revealed as an addict, we kept up with the lie. 'Hannah became addicted to painkillers after a car accident.' This narrative left out the thornier story, the one that explains why a twelve-year-old wants to anesthetize herself, why a sixteen-year-old dreams of death."

And then it stops being under control. And you see the real shit going down because of you. You see your parents go into debt. You see your brother's life getting shanked. And you think you should stop. You think you can stop. And you try to stop. And you try again. And again. And again. And you can't. And you don't.

"But I was ignoring the real work of my recovery. The hard part of it, which for me is not giving up the dope—though that is hard—but letting go of that good girl my parents raised me to be. Understanding that *she* was making me sick."

The Big Book tells us that addicts are not selfish. We just lack humility. We overestimate our power, which trust me, is not a new concept to me. I stand before you thinking that maybe this is the time I don't fall back down but knowing it might not be. But I really hope it is. Because the hard part of falling down is not the falling, or the getting back up. It's seeing what happens to the people you fall on. You get bruised; they get flattened.

"I know you're not supposed to move to a new place when you're newly sober, but I also knew that if I didn't leave home, leave that lie, I would never get better, so I left. And I moved here, to find a new home, create a new family, figure out who I really am, who I want to be." Here Hannah looks at Jax, who nods, and then, for a second, at me.

And every time they get flattened, so do I, killing me, cut by cut.

And I know we're supposed to get better for our own sake, but damn, I want to get better for theirs. And here Sandy looked directly at Ira, at Mom, and then at me. He didn't stop looking at me for the rest of the meeting.

"So here I am," Hannah continues, "on the cusp of my first year of sobriety, about to travel home to my family of origin for the first time. I'm terrified, but I'm oddly grateful to be terrified. It feels like that means something. Like, I've heard it said that in destroying ourselves, we also learn to create ourselves. So maybe that's what's happening. And whatever is happening, thanks for helping me get here."

Thanks for catching me no matter how many times I fall. And here's hoping, with all the humility in my heart, that I can learn to fall without flattening anyone else.

///

That meeting, Sandy got his three-month chip. Afterward, we went out for ice cream to celebrate. Mom held his hand, eyes shining. "I'm so proud of you."

"Me too," Ira said.

I said nothing. I wasn't proud. I was disgusted. Because I just knew their hope was misplaced. Sandy was gonna yank the football. On all of us. Like he always did.

Later, as Mom and Ira were settling up the bill, Sandy looked at me. "Are you gonna say anything?"

I shrugged. "You want a medal from me?" I asked. "How many times do we have to do this? How much more debt do we have to go into? How much more misery do you have to put us through?"

"Hopefully, none," Sandy replied.

"I don't believe it, and you know what, I don't care. I'm so tired of this. So sick of waiting for the inevitable. If you're gonna die, just get it over with already!"

I'd just wished my brother dead, but he barely reacted. Instead, that next morning, he went to the hardware store, the lumber yard, and built his bins. Locked away his precious albums.

"You gotta promise me you won't let anyone sell them," he said. And then he handed me the one and only key.

"Why are you asking me?"

"Because you're the only one who hates me enough to keep the promise," he replied.

I accepted the key. I sealed the promise.

Five months later, Sandy was dead.

⁂

After the meeting, people gather around Hannah, just like they do at shows, sharing their stories, or telling her how inspiring she was. I watch from the wings, trying to re-inflate myself because I don't want Hannah to see me flattened.

"It's always like this with Hannah," Jax tells me. "Always has been." They check their phone and smile, and I know it's a text from Chad but I don't say anything. "I'm gonna pull an Irish good-bye," they say. "Tell Hannah I love her and I'll call her tomorrow."

Eventually the crowd thins, and the people start to pack up the remaining donuts, empty the coffee samovar, sweep the bits of

Styrofoam that litter the floor like chemical snow. Hannah talks to Fran quietly and they hug for a long time before she comes over to me.

"I thought you might bolt," she says.

"I'm not the bolting type." I glance at the other addicts. "Just waiting my turn with the groupies. You're popular."

"It's a good room. So, what'd you think?"

"What I always think. That you're amazing."

"That's not what I'm asking."

"What are you asking?"

She sighs. "I want to know how you feel. About this. About me. About us."

"I'm in love with you."

She rocks back from side to side, as if she doesn't believe it. But I do.

"You've known me like a month."

"So what?" It was a matter of hours between the time Ira picked up Mom and dropped her off, and by then, they both knew. "Time is not a measure of love. You said that yourself," I remind her. "Feelings aren't facts."

She nods, her ponytail bouncing. Then she looks at me, her face so open and vulnerable it makes my heart split open. "I haven't done this sober. It feels terrifying. Like I'm a newborn. I have to relearn everything."

"Well, I haven't done it, period. So we're in the same boat."

"Except I'm an addict and you're not and your brother was and he died of his addiction."

"That has nothing to do with us."

"But it does," she says. "He does. It's a part of you. And I want to know all the parts of you and for you to know all the parts of me."

"I can think of better ways for you to know all the parts of me."

She rolls her eyes but the smile spreading across her face gives her away. "I'm serious."

"I am too and I promise I will tell you anything you want to know. I am an open book." I spread my arms wide.

Hannah chuckles. "This is a lot for a first date, isn't it?"

"So let me get this straight. This is our first date, and before you said we're in a relationship? Slow *your* roll, girl."

But I don't want to slow anything. I want to catapult into a future with Hannah. I pull her to me and I kiss her. She's tentative at first, but then she opens to it, opens to me, drawing me closer, running her hands through my hair, gasping. I kiss her back, trying to lose myself in it, in her, trying to banish the ghosts banging around my heart, and almost succeeding.

※

Hannah rents a room in a sober house. It's a drab, ranch-style place with ugly brown siding, but her room feels like a nest. It's small, with a queen bed, a zillion throw pillows, lights strewn along the frame. On the giant bookshelf—wood, Ike would be pleased to know—books compete for space with records, CDs, and cassette tapes.

Mind you, I don't notice any of this until the next morning.

"See?" Hannah teases me when we wake up and I go straight to the bookcase. "Books and music can coexist."

"I'd say last night showed they can do way more than coexist," I tease, reaching for her again.

She smacks me with a pillow. "Not now. I have to finish a transcription project before noon," she says. "But that will only take an hour or two."

"A what?"

"Transcription. Typing up what people say. That's my job these days. Until I figure out what I want to do when I grow up."

"You don't want to make music?"

"I already do make music," she says. "But making a living from it . . . I wouldn't bet on it."

"What are your plans after the transcription?"

"I just have to pack for Arizona." She smiles. "But other than that I'm free. What about you? Do you have things you need to do?"

A long list of them. Now that selling to Lou's boss is out, the store is Penny's. I've got to break the news to Ira. And the Lumberjacks. And Chad. Send the bulk buyers the inventory Chad is working on. Put the records in storage. Figure out where Ira and I are going to live. I'd planned to go somewhere sunny but now I'm not so sure I want to be far from Hannah. Or Chad, for that matter.

Hannah's hair is down, fanning across her shoulders. Her silk kimono keeps slipping, revealing the star-shaped mole on her clavicle that I can't stop kissing.

There is nowhere else I'd rather be. No one else I'd rather be with. All my problems will be there tomorrow, but for today, there's this.

I pull at the belt of her robe, bringing her close, kissing her again. "Nothing that can't wait."

///

I text Ira that I'm going to be away for two days and where he can pick up the car if he needs it, but he tells me not to worry and have fun. And so I turn off my phone and just try to let myself have this.

Because this—Hannah and me cooking omelets side by side in her kitchen—feels like a miracle.

Because this—Hannah and me reading chapters aloud from her old copy of *The Lion, the Witch and the Wardrobe*—feels like happiness.

Because this—Hannah and me, together—feels like inevitable.

///

At the end of the second day, Hannah pulls down a suitcase and starts to pack.

"Stay," I tell her.

"Trust me, I wish I could."

"Then don't go. We'll make Thanksgiving dinner and eat in bed."

She kisses me, casually, because that's what Hannah Crew does now. "Tempting," she says. "But I have to face the music."

She pads to her shelf and rifles around; the zigzag scar down her hip from the accident that got her addicted to painkillers peeks out of her robe. When I saw it for the first time, and she told me the full story of the accident, I felt such tenderness, and relief. She is not Sandy. Her addiction was not her own choice.

"I have something for you," she says. "I made it last night when you were sleeping." She opens a desk drawer and pulls out a tape. "Old school. Seemed more your vibe."

"What is it?"

She hands me the cassette. AARON'S PERFECT SONGS? is written in block letters across the spine of the case.

"It's from the playlist I made you, plus a few new additions." She nibbles on her thumbnail. "I told you I wouldn't rest until I found you a perfect song."

There's a part of me that never wants her to find the perfect song because that way Hannah will have to keep looking. And if she has to keep looking, we won't end.

But there's another part of me that needs to tell her—prove to her—how meant to be we are.

"You already found me a perfect song," I say.

"I did?" She lights up. "Which one?"

"Talking Heads, 'This Must Be the Place.'"

"Really?" Her eyebrow—the one with the scar on it that I now know she got in an ice-skating accident when she was nine—quirks up. "I almost didn't put that one on. I'm not sure why I did."

"I am," I say, pulling her to me. "I knew it from the moment we met."

"And what did you know?"

"That you and me, we are inevitable."

The 2010 Rand McNally
Road Atlas

Since I've never been drunk, I've never been hungover, but Chad has explained how it all works. Not just the headaches, or feeling simultaneously ravenously hungry and needing to puke, but the correlation between pleasure and pain.

According to Chad, there's a direct link between how much you overindulge and how shitty you feel. "It's like bricks," he explained to me. "Drink a brick, get hit with two. Drink a dozen bricks, and it's like a house fell on you."

The first brick hits as I drop Hannah off at the airport shuttle bus. I won't see her for five days. Rationally, I know five days is nothing. We've known each other barely a month. Have spent all of five days together in that month. But it's a brick just the same.

The second brick smashes down when I pass the sign at the edge of our town. In one week, we lose the store. And I haven't told Ira.

The third brick lands when I realize I'm telling Ira right now. There is no more putting it off.

The fourth brick lands when I pull up to the store and see both Ike's and Chad's trucks parked out front. It's Thanksgiving week. Ike's supposed to be in Walla Walla.

When I open the door, it's like I've stepped through the ward-robe into Narnia. The store is unrecognizable. The shelves have been patched and repaired. The floors are leveled, the planks sanded and varnished. The Sheetrock plastered, primed, and painted. There's now a small area by the café with two bistro tables. And a new sofa in the corner where Ira's armchair once lived. In the back of the store is a freshly oiled butcher-block counter with Gaga situated in the middle like a queen. Next to her, a case full of Angelica Silvestri's pastries, and beneath that, a minifridge with yogurts and juices. Next to the front counter, where I usually sit, is a brand-new computer, the browser page open to a website that reads BLUEBIRD BOOKS & CAFÉ.

"He's back!" Chad shouts.

And then everyone—Ira, Bev, Ike, Richie, Garry, Jax, Angela Silvestri, and an older woman with a walker who I recognize as Beana—all turn to me. "Surprise!" they shout. As if it's my birthday. As if, like the store itself, this is a gift I want.

Ira bounds up, coffee-cake crumbs clinging to his beard. "Can you believe it?"

No. I can't. I shake my head.

"When we heard you were with Hannah," Chad says, throwing a glance at Jax, "we figured you'd be together till she left and we wanted to have it all ready."

"It was Penny who gave us the idea," Ira says.

"Penny?" I croak.

"When she asked about our opening, we realized we should try to be ready for the holiday season," Ira explains. "We went on a spree and now we're aiming for Black Friday. All we have to do is let things dry and put out the books, but Chad's nearly finished organizing them all."

"A spree?" I ask, my head spinning.

"And now we were thinking," Ike continues, "we ought to have a grand reopening around the holidays. Like maybe get some Seattle authors to come up. Have a party. With music, even." He looks at Jax.

"Yeah, I'll talk to Hannah," they say. "We can play an acoustic set."

"What do you think?" Chad asks. "Do you love it?"

I can't answer. I'm buried under a house of bricks, suffocating from all my lies.

"How?" is all I can manage to ask.

How did I let it go this far? How do I wreck everything I touch? How do I keep hurting the people I love?

"Easy," Chad replies. "Teamwork. And a little bit of cash."

"How much cash?" I ask.

Chad shrugs. "A few grand. But it's an investment, not a loan."

"Is that why you withdrew all the money from your bank account?"

"Yeah," Chad says. "Wait, how'd you know about that?"

"What about the Stim?"

Chad looks sheepish. "I backed out of the Stim."

"What? Why?"

"I changed my mind."

"What about your deposit?"

Chad shrugs. "I lost it."

"Why? Why would you do that?"

"My priorities changed."

"Chad, you shouldn't have done that!"

"I thought you of all people would be glad."

Penny was right. Chad emptied his bank account for the store. And he backed out of the Stim. To invest in the store. To think I warned Chad about being scammed by Frederic. I should have warned him about being scammed by *me*.

"I know I should've checked with you," Ira says a bit bashfully. "But we wanted to surprise you. After everything you've done, we wanted this for you."

"Everything I've done?" I scoff. "You have no idea what I've done."

"Of course I do," Ira says, smiling. "We all do."

"No. You don't. Because what I've done is sell the store."

Ira's still smiling, as if he doesn't or can't comprehend what I just said. So I repeat it. "I sold the store. To Penny Macklemore."

"No," Ira says. "You'd never do that."

"I would and I did, Ira."

"But you love the store," Ira insists. "You love books."

"No, I don't. I don't even read anymore. This place has made me hate books. And I used to love books. I used to think they were miracles like you do. But now they make me sick, like strawberries do."

When I mention strawberries, Ira's face goes white. His lips form a fish shape. "You don't want the store?" he asks in a tattered voice.

"No," I say. "I never did. And that's why I sold it to Penny."

"Buy it back," Chad says.

"I can't. And I don't want to."

"When did you do this?" Ira asks.

"After the shelf broke. When I found your credit-card stash and it was just so obvious, it's been so obvious for so long, that it wasn't coming back. And I just wanted it to end. Because the waiting for it to end . . . I can't go through that again."

I spin around, jabbing a prosecutorial finger at Chad. "And then *you* showed up with your ramp idea." I swivel toward Ike. "And then *you* built a better ramp. I kept telling you to stop but you went ahead anyway and then you brought the paint and then you . . ." I pivot back to Chad. "Built your database and started talking about partnerships and it got Ira's hopes up . . ." I turn back to Ira. "And you were so happy. I haven't seen you like that since Sandy died, since Mom left . . ." My voice breaks again but I push through. "And I thought, maybe I could change Penny's mind, get the store fixed up, to how it used to be, and you could take it over. I tried to back out. I tried. So many ways. But it didn't work. Because it can't work. Because there's no coming back from extinction. Can't you see? We're dinosaurs. The asteroid has hit. It's time we accept that and move on."

Ira sinks onto his haunches, eyes bulging, the panic returning as the room erupts into pandemonium, everyone yelling at once. Ike is shouting about selling the store. Garry and Richie are shouting about all the work they did. Angela is shouting about whether or not her crumb cake is needed. Beana and Bev are shouting for everyone to stop shouting.

My head is spinning and my heart is racing and my ears are ringing and it's loud as shit in here but somehow I hear Chad's quiet voice cut through it all. I have never heard him sound so angry.

"Don't you dare," he says. "Don't you fucking dare call *me* a dinosaur."

///

I run out of the store without looking back. I jump into the Volvo and take off, tearing past C.J.'s and the hardware store and the used-car lot, blowing through the traffic light, not stopping until I see a blur of blue.

Denim Blue. That was the name of the paint color Mom used on the porch swing. She used to repaint it every few years, so it would stay bright. "You have to take care of the things you love," she said. Which she did. Until she couldn't.

There it is, on the side of the road. Bart must have dumped it here. Like I told him to.

I stop. I load the porch swing in the back of the car. And then I keep going.

///

I have no idea if Daryl Feldman is going to be in his office. It's Thanksgiving week. People have places to go to. Family to visit. But I'm flying blind here. The assistant is in, surprised to see me. "Did you have an appointment?" I shake my head. And maybe it's the desperation reeking off me or maybe she knows her boss is an asshole or maybe it's the Thanksgiving spirit, but she says, "Let me see what I can do."

Five minutes later, I'm ushered in. Before Daryl speaks, I do. "The records are worth way more than forty-five hundred dollars. I left the index here last time, and if you looked up any of the albums, you'll see how valuable they are."

Daryl Feldman stares at me from his modern and uncomfortable-looking and obviously very expensive desk chair.

"There's a Pink Floyd *Piper at the Gates of Dawn* in there, first pressing, worth two fifty. A Replacements *Stink*, first pressing, two hundred. And more like that. Thousands more. They're worth, ballpark, fifty thousand dollars."

Daryl swivels back and forth in his chair.

"But I'll sell them to you here, now, for twenty grand. At twenty grand, you're still gonna make a shit ton of money."

Daryl swivels some more. "Eight grand," he counters.

If Penny were here, she would keep going, recognize this as an opening bid, part of the negotiation dance. But I don't want to dance. I just want it to be over. And eight grand solves my most immediate math problem. It'll pay Chad back for most of the deposit he lost because of me. I can take the $1,200 I've made off record sales and pay the guys for their work. We still lose the store. But once the asteroid hit, we were always going to lose the store. Like we were always going to lose Sandy. Like we were always going to lose Mom. Some things are inevitable.

"Deal," I tell Daryl.

"When can I pick them up?"

"Today if you want." I write down the store's address and instruct him to make out the check to Chad Santos. Then I pry off the key Sandy gave me after I promised I would not sell his records. I slide it across Daryl's desk. "Show this to Ira. Tell him you came for the vinyl. He'll understand."

///

Ira still keeps an old Rand McNally Road Atlas in the seat pocket. According to a distance chart in the back, the drive is fifteen hundred miles. I plot my course, running my fingers down and to the right, along the thick blue interstate lines, the way Ira must have done when he traveled from one end of the country to the other, not knowing what he was looking for until he saw her standing on the side of the road.

The Magician's Nephew

Phoenix is the fourth sunniest place in country, the sun shining eighty-five percent of the time. I know this because I've Googled it as I've thought about places to live where the sky does not constantly cry. In my fantasy version, these places all have bright blue skies, open vistas, sunlight burnishing a copper Georgia O'Keeffe landscape.

But as I reach the outskirts of the city, the sights are oddly familiar: big-box stores, car dealerships with inflatable tube balloons, gas stations, fast food chains. Instead of damp and cloud-shrouded, it's sun-bleached and violently bright, but otherwise, it feels the same.

Except for one crucial difference. Hannah is here.

I pull into a Circle K off the highway and use some more of my record-sale stash to gas up again and buy a travel pack of toothpaste, some deodorant, a new pair of boxers. I lock myself in the bathroom and clean off as best I can. When I feel halfway human, I extract my phone from the seat pocket where I've buried it and turn it on for the first time since I left home. It whooshes back to life with a cacophony of alerts, missed calls, voicemails, and texts. I ignore them all, and call Hannah.

She picks up right away. "Hey, baby," she says. "I was just thinking of you."

She was thinking of me. She called me *baby*. It's going to be okay.

"I was thinking of you too," I rasp.

"Are you sick? Your voice sounds hoarse."

Somewhere outside Bellevue when the silence was already starting to make me crazy, I remembered the tape Hannah made me and popped it in. I listened to it, on repeat for twenty-nine hours, through Eastern Washington, across Oregon and Idaho, and into Nevada. I sang along, at first making up nonsense words and then, after repeated listenings, the real ones. I sang at the top of my lungs, even to the songs like "Clair de Lune," which has no words. I sang louder than the wheeze of the Volvo's beleaguered engine, louder than the voices in my head.

"I'm fine," I reply. "What are you up to?"

"Making coffee."

"And after that?"

"I don't know. Probably staying out of the way while my mother cooks."

"Can you hang out for a while?"

"You want to fool around on FaceTime at ten in the morning?"

"Definitely." I pause. "But I thought today we could hang in person."

The line goes quiet. In the background the coffee maker gurgles and hisses. "Where are you?" she asks.

"In Phoenix."

"You flew to Arizona?"

"Drove, actually."

"Why?

"To see you." In the ensuing silence, my phone beeps with two new incoming texts. I flick them away without looking. "So when can I see you?"

"Aaron," she says in a measured tone. "I'll be home in three days."

"I know, but I'm here. I want to see you. Don't you want to see me?"

"I do want to see you. But back at home."

"Hannah, I drove thirty hours to see you."

"I didn't ask you to do that."

"I know! But I'm here. Surprise!"

Hannah sighs.

"I really want to see you." I try to sound bouncy, a guy in love doing something romantic and spontaneous. But I can't even convince myself, let alone her. "I *need* to see you," I add, voice breaking, unmasking my desperation.

Another sigh. But then:

"Come on over."

※

I get lost on the way to Hannah's house, which is in some gated community. I mistakenly pull into Desert Pines Estates and Sandpiper Estates before I finally see Hannah waiting at the gates of Mirage Estates. The guard lifts the rail and Hannah slides into the seat next to me, but when I turn to kiss her, she is saying something in Spanish to the guard and so I wind up kissing mostly hair.

"I didn't know you spoke Spanish," I say.

"There's a lot you don't know about me."

"That's why I'm here." I paste over the awkward silence that follows with a jolly "Happy Thanksgiving!"

"Thanksgiving is tomorrow."

"Happy early Thanksgiving. Here." I grab a melting maple bar I bought at an earlier pit stop.

She shoves the candy into her hoodie pocket and looks into the back seat.

"What is all that?"

"Oh, nothing. I mean, it's our old porch swing."

"You drove your porch swing down to Phoenix?"

"It was sitting by the side of the road and I couldn't leave it there, so here it is . . ." I trail off. "Do you want it?"

"No," she says. "But I do want to know what you're doing here."

"I told you. I came to see you."

"You drove a thousand miles to see me?"

"Fifteen hundred, but who's counting?"

"Why?"

"Do I need a reason?"

"Yeah, you kind of do. This is weird, Aaron. I've been gone two days. And I'll be home in three."

"Look. I know it's spur-of-the-moment, but my family doesn't really do Thanksgiving anymore and I had a few days to kill and I thought I'd come down here and see you. So we could get to know each other more. I could see where you grew up. Where you went to school. That kind of thing."

"You drove down here to get to know me better?"

"Yeah!"

She mulls this for a bit. "Okay," she says. "Pull a U-turn and go back out the way you came."

"I thought you lived here?"

"No, Aaron. I live in Washington. My parents live here."

Right. They probably don't know Hannah is involved with me yet. I hadn't thought about that.

"Anyhow, you came down here to get to know me, so that's what we'll do. Go out to the street and turn right."

I do as she says and we're back on the wide boulevard full of landscapers trimming the flowering hedges. Her tape is still playing on the stereo but suddenly I'm a little embarrassed, so I turn it off and we drive in silence past several more gated communities, past several more strip malls, until she tells me to slow down. "See that?" Hannah points to an anonymous storefront. "That's where I did modeling class when I was younger."

"You took modeling classes?"

"For six years. It taught me good posture, how to saunter down a catwalk, and which diuretics will help keep your goal weight."

The edge in her voice is subtle but unmistakable. "Are you mad at me?"

"Take a left at the light," she says, ignoring the question. We drive in silence, my mind spinning with what to say to make it better.

Hannah points to an adobe building with a massive parking lot and a marquee reading HILLSDALE LIONS. "This is where I went to high school." She points to the football field. "That's the field where I cheered at games." She points to an adjacent cinder-block building. "And there's the locker room where I gave my first blow job to my boyfriend, who was, naturally, on the football team. He told all his friends and that got me the nickname Hannah Blew. Which I pretended to be cool with. I still run into guys in town who call me Hannah Blew. Good times. Okay, now follow the signs for 101." She points to a highway entrance.

"You *are* mad at me," I say as I merge onto the highway.

"Why would I be mad at you? You came here to get to know me, so I'm giving you the super cuts of my life."

We drive a few miles in silence, then she guides me off a ramp and down a dusty road full of mature oak trees. "See that one?" she says, pointing to a tree indistinguishable from the rest. "I wrapped my dad's car around that tree."

"I thought your accident was on the way home from a ski trip," I say.

"The accident where I shattered my hip was on a drive home from Taos. This is when I crashed my father's car while high on Adderall."

"Oh," I say, swallowing. "I didn't realize you had two accidents."

"I'm not sure why," Hannah replies coolly. "I told you about it at the NA meeting. Were you even listening?"

"Of course I was."

"What did I say?"

"I didn't memorize it."

"I don't need it verbatim, Aaron, but what was the gist of it?"

I scramble to come up with something that will appease her, that will undo the damage I've seemingly done. But I can't remember anything. It's all muddied up with memories of Sandy. "You got in the accident. You got addicted to painkillers."

"That's it?"

"No. No. Your parents didn't want to face up to your addiction. They wanted to think you were perfect."

"What else?"

"I don't know what else. What else is there? Oh, I forgot the most important part. You've been sober almost a year."

"Why is that the most important part?"

"A year. It's a big accomplishment."

"You make it sound like I've crossed some finish line."

"Well, maybe not that. But getting closer. And a lot of people don't make it that far. My brother sure as shit didn't."

At the mention of my brother, Hannah quietly curses, shaking her head.

"What?" I ask.

"Pull over, please."

"Where?" We're in the middle of nowhere. Just miles of dry, dusty road.

"Anywhere. I'm getting out."

"Why?"

"Stop the car, Aaron."

"Hannah, if I said something wrong . . ."

"Stop the fucking car, Aaron." Her voice is a quiet growl.

I pull over. "Look," I begin. "I clearly did something wrong. Maybe I shouldn't have come down, so soon into our relationship, and without asking. I see that it seems a little nuts—"

"Why are you here, Aaron?" she interrupts.

"I told you. I came to see you. To know you."

"If you really came to see me, if you knew me, even a little bit, you'd have understood that this is my first visit with my family since I left. How hard that is for me. And you wouldn't have made it harder."

"No! That's the last thing I want to do." I reach for her hands. In spite of the heat, they feel cold.

"Then why are you here?" she repeats.

"I came to see you."

"Why are you here?"

"Because I'm in love with . . ."

She silences me with a slice of her hand in the air. "You don't know me well enough to be in love with me."

"Don't say that! I've been in love with you since the minute I saw you. And you felt it too. Our connection. You said so."

She shakes her head.

"You can't deny it. We just had the most amazing two days together. You found me my perfect song."

She takes off her seat belt and turns to me. "Tell. Me. Why. You're. Here."

"Because I love you."

But Hannah knows something can be true and still not be the truth. She says, "You know, I've been around addicts long enough to know when someone's hustling me."

"I'm *not* hustling you. And *I'm* not an addict. My fucking brother was the goddamn addict!"

I see the words come out of my mouth, like a poison vapor. I can see them enter Hannah's bloodstream.

"Like I am a goddamn addict."

"No! You're nothing like him. You didn't *choose* to become an addict. You didn't ruin your family's life."

"No one chooses to become an addict."

"Sandy did! Over and over again! He chose drugs over us. You want to know why I'm here? I'm here because you're the first good thing that's happened to me since my brother got sick. Since our family business went under. Since my mom was so broken she had to leave and my father came apart. You're the one good thing, Hannah. And I'm so tired of bad things. I know they're inevitable but I want a good inevitable thing. And that's you."

And then the dam breaks and all the years of anger and fear and sadness and loneliness and guilt come pouring out of me in a torrent of tears and snot.

Hannah gathers me in her arms. "Oh, baby," she croons as she rocks me back and forth. All I want is to stay in this embrace. Never go back to the store, to Ira, the Lumberjacks, Chad.

We stay that way for a while and then I guess the relief of it, and the exhaustion of the past few days, catches up with me because I fall asleep.

When I wake up, the light's different. Softer. The air in the car feels warm, intimate, the two of us enclosed in a bubble. If we could stay here forever, I would.

"Hey," I say, wiping some drool from my cheek. "How long have I been out?"

"A couple hours," she says.

There's a crick in my neck that I try to massage out.

"Here," Hannah says, reaching over to rub it for me.

I close my eyes. "That feels good." Hannah massages a bit more. "I'm sorry about losing it before. Laying all that on you. There's just a lot going on right now."

"I can see that. And I'm glad you were honest with me. It clarified some things." She stops rubbing and I open my eyes.

"Like the guy you got involved with is clueless when it comes to romance and relationships?"

"Oh, that was clear from the jump," she says with a rueful smile.

I lean in closer, wanting to bridge any distance between us. I kiss her. Her lips are warm and soft, but after a second she pulls away. "I have to tell you something."

I might be new to the girlfriend thing, unpracticed in relationships, but I know *I have to tell you something* is a precursor to an asteroid. *I have to tell you something* is what Ira told me when they put Sandy in rehab the first time. What Mom told me when she had to leave.

"Please, don't say it."

She says it: "I can't be involved with you."

"No. NO! You're the one thing in my life that makes me feel good."

She reaches out to touch my face. "Funny. That's how I used to feel about heroin."

"It's not the same. You're not a drug."

"Aren't I? You're using me to run away. And you're keeping so many secrets. The fact that I didn't see it, or chose not to see it, proves I'm not ready for a relationship." She looks at me. "And neither are you."

"We'll get ready together. To be ready for each other."

"That's not how recovery works."

"Don't do this! Don't throw this away. We're meant for each other."

"Why? Because I was reading some book?"

"Not some book! You were reading *The Magician's Nephew.* You had 'This Must Be the Place' on your perfect-song mix."

"What's that got to do with anything?"

"It means we're inevitable."

"How?"

"Because that song," I say, my voice breaking. "That was the song."

"What song?"

And then I tell her the story. Of Mom and Ira meeting by the side of the road. The song that started our family. The inevitability of them. The inevitability of us.

When I finish, Hannah starts laughing. Like hardcore, holding her sides, tears down the face, laughter. "All this time," she says between hiccups. "You've said you don't like music." More chortling. "But music is your *origin*. You literally would not exist without it." She wipes the tears with the back of her hand and kisses me good-bye before opening the car door and turning to me one last time: "Aaron Stein," she says. "You're the most unreliable narrator I've ever met."

A Grief Observed

It's dusk when I pull into Silver City, but the light is blue, peach, purple. It's Georgia O'Keeffe light. We don't have skies like this in the Northwest. Not ever.

After Hannah left me on the side of the road, I grabbed the atlas to figure out where I was and how to get home. Then remembered I couldn't go home.

And that's when I saw how close I was to New Mexico. How close I was to the thing I've been running from. Turns out, no matter how fast or far you go, the inevitable always catches up with you.

I picked up my phone. And for the first time since she left, I called my mother.

///

The dogs start barking as soon as I pull into the driveway and get more frenzied as I come up the front walk. My olfactory bulb starts firing the minute Mom opens the door. It's not just her smell—lavender and sandalwood—but the aroma of chicken soup wafting from the kitchen. Jewish penicillin, what she would feed us whenever we were ailing. I stand in front of this strange house, with these strange dogs, and it's like I'm there and here, then and now, all places at once.

"Hello, my love," she says.

"Hi, Mom."

We just stand there, neither of us knowing what to do. Mom used to be a hugger, but we all used to be things we're not anymore.

"Do you want to come in?"

I nod.

As soon as I go inside, the dogs switch from fierce guardians to adoring lap animals. Mom introduces me: "This is Terrence," she says, petting an oddly shaped mutt. "He's half Siberian husky, half Welsh corgi, and mostly blind, not that he lets that stop him. And this is Mindy," she says, tickling a poodle under the chin.

Mom, Terrence, and Mindy lead me down a hallway decorated with Southwestern style paintings of buffalo, hawks, coyotes. The chirp of birdsong is everywhere.

"Noisy little shits, aren't they?" she says. "They're always like this before bedtime. You want to meet them?" Keeping the dogs at bay, she opens the door to a small bedroom full of large cages and a pull-out couch, the bed made up. "Getting their ya-yas out. Reminds me of how you boys used to be. So riled up, I'd have to sing you to sleep." She stops, lost in the memory. "Sometimes the birds sing me to sleep."

I step toward one of the cages; five colorful parakeets flutter about inside. I stick my finger through the bars. They all ignore me save for one, a small yellow bird with orange spots and a baby mohawk, who gently pecks at my finger.

"That's Ramón."

"Hi, Ramón," I say.

"Want me to open the cage? He likes to perch on fingers."

I nod.

Mom unlatches the little opening, whistling and warbling like she's become fluent in bird-speak. It wouldn't surprise me. She always knew how to talk to anyone.

Most of the birds ignore her, happy with their birdseed. Ramón stares right at me, eyes flashing.

"He's pinning," Mom tells me.

"Pinning?"

"Dilating and contracting his pupil. It's a sign of how parakeets are feeling."

"How's he feeling?"

"Curious, I suspect." And then, as if to confirm Mom's hunch, Ramón flies out of his cage, landing on my shoulder.

"Wow," Mom says. "I've never seen him do that before."

"What do I do?"

"Nothing. Unless you want me to get him off you."

I feel Ramón's tiny claws clamping on to my flesh, like he's holding on for dear life. "Leave him."

"He must like your aura," Mom says.

I roll my eyes.

"Laugh if you want, but the people who live here have a ton of animal behavior books. One I read said that parakeets can see UV light, which allows them to see people's auras." Mom pauses and reaches her finger toward Ramón, who gently pecks at her nail. "He must like yours."

"Then clearly Ramón has terrible taste. Because if I have an aura, it's puke green."

"Well, if it is, Ramón likes it, don't you?" she chirps.

"You've become a bird person," I say.

"I suspect I always was. I did name the store Bluebird Books."

At the mention of the store my stomach clenches. Ramón flaps his wings in sympathy.

"But I never lived with birds before," she continues. "I find them endlessly fascinating. We say *birdbrain* like it's an insult, but as tiny as their brains are, they are remarkably intelligent animals. They can predict earthquakes. Storms. They go quiet in the moments before a cataclysmic event."

Mom whistles and holds out her finger. Ramón jumps on, and she returns him to the cage. "It's funny because the day I found your brother . . ." She trails off, latching the cage and unfolding a white sheet. "I woke up at dawn. Usually the birds are making a racket at that time, but they were eerily quiet." She shakes the sheet out a few times before gently laying it over the cage. "I went into Sandy's room, even though he hadn't been home in days; if he had, I'd have been checking on him. I could never sleep when he was in the house. But he must have come in late, after we went to bed. When the birds were quiet, I just knew." She pulls down the sheet and the birdsong falls silent. "I just knew."

I can still hear the sound of her screams when she found him that morning. I'd known straightaway too: the inevitable had finally happened.

And I was relieved. The end had finally come.

But it wasn't the end. Mom kept screaming. At the hospital

where they pronounced him dead. At the morgue where they took his body for an autopsy. At the memorial service hardly anyone attended. Every morning she woke wailing, as if his death was happening to her over and over again.

"She needs time," Ira told me. "She'll get better in time." But she didn't. And every day that she didn't, Ira got worse. He'd kept it pretty together through Sandy's sickness, and even his death, but when Mom started to unravel, so did he.

A new dread descended over me, thick as the December skies. If this carried on, I was going to lose all of them. Not just Sandy, who was already gone. Not just Mom, who was halfway gone. But Ira too.

I began to wish Mom would just leave, the way I'd wished Sandy would just die.

And then she did.

And nothing got better.

Ira may be the Giving Tree, but the boy with the ax who chops him down, branch by branch—that's me.

///

I fall asleep in my clothes without eating and wake the next morning to the sounds of the birds chirping away. I blink. The clock reads 10:34. Ramón is staring at me, his eyes pinning.

"You know the truth, don't you, little buddy?" I ask him.

His eyes grow larger, smaller, larger, smaller.

I shuffle into the kitchen. Mom is staring at the refrigerator. "It's Thanksgiving," she says, pulling open the empty drawers. "I sort of forgot it was happening and now all I have is chicken soup and hot dogs. I suppose we could go to the market and see if there are any turkeys left."

"That's okay," I say. "I'm not feeling very thankful."

She turns to me. "Funnily enough, today I am."

My stomach lets out a gurgle. I haven't eaten since the Circle K in Phoenix. "Wouldn't mind some chicken soup."

Mom pulls out a Tupperware container and ladles some into a bowl, popping it in the microwave. As it heats, the smell fills up the kitchen, but this time it doesn't transport me anywhere. I stay here. The microwave dings. She pulls out the bowl and plops it in front of me. "Eat up and have a shower. I borrowed some of the owner's clothes for you because I couldn't find any suitcase in the car."

I swirl my spoon into the soup, chunky with carrots and onions and hunks of white meat, but no noodles. Ira is a firm believer that the only starch that should adorn chicken soup is a matzo ball.

"By the way, what's my porch swing doing in the car?"

I take my first bite. It is salty and fatty and warm and it goes straight into my bloodstream. Immediately, I feel a bit better.

"That's a long story."

"Finish your soup. We'll take the dogs out for a walk and you can tell it to me."

The house is in the foothills of the Piños Altos, and we set up a steep, rocky trail. As we walk in the brisk, clear air, I let the story unspool backward, starting with the porch swing in the car, to the record selling, to the renovation, to the building of the ramp, to the night I met Chad and went and sold the store to Penny Macklemore.

Mom's face stays neutral as I talk. Clearly, this is old news.

"Ira told you?"

"You sold the store out from under him. You think he wouldn't tell me that?"

A fresh fist of guilt socks me in the gut. "I figured he might. The next time you called."

Mom gives me a look. "Your father and I talk almost every day."

"You call once a week."

This time, Mom rolls *her* eyes. "I call *you* once a week, my reticent son. But I speak to Ira frequently. He calls me when he's on his walks."

"He does? I thought he was smoking pot."

"Ira?" She laughs. "He's too paranoid for that."

"So if you talk to Ira every day, do you know about . . . ?"

"Bev? Of course."

"And you're okay with it?"

Mom unleashes the dogs. Mindy bounds up the hill, but Terrence stays by our side until Mom pulls out a bright yellow rubber ball. "I want your father to be happy," Mom says as Terrence trots off after the ball. "He wants me to be happy. And we both want you to be happy. But when you've been through what we have, you start to understand that happy doesn't always look like it used to. Family doesn't always look like it used to. But it's still family."

"That's what Ira says."

We reach the top of the hill. Off to the side is a rocky promontory, a series of boulders jutting out from the craggy hillside, as if in defiance of gravity. Mom whistles and the dogs come running. She leashes them and ties them to a pine tree, which is gnarled but strong, reminding me of Ike. She plops down at the edge of a flat rock, her legs dangling into the canyon.

"Why didn't you say something? Tell anyone?" she asks as I sit down next to her.

"I don't know," I admit, throwing a rock into the ravine. "I meant to. But then things just sort of got out of control. I sold to Penny and the Lumberjacks came and I tried to get out of it, I tried to tell the truth, but I just kept digging myself deeper. And every day I'd wake up and think: 'Today is the day I'll fix it.' But then the day passed and I couldn't do it."

"You know who you sound like?"

"Ira," I reply.

"No, Sandy."

"Why do people keep saying that? I'm *nothing* like Sandy!"

"Aren't you?"

"No! I like books, not music. I look like Ira, not you. And I'm not an addict. I've never even had beer."

"The secrets. The lying. The justifying. Making and breaking promises to yourself. That's your brother in a nutshell."

"Yeah, but at least I didn't ruin anyone's life . . ."

As soon as I say this, I see Ira's broken face after I told him I'd sold to Penny. And Ike's hopeful face as he vowed to not be the termite that destroyed the wood. And Chad's betrayed face when I called him a dinosaur.

Suddenly, I see it. A flaming piece of rock hurtling through the atmosphere.

Oh my god. *I'm* the fucking asteroid.

"But I never meant for this to happen," I say. "Things, they just, I don't know, spun out of control."

"I imagine your brother felt the same way."

Instead of objecting, drawing a Kryptonite line between me and Sandy, as I have done for years, I let myself feel how Sandy must have felt: caught in the undertow of his mistakes, trying with everything he had in him to set things right—and still failing.

And with that, I begin to understand. He didn't mean to destroy our family any more than I chose to destroy the store. He got caught up in something he couldn't control.

Same as me.

***

The next day, we go out to lunch at a diner in Silver's City's tiny downtown. The place is a lot like C.J.'s, the same well-worn booths, laminated menus, whipped-cream-laden pies in the display cases. Donna, the waitress, already knows Mom's name and her order. "The usual?" she asks.

"I'm celebrating Thanksgiving a day late with my son," Mom says. "We'll have two hot open-faced turkey sandwich platters, please."

"Turkey's always better the next day anyway," Donna says, scratching the order onto her pad.

"I'm going to hit an Al-Anon meeting after lunch," Mom says

after Donna drops our food. "If you want to come. I think it might do you good."

"Maybe another time," I say. "I went to an NA meeting last week and I'm still in recovery from that."

"You went to an NA meeting?" Her look is more amused than concerned.

"I went with Hannah, the girl I was seeing."

"Was?"

"She dumped me."

"How come?" Mom asks.

I scoop up a hunk of mashed potatoes and splat them against the plate. "She said I had some shit to deal with, if you can believe that."

"Don't we all." Mom swirls the gravy into the cranberry sauce. "I have a crazy idea."

"Yeah?"

"You could stay here. Work out your shit. With me. Silver has three bookstores, a public university, and three hundred sunny days a year. Not the worst place to make a home."

"You're gonna stick around?"

She nods. "I think so. I feel at peace in the mountains. The animal shelter where I volunteer has offered me a job. Also"—she glances at me and smiles—"I have a porch swing now, so I need somewhere to hang it."

"What about Ira?"

"Ira wants you to be happy. And he has Bev now."

"Can I think about it?"

"You can do whatever you need to, my love."

When Mom heads off to her meeting, I walk toward downtown, a cluster of low-rise brick buildings dwarfed by the mountains behind them. I find the bookstore immediately and as soon as I step inside, my olfactory bulb kicks into gear. I'm transported to Bluebird Books, and in that moment I yearn to be back there. And then I remember that there is no more *there* to go back to.

"Can I help you?"

The man behind the counter looks nothing like Ira—he's short, brown-skinned, and balding, wearing a bunch of turquoise rings—except I can tell right off the bat, they are brothers of a sort. If there were such a thing as a bookseller covenant, this man would be a signatory.

"I'm looking for a book." I used to scoff at people who said that. What else would you come to a bookstore for? But I think Mom always understood that bookstores were about the people inside them, the ones on the pages, and off the pages too.

"You've come to the right place," he says. "Would you like help finding one?"

"I would."

"Tell me: What's the last book you read that you loved?"

The question stumps me at first. I've reread *The Rise and Fall of the Dinosaurs* multiple times, but I'm not sure that's a book I loved so much as clung to. But then I remember Hannah and me, a few days ago, reading aloud from my first love.

"*The Lion, the Witch and the Wardrobe.*"

"Ah yes," he says. He looks at me for a long moment, sizing me up, the way Ira used to with customers. "I think I have just the thing for you." He disappears into the stacks. When he returns, I expect to get another of the Narnia books. Or another fantasy series. Harry Potter. His Dark Materials. But he hands me a slender volume, its cover a sketch of three red birds.

"*A Grief Observed* by C. S. Lewis," the bookseller tells me. "He wrote it after his wife died, trying to reconcile his faith with his loss before coming to realize the two aren't at odds; they're bedfellows. It's nothing like Narnia, but I thought it might be of interest."

I look at this man, who doesn't know me, or anything about me, but who knows, like Ira always knew, like all the best booksellers know, not just what their customers want, but what they need.

※

No one ever told me that grief felt so like fear. I read the opening lines of the book, and it's like my own pages are coming unstuck. For so long, all I've felt is fear, and all this time, it was grief. I continue reading, remembering why I used to love books. Because they show us, in so many words, and so many worlds, that we are not alone.

A miracle, in twenty-six letters.

※

I'm reading the book when Mom finds me that afternoon. I read it the rest of the day as the long shadows fall, Ramón occasionally perching over me, as if he's reading over my shoulder the way Ira sometimes does. By the time I finish, I know that I will not stay here with Mom. I will go back and face up to the fear and the grief, that which I've caused and that which I've been the victim of.

"Do you want me to drive up with you?" Mom asks when I tell her before bed that I'll be leaving in the morning.

I shake my head. She's stopped running away. Let her stay, with her birds. I'll come back another time. Figure out a way to be family.

She tucks the covers around me. "Want me to sing to you?" She's half joking, unsure.

But I do. "Please."

She sits down on the edge of the bed. When she begins, the years fall away, as she sings us all the way back to that day that started us all.

Home is where I want to be, but I guess I'm already there.

My Brother

Mom insists I stop somewhere along the drive, so arrangements are made for me to spend the night at a motel in Boise. When I pull up, the clerk tells me the room has already been checked in by the other party.

"What other party?" I ask, even though I know the answer to that even before I see my father through the window, reading a book by lamplight.

I have so many questions. What is he doing here? How did he get here? Does he forgive me? What about Chad and Ike and the Lumberjacks? But instead I speak in the language that's always come most naturally to us. "What are you reading?"

"Funny you should ask." He holds up his book. Something by Jamaica Kincaid. It's called *My Brother*. "It's a memoir," Ira explains. "Kincaid processing the grief after her brother died of AIDS." He shakes his head. "Not processing. That's the wrong word. Processing makes it sound like you digest your grief. It reminds me of the mourner's kaddish, somehow. Like she's singing her grief, because words are not sufficient. Maybe that doesn't make sense."

Mom, singing me to sleep. Hannah, singing to tell a story. Bev, singing away her panic attacks. "Actually, it kind of does."

"I thought it might be of interest to you." He pauses. "But only if you want." He looks pained. "Are you really not reading anymore?"

"I haven't really been able to read since Sandy died."

"And all the books I assigned you . . . ?"

"I've been faking. About that. And a lot of stuff." I take a deep breath, forcing myself to keep going. "I'm sorry I didn't tell you about selling the store. I sort of did it in a panic, after I saw your credit cards, but the truth is, I just wanted out."

"Out of what, exactly?" Ira asks.

"The store."

"Hmm." Ira strokes his beard. "See, the thing that perplexes me is, if you wanted out of the store, you could've sold it months ago. And after you did sell it, you went to a lot of trouble to try to get it back." Ira shakes his head. "I might be bad at running a business, but you're terrible at shuttering one. So you'll forgive me if I don't quite buy this."

Hannah called me an unreliable narrator. And maybe I am. The thing with unreliable narrators is that sometimes even they don't know why they do what they do.

"I ask again: What is it you want out of?" Ira asks, leading me to an answer he already knows.

I think of Chad, falling off the cliff, those three seconds when he was sure he was going to die. It's like I've been suspended in those three seconds ever since Sandy got sick.

"I want out of inevitability," I tell Ira.

"Inevitability?" Ira asks.

"Knowing that something bad is going to happen, whether you

want it to or not, to the point that you just want it to happen so you can stop dreading it."

"You mean like your brother dying?"

I swallow the lump in my throat and nod. "And Mom leaving. I knew that was coming, and I just wanted it to be over. Same with the store."

"And you think you have the power to make people live or die? To impact consumer trends?" Ira chuckles. "I didn't realize I'd fathered a god."

When he says it like that, it does sound kind of ridiculous.

Ira continues. "You should also know something: I told Annie to leave after Sandy died."

"You did?"

Ira nods. "She was flailing, caught in this loop of grief. I was afraid what would become of you if she stayed."

"I wanted her to leave because I was afraid what would happen to *you* if she stayed."

Ira strokes his beard and smiles sadly: "How very 'Gift of the Magi.'"

"What do you mean?"

"It's that O. Henry story where the husband sells his pocket watch to buy his wife combs for her hair, and she sells her hair to buy him a chain for his pocket watch." He pauses. "They both try to do something for the other but they kind of lovingly blow it. Like us."

"Like us," I repeat. "Are the answers to all life's questions in books?"

"Of course," he says. "That's what makes them miracles."

//

The next morning, I wake to a call from Penny Macklemore. It's Sunday at eight thirty, but tomorrow is D-Day. December 1. "Just reminding you we have an appointment at my office at ten o'clock."

"I'll be there."

I wake Ira, an idea forming. "Did some guy come for the records?" I ask him.

"Huh?" he asks. Bleary-eyed.

"I sold Sandy's records. To a guy named Daryl. He was supposed to drop off a check for Chad and get the records. Did he come?"

"Oh, that fellow. He came." Ira yawns. "I sent him away."

"Why? He was gonna pay eight grand for the records. I was going to pay back Chad and the guys. I need to make amends."

"That you do, but the records are worth at least five times that."

"How do you know that?"

"Your brother had the collection appraised."

"He did?"

"What do you think that index is for?"

"If you knew how much they were worth, why didn't *you* sell them?"

"They aren't mine to sell," Ira says.

"But they could've saved the store!"

"Sandy didn't leave the records to me. Or to the store. He left them to you."

"He didn't leave anything to me. He gave me the key and made me promise not to sell them."

Ira cups his fingers. "I think he meant not to sell them when he was alive," he says in a soft voice. "It wasn't lost on him that we mortgaged your future to try to save his. I think he wanted to set something aside for you in case the worst happened. I always assumed the records were his legacy to you, and when you were ready, you'd do something with them." He kicks off the sheets and gets up. "But not for eight thousand dollars."

I let this sink in: Inheritance? In case the worst happened? Had Sandy seen the asteroid? Did he know his days were numbered? And if so, when did he know? And why didn't he say anything to me?

But as we get into the car to head home, I realize I need to let this one go. My brother's thoughts on his own extinction are—like the dinosaurs' thoughts on theirs—a mystery that will never be revealed to me.

The Great Good Place

Though the store has been all fixed up, when we walk in that night it feels as empty and desolate as it's been these past few years. Chad and Ike and the Lumberjacks have been fixtures for only a few weeks but their absence is as glaring as the now-fixed broken shelf was. Hannah was right: time is no measure of something like love.

"You want dinner?" Ira asks.

"In a bit. I have to go see Chad."

Ira puts a hand on my shoulder. "He might need some time. He's pretty hurt. They all are."

"I gathered that." On the drive up, I texted him a dozen times but got no response. "But time is the one thing we don't have."

⸝⸝⸝

Aside from that day I was tricked into building the ramp, I've never been to Chad's house. His mom knows exactly who I am and leads me down a wide hallway to the converted garage that's now his lair. The floor is full of books, our books.

"Your mom let me in," I say when he greets me with silence.

He grunts in response.

249

I gesture to the books. "How's the indexing going?"

"Like you care."

I walk toward him, stumbling over a copy of *Pride and Prejudice*. "I do care. I'm so sorry, Chad. If I'd known you were pulling out of the Stim for the store . . ."

"You think *that's* what I'm pissed about?" He shakes his head. "Man, for someone who's supposedly so smart, you can be hella stupid. I pulled off the waitlist because I changed my mind."

"You did? Why?"

"Because it's risky and unproven and maybe love is not dependent upon a person's genitalia."

"So what are you pissed off about?"

"Aside from you lying to me for weeks on end?"

"Yeah," I say, chastened. "Aside from that."

"You got my hopes up, dawg." He fiddles with the seams on his gloves. "You got me believing in a great good place."

"What's that?"

"Damn, don't you read your own books?"

"Not all of them."

"You should read this one." He wheels over to his side table and pulls out a paperback titled *The Great Good Place*. "It's about these spaces, like bookstores, like coffee shops, where people can come together. How important they are. And I thought the store was going to be my great good place. Not just a bookstore but a musical venue, and a place to have your dad's tai chi classes, and Bev to have her Knit and Lits, and Jax's twelve-step meetings and my support groups." He holds up the book. "It coulda been so great.

A place for everyone. You let me believe we could have that." His voice breaks. "You let all of us believe that."

"If it's any comfort, I let myself believe it too."

Chad's head whips up. "But you said you don't want the bookstore. You sold it."

"I don't want to *own* the bookstore," I tell Chad. "But I do want to be a part of a great good place. I just didn't think it could happen here. I've lived above that bookstore all my life but it never felt like a great good place . . . until you showed up and made us build you a ramp."

Chad nods slowly. "*Conned* you into building me a ramp, you mean."

"*Con* is a strong word, wouldn't you say?"

When Chad cracks a small smile and says, "Swindle?" I know I haven't lost him.

"Look, Chad, I came here to say sorry. But also because I have an idea. Did you spend all the money you had in the bank?"

"Not all of it."

"So how much do you have?"

"About six grand."

I do the math. I can almost make the numbers work. "Can I have it?"

Chad raises an eyebrow. "Hell to the no!"

"Hear me out. I have about a thousand left from selling the records. If we add in six grand of your money, I think it might work. But only if . . ."

"If what?"

"If you really want to be a partner." I feel shy, like I'm making a promposal, not that I ever did that kind of thing. "Do you want to?"

Chad paces back and forth in his chair. "I mean, it's crazy, right? I hardly read books."

"You'll start."

"And I don't know which movies were books first."

"You'll learn. And you have more business acumen than Ira and me combined."

"True, but that's a low bar."

"I have a meeting with Penny tomorrow morning. If I go in with your money and mine, that's seven grand. And I know I can scratch up the rest quick. I think I can make this work. But there's one catch."

"Ain't there always?"

"You wouldn't be partners with me. I meant it when I said I don't want the bookstore. But Ira does. And you do. So you'd be partners with him."

"I love your dad," he says, scratching his chin. "But if we're partners, what would you be?"

"What I hope I still am," I reply. "Your friend."

The next morning, I wake up and get ready for my meeting with Penny. As I head off, Ira stands up.

"What are you doing?"

"Coming with, of course."

"But we'll have to close the store. During business hours."

Ira shrugs and locks the door behind us. "Hardly seems to matter anymore."

My heart is beating so fast as we walk to the hardware store. I practice what I'll say. Basically, I have to do the opposite of hand-sell. I have to convince her not to buy something.

Chad is waiting at the corner of Main and Alder.

"What are you doing here?" I ask.

"No offense, son, but we're not letting you face Penny Macklemore alone." He glances at Ira. "Historically, that has *not* gone well."

We continue up Alder. Ike's truck is parked in front of the hard-ware store. In itself this isn't so weird, but the sight of Ike, in a suit, is nearly as jarring as hearing him talk about Viagra. He growls at me. "Just so we're clear, we're here for your father and Chad, not for you."

"Understood," I say.

"We're not speaking to you," Richie says as he emerges from the cab, trailed by Garry.

"I can appreciate that. I'll do whatever I can to make it right."

"We'll see about that," Garry says.

"You guys, I'm so sorry."

"You should be," Richie says.

"You coulda told us," Garry adds.

"I know. I was scared."

"Everyone gets scared, Aaron," Ike says. "Don't give you license to act like a mother fudger." He looks at Ira. "Pardon my language."

"Seems warranted," Ira says.

We enter the hardware store. Penny is in the back office with her lawyer. "What's going on here?" she asks when she sees the crowd. "We only need Aaron and me for the closing." She looks at me. "Because this *is* a closing. I didn't receive any other word from you."

"You're receiving it now," I say. "Penny, I don't want to sell you the store. Well, actually, I do. But *they* don't. They want to run it." I point to Ira and Chad and Ike too. "And so I'd like to take you up on your offer of thirteen thousand dollars to back out of our deal."

"Thirteen thousand dollars?" Ike bellows.

"You have a cashier's check?" Penny asks.

"No cashier's check, but I have this." I pull out an envelope full of cash from the record collectors. "One thousand dollars."

"And here's a check for six thousand," Chad says.

"You're still six thousand dollars short."

"Six thousand dollars short of what?" Ike asks.

"Thirteen thousand dollars," Penny replies.

"What's thirteen thousand dollars?" Ike asks again.

I turn to Ike. "Don't worry about the money." Then I turn back to Penny. "I can get the rest of the money by the end of the day." I haven't talked to Daryl yet but I suspect he'll be more than happy to take the collection for the bargain-basement price of eight grand.

"How?" Chad and Ira ask at the same time.

"Will someone tell me what the darn-tootin' is going on?" Ike asks.

I turn to Ira. "I'm selling Sandy's records to Daryl. I know they're worth way more than eight thousand dollars. But if Sandy left them to me, it's up to me to decide what to do with them. And this is what I choose. This is how I can make it right to all of you."

"Can someone explain to me what's costing thirteen thousand dollars?" Ike shouts.

"It's what I have to pay Penny to get out of our deal," I explain. "And I can do it. If I sell all the records now."

"But the records are part of our revenue stream," Chad says. "I put it in the business plan."

"Why? I told you we weren't selling them in the store."

"Yeah, but you say a lot of stupid shit. And anyway, they're mad valuable. And I talked to Lou and he says he would become our buyer, so we could keep up our supply and revenue stream and he gets to shop for records for a living."

"Yeah, but Chad, we need to sell the records to get the money to pay off Penny."

"And we need to sell records to make the store profitable," Chad says, shaking his head. "That's a real catch-22."

"Chad Santos, did you just make a literary reference?"

"I guess I did."

"Well, then, you have to run a bookstore now."

Everyone laughs and the mood in the office is festive and for a moment I think I've won. I've saved the bookstore *and* gotten out from it.

But then I see Penny, who is smiling too. And I know Penny well enough to know that she doesn't smile when she loses. She smiles when she wins.

And Penny Macklemore always wins.

"It's December first," she says merrily. "And you don't have the thirteen thousand dollars, so our deal is closing now."

"But I'll have it in a few hours . . . Tomorrow at the latest."

"Too late. The offer is off the table. The deal is closing now," she repeats. "And if it doesn't, I'll sue you, and trust me, that will get very expensive very fast."

I look at Penny. How did I not see this before? The curled hair. The upturned nose. The small eyes. She's Lucy, at age seventy.

"Were you ever going to let me out of the deal?" I ask her.

She shrugs. "If you raised the money, sure. But I knew if you somehow did, you'd only dig yourself in deeper because a bookstore is not a growth market. Then the property would flounder again and I'd get it all fixed up, even cheaper, and be ten thousand dollars the richer for my trouble." She unclasps her pen. "Either way, I get the store. I've wanted it for years. And when I want something that badly, I don't ever give up."

"It's your Great White Whale," Garry says.

"My what?" she asks.

"It's a book reference," Garry replies.

"Oh," Penny says. "I wouldn't know anything about that."

The room goes quiet, so the only sound is of Penny's pen as she takes possession of the store.

And like that, it's done.

Stone Soup

It's quiet. Too quiet. It shouldn't be this quiet right now. It feels wrong.

I walk through the empty space, my footsteps echoing off the barren shelves: the mahogany one that broke Ike's heart looks, if not new again, old in the right way. The other shelves are all reinforced, restained, and empty. Lady Gaga glimmers in the morning light.

Sandy's record bins, the ones he painstakingly built in that fury of foresight, or fear, or whatever it was that drove him, yawn open, their locks removed, the records gone.

I call Chad. "You're coming, right?"

"Dawg, chill. I said I'd be there and I'll be there."

"It's just we're running up the clock."

Chad guffaws. "Running *down* the clock. Stick to book metaphors, son."

"Whatever," I snap back. "Clock's ticking."

"I'll be there," Chad replies. "We'll all be there."

///

Ten minutes later Ira walks in. "Sorry," he says breathlessly. "Tai chi ran long."

"It's okay," I say. "Where's Bev?"

"Picking some things up. She'll be by later." He looks around the empty room, his face a mix of emotions I can't quite read. "The end of an era."

"We had a good run, didn't we?"

"We did." Ira clasps me on the shoulder as the sputter of Ike's pickup truck nears. "Ready to do this?"

"Ready as I'll ever be."

But neither of us move. We just look around the empty space, which until three months ago had been Joe Heath's scrap shop. It's bigger than our bookstore was. Wide-open, accessible, with room for all the shelves we have, plus several more that Ike's built. It looks so different from how it did when we took possession a few weeks ago. It doesn't seem possible for things to change so quickly, but sometimes they do. Just ask the dinosaurs.

Ike barges in, spitting tobacco into his Diet Peach Snapple bottle. "You two gonna just stand there all day? These boxes ain't gonna unpack themselves."

※

Within the hour, everyone's here: Ike, Garry, and Richie, Garry's girlfriend, Amanda. The now-inseparable troika of Beana, Bev, and Angela. Lou's there. And Jax. And of course Chad. He's christened himself "project director" for the day, because of his mobility challenges, he claims, but we all know that's a ruse. The new space is wide-open by design, so it can be used for Knit and Lits, Books and Brews, support groups, tai chi classes, yoga, open-mic nights, or whatever else they come up with.

There are plenty of low shelves for Chad to stock. But he likes playing God. "If you consult my very clear blueprints," Chad is now bellowing, "you will see that the boxes are all numbered and color-coded to match the appropriate shelves so you don't have to think, just unpack. I measured and everything should fit to the inch."

"Seriously," Jax says. "He has like literally measured every book even though I told him a perfect fit is kind of a Sisyphean task, given that the inventory is always going to be shifting."

"And I know what *Sisyphean* means." Chad grins proudly. "I figure if I'm a co-owner of a bookstore, I oughta understand the literary references."

"It's not really literary," I say. "So much as Greek mythology."

"Ugh. Are you always gonna be like this?" Chad asks.

"Yep!"

"Well, you're just one of the common paying folk now, so I don't have to listen to you."

"Like you ever did."

"Who's ready for another espresso drink?" Ike booms from behind Lady Gaga. "I got cappuccinos, lattes, mochas, macchiatos, espressos, Americanos . . . hot or iced. Cow milk, soy milk, or oat milk." Ike gives Gaga a loving wipe-down. "We got a lot of work to do before the party, so I'm here to power you with caffeine."

"Where do you want the records?" Lou asks as he and Garry begin to cart in the special crates that Lou insisted we store the vinyl in to keep it from getting warped.

"Don't ask me," I reply. "I'm not the boss. Chad, where do you want the records?"

"Where do I want the records?" Chad asks, exasperated. "Check the blueprint. In the record bins. Back by the café."

"Cool. Like in a department store," Lou says, nodding, heading toward Sandy's bins. Ike proclaimed the workmanship solid and the pine standard grade, and therefore the bins did not need to be upgraded. I suspect that Ike would have preferred to rebuild the bins with nicer wood but out of respect to Sandy chose not to.

"I can't wait to get these records on display," Lou says. "It's about time we honored this vinyl."

Lou unpacks Sandy's vast collection, the music he loved more than anything, which he left to me. Which led me to the Outhouse, and to Chad. And the Lumberjacks. And even to Hannah.

Maybe Ira was right. The records are my legacy.

//,

We finish the setup by four o'clock. Which gives everyone about an hour to run home, shower, change, and come right back again in time for the party. There's not really time for speeches or dallying, but when Ira clears his throat and asks everyone to come outside for a huddle, no one objects. Richie and Garry clamber up two ladders alongside the flat, rampless entrance to the store. Ike nods at Ira.

"Some of you were around when we first opened Bluebird Books more than twenty-five years ago." Ira looks at Ike. "The store's been through a lot. The town's been through a lot. We've all been through a lot." He looks at me. "But here we are."

"Here we are!" shouts Chad.

Ira gestures for Ike and Chad to join him under the railing, and then for me too. But I stay behind. The store's not mine anymore. But somehow, giving it up, I gained more than I ever could have imagined.

Ike whistles and Richie and Garry unfurl the new sign. Mom designed it with Amanda, Garry's girlfriend. It has Mom's original lettering and Amanda's illustration of birds flying out of a nest. She painted a similar design on the ceiling of the new space. I look at the sign, old and new, the same and different, like the store, like my family. Ira looks at me. I look at Ira. It's time.

"I now declare Bluebird Books, Music, Coffee, and Community Center open," he booms.

Everyone in town seems to have shown up for the grand opening: Ike's friends from the mill. Bev and Beana's newly assembled book group. The middle school principal and a bunch of teachers Angela knows. Lou's collector pals, all drooling for first dibs. A bunch of small kids are tearing around. Even Penny Macklemore is here, sniffing things out.

"Want me to have her thrown out?" Chad asks. "I'm happy to be the bouncer."

"Let her stay," I say. "Everyone deserves a great good place. Even Penny."

"Also, look how many people are here. Rub her nose in it a bit."

"And that."

The crowd is so thick I can hardly see through it, but when Hannah walks in, I feel it immediately even though I haven't seen her since Thanksgiving. We've texted a few times and I hear about her from Jax, who's always at our place these days. When we closed the old store, Ira decided to rent Joe's house. There was space for me, but I think we both knew it was time for this bird to leave the nest. As I was starting to look for rentals, Chad showed me a listing of an apartment in a new elevator building, between here and Bellingham, totally accessible. "It's nice, but I can't afford that," I'd told him. He'd grinned at me. "Yeah, but *we* can."

Hannah approaches me, awkwardly. I'm not sure what the protocol is for greeting an ex who was really only your girlfriend for two nights, but like everything else in my life, I'm trying to figure it out as I go.

"You came?" I ask, settling for a half hug, half arm pat. My heart still does something funny but it's not like it was before. It's distant, like a fossil of something that was once alive.

"Damn straight I came," she says. "A bookstore, café, record store, community space has to have music at its opening." She looks around. "Is Jax here yet?"

"They've been here all day, helping."

"Helping, you call it?" Hannah gestures to where Jax is canoodling with Chad.

"Anything that keeps Chad happy is helping."

She chuckles. "We have a special set planned. All songs with book references. Elvis Costello, 'Everyday I Write the Book.' Talking Heads, 'The Book I Read.'"

"Not 'Clair de Lune.'"

She looks me straight in the face, and there it is, that echo again. Maybe she hears it too. "Not that."

"I'm sorry, you know. For running to you when I was really running away."

She smiles, nods. "It's okay. How've things been?"

"I keep thinking about what you said at the meeting, about needing to destroy things in order to create something new. I'm somewhere in that process."

"You *were* listening?" I can see this pleases her. "I'm glad. I heard you're going to college."

Jax must have told her, which means the two of them talk about me. Which pleases me. "I'm taking a few classes."

"Anything interesting?"

"A literature course, now that I can read books again. And intro to paleontology."

"Dinosaurs." She laughs. "Some things never change."

Maybe that's true. Because no matter what Hannah and I are now, I will never stop believing we are inevitable. Not just her and me, but me and Chad. Chad and Jax. Ira and Ike. Maybe we are all inevitable.

///

By seven we run out of Angela's crumb cake, by eight the muffins are history, and by nine the espresso's history. "I bought five pounds of beans this morning," Ike says, dismayed. "Thought that would get us through the weekend, but it didn't last the day."

Ira laughs. "If we get a boom of babies in nine months, we'll know it's because no one in town could fall asleep tonight."

"We'll expand our children's section," Chad says, gesturing to two little kids racing around the store like maniacs. "Get a train set. Stuffed chairs. Some other kid stuff. And more books about travel. Your mom was right about that one, which is why I left the travel and parenting books together."

"I saw that," I say.

"Maybe we should start the musical portion," Ira says. "Since we're out of coffee."

"Good idea," Bev says. "I'll tell the musicians. Then we can announce the upcoming events. Because we also ran out of printed schedules."

"The schedule's all up on the website," Chad says as a father chases down a pair of wayward kids, followed by a laughing woman. "Holy shit," Chad whispers. "I think that's the guy who used to be in Shooting Star."

"What's that?"

Chad rolls his eyes. "Only, like, a world-famous band. The lead singer married a famous cellist. I heard they bought a spread around here to turn into a studio. Dude, I think that *is* them and their kids. I gotta go tell Jax. Opening night and we got celebrities in the house!"

Ira sidles up next to me. "You okay with all this?" he asks, giving my hand a squeeze.

I nod. More than okay. "It's the happy ending I couldn't have imagined."

He shakes his head. "I still don't understand how we did this."

"Sure you do," I reply. "*Stone Soup.*"

"You're right. *Stone Soup.* You're the one who got the pot going."

"That tracks. The story does start with an act of fraud."

"Hmm, I never thought of it like that before."

"I did," I reply. "Being the resident con artist and all."

Ira reaches out to hug me. "Thanks for being you," he murmurs in my ear.

I hug him back. "Everyone else was taken."

※

When Hannah and Jax take the stage, I follow Chad to a special spot we've set up where his view will be unobstructed.

"Life is strange, ain't it?" Chad asks. "Who woulda thunk it when I saw you at that first show at the Outhouse we'd end up living together, or that I'd end up a partner in a bookstore, where rock stars apparently shop. Living our best lives now, aren't we?"

"Yeah, Chad. I think we are."

"Hey, I keep forgetting to tell you. I finally read the dinosaur book you were so obsessed with."

"*The Rise and Fall of the Dinosaurs*? Did you like it?"

"Yeah. It was totally not boring. The thing I don't get is how you read that book like a hundred times and still missed the point."

I sigh. One of the drawbacks of selling my stake to Chad is that he now feels no compunction whatsoever to lecture me about books. "How exactly did I miss the point?"

"Well, you're always talking about the dinosaurs being extinct.

Did they know? How did they feel? Blah blah blah. But they're not *really* extinct."

"I think you're confusing the Brusatte with *Jurassic Park*."

"Nah, dawg. I'm not. Because right at the end, he talks about the new breed of flying dinosaurs. They were smaller, bat-sized, able to fly, so when the asteroid hit, these new guys were somehow able to survive. And eventually they . . ." He trails off.

"They *evolved*," I finish.

He reaches an arm around me and pulls me toward him, knocking me on the head as if to tell me what I already know. That I'm dense. And he loves me. And he knows I love him too.

"And what did they evolve into?" he asks, pointing up.

I look to the flock of bluebirds Amanda painted on the ceiling, and then I turn to Chad and answer his question once and for all.

"They evolved into birds."

BIBLIOGRAPHY

BOOKS REFERENCED OR REFERRED TO IN *We Are Inevitable.*

The Rise and Fall of the Dinosaurs by Steve Brusatte

Jane Eyre by Charlotte Brontë

Master of the Senate by Robert A. Caro

Modern Life by Matthea Harvey

The Lion, the Witch and the Wardrobe by C. S. Lewis

The Lord of the Rings by J. R. R. Tolkien

Murder on the Orient Express by Agatha Christie

Death on the Nile by Agatha Christie

Appointment with Death by Agatha Christie

Too Loud a Solitude by Bohumil Hrabal

Sometimes a Great Notion by Ken Kesey

Caps for Sale by Esphyr Slobodkina

The Sorrows of Young Werther by Johann Wolfgang von Goethe

The Rules by Ellen Fein and Sherrie Schneider

Twilight by Stephenie Meyer

The Giving Tree by Shel Silverstein

Peanuts by Charles M. Schulz

Batgirl, Volume 1: The Darkest Reflection (The New 52) by Gail Simone

Batgirl, Volume 2: Family Business by Cameron Stewart and Brendan Fletcher

Fifty Shades of Grey by E L James

Gone Girl by Gillian Flynn

Emma by Jane Austen

The Magician's Nephew by C. S. Lewis

The Last Battle by C. S. Lewis

The Percy Jackson series by Rick Riordan

Ways to Make Sunshine by Renée Watson

The Unicorn Rescue Society series by Adam Gidwitz

Wonder by R. J. Palacio

The Track series by Jason Reynolds

The Dog Man series by Dav Pilkey

Walter the Farting Dog by William Kotzwinkle and Glenn Murray, illustrated by Audrey Colman

A Wrinkle in Time by Madeline L'Engle

The Door by Magda Szabó

The Melancholy of Resistance by László Krasznahorkai

Just Kids by Patti Smith

When You Reach Me by Rebecca Stead

Stone Soup by Marcia Brown

The Scent of Desire by Rachel Herz

The Harry Potter series by J. K. Rowling

The Heart Is a Lonely Hunter by Carson McCullers

Fight Club by Chuck Palahniuk

The Little Book of Hygge: Danish Secrets to Happy Living
by Meik Wiking

The Art of the Deal by Donald J. Trump and Tony Schwartz

War with the Newts by Karel Čapek

Goldmine Record Album Price Guide, 10th Edition
by Dave Thompson

Beethoven's Anvil: Music in Mind and Culture by William Benzon

The Complete Idiot's Guide to Starting and Running a Coffee Bar
by Susan Gilbert, W. Eric Martin, and Linda Formichelli

Eat, Pray, Love by Elizabeth Gilbert

Tuesdays with Morrie by Mitch Albom

Moby-Dick by Herman Melville

Lost Horizon by James Hilton

Moneyball by Michael Lewis

Alcoholics Anonymous: The Big Book by Bill W.

The 2010 Rand McNally Road Atlas

His Dark Materials series by Philip Pullman

A Grief Observed by C. S. Lewis

My Brother by Jamaica Kincaid

"The Gift of the Magi" by O. Henry

Pride and Prejudice by Jane Austen

The Great Good Place by Ray Oldenburg

Catch-22 by Joseph Heller

Mythology: Timeless Tales of Gods and Heroes by Edith Hamilton

Jurassic Park by Michael Crichton

ADDICTION NOTE

In *We Are Inevitable* Aaron repeatedly says that Sandy's addiction is his own doing, that he chose his addiction over his family, that if he'd wanted to, he could've kicked the habit.

I want to start this note by emphatically debunking this idea, which has been proven untrue by scientists and substance-abuse experts. Addiction is not the fault of the addict. We authors often make characters say things we know to be untrue—and, spoiler alert, by the end of the book Aaron begins to realize that his blaming of Sandy is a way to shield himself from the pain of losing his brother.

The opioid addiction sweeping the country is not the fault of weak-willed addicts, lack of willpower, etc. If you feel the need to assign blame to for the crisis, one place to look is the pharmaceutical industry itself, notably companies such as Purdue Pharma that have knowingly heavily marketed products like oxycodone as non–habit forming even though these synthesized drugs' chemical makeup is nearly identical to morphine, the highly addictive opiate from which heroin is derived. This is a travesty and a public-health nightmare, and if you'd like to read more about it, I highly recommend Sam Quinones's *Dreamland: The True Tale of*

America's Opiate Epidemic. An adult and a YA version is available.

Here's what you need to know about addiction. It is a potent combination of physical and psychological dependencies, and if it were easy to kick, millions of people in this country would not be losing their livelihoods, homes, and lives to addiction.

And yet recovering from addiction is possible. For every Sandy, there are a hundred Hannahs.

If you believe you have a substance-abuse problem, SAMHSA (Substance Abuse and Mental Health Services Administration) has a 24-hour-a-day, 365-day-a-year information-service hotline for individuals and family members facing mental or substance-use disorders. Call 1-800-487-4889 or visit samhsa.gov. The calls are confidential—no one will tell your parents, your doctors, etc.—and can help you figure out the next steps, such as rehab options or twelve-step meetings, or offer support so you can tell the trusted adults in your life. According to several studies, many people with substance-abuse problems have underlying untreated conditions (like anxiety and depression), and SAMHSA can help you find mental-health support as well.

If you have a friend or family member who has a substance-abuse problem, you can also reach out to SAMHSA. You might also think about joining an Al-Anon (al-anon.org) or Nar-Anon (nar-anon.org) group, which supports friends and relatives of people struggling with substance abuse. (Al-Anon focuses on alcoholism and Nar-Anon on narcotic addictions, but the struggles with substance abuse transcend the substance, so you would be able to find support in any such group.)

Anyone can attend a twelve-step meeting anytime. So if you

think you might have an issue, Google "twelve-step meeting near me." There are meetings happening all the time—most of them virtual until the pandemic ends—and you can attend nearly any of them.

According to SAMHSA, in 2016, of the approximately one in thirteen people ages twelve and older who needed substance-abuse treatment, only about 18 percent were able to access it. Other studies suggest that only 11 percent of those needing treatment can access it. There are many reasons for this—stigma, denial, proximity to facilities (particularly a problem in rural areas)—but one major obstacle is the scarcity of publicly funded rehab facilities. This is not an accident. Many states have defunded public-health programs that pay for rehab, leaving families like Aaron's to fend for themselves. If you are of voting age, you should vote, and especially you should vote for candidates, particularly in state government, who support funding necessary public-health services, including rehab.

Whether it's you or someone you love dealing with substance abuse and addiction, understand that you are not alone. And as you move forward on your journey, whatever it is, try to walk with compassion. Forgiveness is hard. Forgiving others for their stumbles is harder. Forgiving ourselves can be hardest.

—Gayle Forman, January 2021

ACKNOWLEDGMENTS

This book is a love letter to books, and to booksellers, so I want to begin by thanking all the booksellers I have had the pleasure to know and those of you I have yet to meet, those of you who have hand-sold me (and millions of other readers) books, and those of you who have hand-sold my (and millions of other authors') books.

I will not try to gloss over how difficult this past year has been for you all. What I will say is that it has reminded me and so many others how much we rely on you, not just for the books you sell but the great, good places you provide. That so many of you managed to create great, good places in the virtual world speaks to your power. That said, I look forward to seeing you again in the crowded aisles.

Along those lines, I want to thank librarians, teachers, and other educators. I cannot imagine how challenging a year this has been for you, but I have seen firsthand the way you have risen to the occasion, turned destruction into creation. Words alone cannot express my gratitude. But words are all I've got.

Writing outside your own experience is both a necessity of fiction and an act of humility, and I want to thank all of the people who educated me and helped me, particularly on disability issues. Thank you to Andrew Skinner of the Triumph Foundation, to Jennifer Korba, who read carefully and thoughtfully, and to Dean Macabe, who did not blink when in our first conversation, I brought up erections and catheters. Thank you to Zoey Peresman for guidance and insight on addiction and recovery issues. Thank you, Andreas Sonju, for helping me make sure I got my lumber lingo and sandpaper grits just right. And to Heather Hebert for reading this book with an open, honest heart and for being everything I love about booksellers in one human.

Thank you to Leila Sales, who pushed me hard on this one. Every time I would hot-potato it over to her, claiming (wishing) I was done, she'd send it back and kick my ass a little further. If you cried at the end of this so-called comedy, blame Leila.

At Penguin Random House, thank you to my amazing team, Christina Colangelo, Felicia Frazier, Alex Garber, Carmela Iaria, Brianna Lockhart, Jen Loja, Lathea Mondesir, Shanta Newlin, Claire Tattersfield, and Felicity Vallence. Tip of the hat to Theresa Evangelista for the striking cover design and Anna Rupprecht for the spot-on illustration. Thank you to Eileen Kreit for ongoing support and good cheer. Finally, a bear hug of thanks to the ringmaster of it all, the incomparable Ken Wright.

I also want to thank the PRH book reps: Susie Albert, Jill Bailey, Maggie Brennan, Trevor Bundy, Vicki Congdon, Sara Danver, Nicole Davies, Tina Deniker, John Dennany, Cletus Durking, Joe English, Eliana Ferrier, Drew Fulton, Sheila Hennesesy, Todd Jones, Doni Kay, Steve Kent, Vance Lee, Mary McGrath, Jill Nadeau, Tanesha Nurse, Deb Polansky, Mary Raymond, Colleen Conway

Ramos, Talisa Ramos, Jennifer Ridgeway, Samantha Rodan, Christy Strout, Judy Samuels, Nicole White, Allan Winebarger, and Dawn Zahorikm. Many readers might not realize that reps are on-the-ground champions of books, the conduit between author and bookseller. I'm not sure how they all managed to keep the train on the tracks when there was no actual train but they did, and for that, and so much more, I am grateful.

Thank you to Michael Bourret and Lauren Abramo, and everyone at DGB. To Mary Pender, Alyssa Lanz, Gregory McKnight, and everyone at UTA, and to Suzie Townsend and Dani Segelbaum and everyone at NLLM. Thank you to my foreign co-agents and publishers for signing up for another ride.

Thank you to Amy Margolis for the encouragement on that frigid day at the beach when I thought I'd never finish this book! Thank you to Raquel Jaramillo for support and encouragement and help figuring out what to call this thing! Thank you to Tamara Glenny, who is always among my first readers. Thank you to my trio of sister-wives: Emily Jenkins, Libba Bray, and Marjorie Ingall, who, respectively, helped me figure out the head, the heart, and the funny bone of this book and who kept me sane during the pandemic. And thank you to my actual spouse, Nick Tucker, who continues to be my muse, this time informing not just the record- and book-collector traits and indie-band ethos, but also the more obscure literary references. I probably never would've heard of Hrable were it not for him.

Thank you to my family, of course, in particular my two girls: Denbelé, my big-hearted partner in crime, and Willa, who showed me that a teenage reader could love Ike as much as I do.

And finally, thank you, my dear reader. It's not always an uncomplicated love affair, this reading thing, with our collective attention pulled in so many directions. That you dedicated yours to a book, *this* book, and made it all the way to these final pages, it makes me (and, I like to imagine, Aaron, and Ira and Chad and Ike) very, very happy.